Death on Milestone Buttress

An Abercrombie Lewker climbing mystery

by

Glyn Carr

Introduction by
Tom & Enid Schantz

The Rue Morgue Press
Boulder, Colorado

Death on Milestone Buttress

P.O. Box 4119
Boulder, Colorado 80306

ISBN: 0-915230-29-1

FIRST AMERICAN EDITION

PRINTED IN THE UNITED STATES OF AMERICA

From *Death on Milestone Buttress*

That wouldn't do. She forced herself to think calmly. Raymond had fallen. He was hanging on the end of the rope, unconscious, perhaps badly hurt. She must first try to see what had happened, then call for help. Tentatively she eased her grip of the rope. The crack held it, tightly jammed by the weight on its other end. She made a loop and put it over a rock spike in case it slipped. Then, shaking a little but with tight-set lips, she clambered very cautiously to the crest and holding on with every nerve and sinew tense peered over the edge.

She was looking down a vertical wall. A narrow ledge ran up it to the right. Beneath the ledge was a sloping earthy gully falling at its lower end into space. The rope, vibrating slightly, led down and over the edge of the gully; but Cauthery was suspended only just below that edge. She could see his head, but not his face. And what she could see of his head was a ball of wet crimson: the color of the handkerchief he had flung away.

Sick and shaken, she lowered herself back again into the safety of the niche. Her fingers trembled so that she had difficulty in taking off the rucksack and getting out the whistle. What had the professor said?—"Six blasts in a minute."

She put the whistle to her lips.

Abercrombie Lewker
Detective Novels as by Glyn Carr

Death on Milestone Buttress (1951)
Murder on the Matterhorn (1951)
The Youth Hostel Murders (1952)
The Corpse in the Crevasse (1952)
Death Under Snowdon (1952)
A Corpse at Camp Two (1954)
Murder of an Owl (1956)
The Ice Axe Murders (1958)
Swing Away, Climber (1959)
Holiday with Murder (1960)
Death Finds a Foothold (1961)
Lewker in Norway (1963)
Death of a Weirdy (1965)
Lewker in Tirol (1967)
Fat Man's Agony (1969)

Abercrombie Lewker
Thrillers as by Showell Styles

Traitor's Mountain (1945)
Kidnap Castle (1947)
Hammer Island (1947)

Introduction
Glyn Carr, Showell Styles and Abercrombie Lewker

IF YOU LOOK UPON a mountain climb as taking place in a large, open-air locked room, then Showell Styles was right to choose Glyn Carr as his pseudonym for fifteen detective novels featuring Abercrombie Lewker, all of which concern murders committed among the crags and slopes of peaks scattered around the world. There's no doubt that John Dickson Carr, the king of the locked room mystery, would have agreed that Styles managed to find a way to lock the door of a room that had no walls and only the sky for a ceiling. In fact, it was while Styles was climbing a pitch on the classic Milestone Buttress on Tryfan in Wales that it struck him "how easy it would be to arrange an undetectable murder in that place, and by way of experiment I worked out the system and wove a thinnish plot around it."

That book was, of course, *Death on Milestone Buttress,* and upon its publication Styles' English publisher, Geoffrey Bles, immediately asked for more climbing mysteries. Over the next eighteen years, Styles produced another fourteen Lewker books before he halted the series, having run out "of ways of slaughtering people on steep rock-faces." But before Lewker put away his ice axe and ropes for good, Styles managed to send him to Switzerland (*Murder on the Matterhorn*), the Himalayas (*A Corpse at Camp Two*), Austria (*The Corpse in the Crevasse* and *Lewker in the Tirol*), Scandinavia (*Lewker in Norway*) and Majorca (*Holiday with Murder*). The rest of the books were set in the place Styles no doubt loves the best, Wales, where, now in his early 90s, he still makes his home.

The foreign locales included some of the places Styles had himself visited, first during the period he refers to as his "tramp" days from 1934 to 1937, and later as the leader of a Himalayan climb in 1954. Somehow he never managed to find a way to send Lewker to the Arctic, where he led expeditions in 1952 and 1953.

While Lewker professes to be new to detective work in *Death on Milestone Buttress,* he certainly was no stranger to danger and adventure, having served in Department Seven of the Special Commando Branch of British Intelligence during World War II. In fact, when Styles was searching for a character to solve murders among his beloved mountain peaks, he needed look no further than to three of his thrillers, published a few years earlier under his Styles byline. Abercrombie Lewker debuted in *Traitor's Mountain* (1947) when he revealed himself, in the guise of a tramp, to another British agent: "He was immensely broad, in general shape resembling a pocket-flask, and his rusty elongated bowler crowned a rather pouchy countenance fringed with a bush of black whisker. His expression was the expression of a dictator travelling incognito. His stained and bulging raincoat was buttoned to the neck with six buttons."

Although the events in that novel were based on Styles' own experiences in the Royal Navy during the war, the author and his fictional creation bore little physical resemblance to one other. Styles' jacket photos from the period show a lean, very fit-looking man, obviously capable of taking on the most arduous of climbs. Lewker, on the other hand, is described as short, bald and fat, and people are always amazed to learn of his climbing feats. Yet, size notwithstanding, Lewker is an imposing figure, perhaps the finest Shakespearean actor of his day, with a booming voice and an often irritating predilection for quoting the Bard at the drop of a hat or a corpse. His wife Georgina is obviously deeply in love with him—and he with her—but she knows that one of her primary roles is to keep his pomposity from running away with itself and getting him into trouble. Ego aside, "Filthy," as his friends punningly call him, is generous to a fault and always willing to lend a hand to friend and stranger alike.

Filthy is also a man of old-fashioned (or perhaps time-honored) values, and chivalry is one he holds most dear, which explains, in part, why he turns detective to solve young Hilary Bourne's moral dilemma. Other aspects of *Death on Milestone Buttress* may puzzle or amuse modern readers grown used to the casual sex that permeates today's books and movies, not to mention television programs. In 1951, it was still possible for a proper girl to be ruined—or at least think of herself as being ruined—by having sex outside of marriage.

The attitudes toward politics in *Death on Milestone Buttress* may also puzzle readers for whom the Soviet Union is rapidly becoming a distant memory. Although published in 1951, the events in *Death on Milestone Buttress* take place a couple of years earlier, when Russia still posed a threat to the free world and the atomic bomb was still in its infancy. On the other hand, World War II was recent enough that people had not forgotten that Russia had been an ally against the Nazis. British communists were suspect in some circles but, on the whole, belonging to the party did not automatically brand one as a traitor. The Red Scare had not yet occupied the full attention of the political witch-hunters, especially in the United Kingdom. Indeed, one of the village girls is proud to claim that her sheepherder intended is the only member of the party in their entire valley. Lewker himself is more amused than scandalized by his encounters with the two or three party members who find themselves suspected of murder.

Besides, Filthy and Hilary are too busy sorting through clues and working out timetables to worry much about either sex or politics. Reference is made to Dorothy L. Sayers, the chosen reading matter (the other being *Das Kapital*) of one of the communists, but Styles actually owes as much to the alibi-busting tradition of Freeman Wills Crofts or Christopher Bush as to Sayers, although Filthy's larger-than-life characterization may remind some readers of a—shall we say—less handsome Lord Peter.

But the real fun of the Lewker books lies in their depiction of life in rural Wales and in the love Lewker and his fellow climbers share for their chosen sport. Lewker is a little reluctant to embrace the kind of extreme technical climbing that was an outgrowth of Hitler's desire to see Germans demonstrate Aryan supremacy by climbing many of Europe's impossible North Faces. Nor is he willing to use words like "hiking," preferring to call such treks walks or tramps. If Shakespeare didn't use the word, why should he?

In addition to being an accomplished climber himself, Styles has written scores of books on the subject, ranging from guides to climbs in Wales to a full-fledged standard history of the sport, *On the Top of the World* (1967). Styles' love for the mountains and climbing comes through so strongly that it is almost impossible to resist the urge to put down one of his climbing mysteries and head for the nearest mountain trail, though those of us who live in places like Colorado can't help but be amused when Lewker appreciatively sniffs the clean mountain air at a thousand—or even three thousand—feet above sea level.

But even the most sedentary readers can enjoy these stories. Those who prefer to do their mountaineering from the comfort of an armchair need not worry about being unfamiliar with the terminology or techniques of the sport. Styles is first and foremost a storyteller, having written many books for children as well as historical novels, and he never forgets that the first role of the professional writer is to entertain.

Tom & Enid Schantz
Boulder, Colorado
5,430 feet
April 2000

Diagram to illustrate this story
drawn by Abercrombie Lewker

TRYFAN, 3,010 feet

X—Grooved Arête
B—Bwlch Tryfan
G—Green Gully
Y—Top of Nor' Nor'
T—Track from Heather Terrace to Milestone Buttress
H . . H—Heather Terrace
N . . N—North Ridge
C—Ogwen Cottage
O—Llyn Ogwen
D—Dol Afon
M—Milestone Buttress

CHAPTER ONE

Without the which this story
Were most impertinent.
THE TEMPEST

" 'AS YOU FROM CRIMES would pardon'd be, Let your indulgence set me free,' " boomed Prospero, from the stage, and flung out his arms.

As the curtain fell on the last lines of *The Tempest* Hilary Bourne, applauding wildly in the gallery, prayed fervently that the auditorium lights would not go up before she had removed the traces of weeping from her cheeks. Hilary was one of those fortunate unfortunates who are moved to tears by sheer beauty of scene or of language, and Shakespeare's loveliest piece of escapism, as presented by the Abercrombie Lewker Players at the Manchester Repertory Theater, had been rich in both. "Consider what a great girl you are!" she said to herself disgustedly in the White Queen's words; but for all her nineteen years the old ridiculous nostalgia for the land of make-believe continued to prickle behind her nose, exactly as it had done at pantomimes when she was six. She shook her straight fair hair angrily round her face and went on clapping.

The curtain, having paused for a moment as though to give the enthusiastic audience time to spit on its hands, had risen again to reveal the dukes, nobles, sailors and sprites arrayed to receive their well-deserved tribute. Prospero, his shortness of stature apparent for the first time now that he had put off his actor's magic, was in the center between pretty Miranda and handsome Ferdinand. The audience redoubled its acclamations, and a reporter in the pit crossed out "due meed of applause" in his notebook and substituted "something approaching an ovation." Mr. Abercrombie Lewker, who was his own producer, appeared to have found the way to please those who consider a Shakespeare play an entertainment as well as those who regard it as merely a vehicle for great poetry. Up and down and up swept the curtain, until, choosing the exact second before the peak of the hand-clapping, Prospero stepped forward and held up his hand.

Hilary rested her tingling palms on her knees in an unladylike manner and leaned forward eagerly. Others were leaning forward eagerly too; even the best of Shakespeare cannot command such attention as can an actor-manager's speech from the stage at the end of a successful repertory season. But Hilary Bourne felt an additional, almost proprietary interest in Mr. Abercrombie Lewker as he stood waiting in his ducal robes for the applause to cease; for though she had never met him she knew a good deal more about the famous actor than most of the people round her. Her cousin Myfanwy Todd had been associated with Mr. Lewker (Myfanwy called him "Filthy") in his incredible and off-the-record adventures during the war, when he and his friend Gideon Hazel, the poet, had worked with the British Intelligence to the undoing of Herr Goebbels' cherished Fifth Column; and Hilary knew from her cousin's stories that she was gazing at one who was not only a notable actor but also a notable man of action.

Mr. Lewker hardly looked the part. He had removed his tall ducal headdress and flowing wig, revealing a large bald bead fringed with black hair. He looked rather comically pompous as he stood with wig and crown held across his breast with one hand and the other tucked Napoleonically behind his broad back, displaying a decided paunch.

"Ladies and gentlemen," he boomed in a voice remarkable for its depth and carrying power. " We thank you. To present Shakespeare faithfully, to bring to our audiences that well of English undefiled, is the work of the Abercrombie Lewker Players, and we love our work. Our greatest reward is to play to an intelligent audience. Your appreciation of our efforts has proved your intelligence, and we are rewarded."

"Well, I'm damned!" muttered a man behind Hilary with a chuckle. Several people said "Ssh!" angrily.

"As you know," continued the actor-manager, "tonight is our last performance in Manchester. Tomorrow my company—and I myself—begin a much-needed holiday. Let me assure you that with the memory of Manchester's appreciative audiences behind us, we shall all enjoy our holiday the more. Once again—we thank you."

The curtain came down for the last time. Half the audience stood rigidly while the first six bars of the National Anthem were played, frowning down their noses at the other half who were openly or surreptitiously gathering up bags and wraps and maneuvering for the assault on the exits. Then Hilary, hastily removing the traces of her shame under cover of blowing her nose, was shuffling with the rest of the galleryites towards the door. The warm illusions of Prospero's island faded as the air of the April night cooled her hot cheeks; she felt a sudden little thrill as she remembered that the reality of the future was just as exciting as the dream-world of the evening. Tomorrow would be the first day of her own holiday.

In a way tonight had been the beginning of the holiday, and a lovely beginning too. But tomorrow would see her setting out, rucksack on back, for the mountains of North Wales, free for at least one week of spring. No longer would she be Miss Bourne of Number Three Calculating Machine in the Inland Bank, Deansgate; no longer would harassed clerks come rushing up to her every five minutes demanding immediate and up-to-date "statements;" no longer would dull but kindly Aunt Emily, with whom she lived, cross-question her every evening until she had extracted the minutest details of the tiring day. These things would begin again when the week was over, of course—but one tried not to think of that. For seven days—no, eight, really—she would be just Hilary, living just where she liked and doing just what she wanted; which, respectively, were in a Welsh farmhouse and scrambling over the Welsh mountains. And—there would be Michael.

It was drizzling with rain when she came out of the theater into the shiny dark streets. But Hilary Bourne, sprinting for the nearest tram, told herself that not even the gifted Abercrombie Lewker could possibly have such a lovely holiday as hers was going to be. . . .

At that precise moment Mr. Lewker's holiday was being made the subject of a speech.

"We all feel we've earned our holiday, Filthy," the handsome Ferdinand was saying, "but we all recognize that but for you we might not have had the chance to earn it, and we hope you'll have—um—the holiday—er—the holiday you deserve."

He looked round the now modestly lit stage, where the Abercrombie Lewker Players were grouped in their glittering costumes, most of them with bottles of beer in their hands. There was a chorus of approval and a voice adjured him to carry on and stop fluffing. Thus encouraged, Ferdinand once more faced the object of his address, who with his ducal crown on back to front was opening his third bottle.

"We are given to understand," he went on, "that you intend to spend a week rock-climbing in the Lake District. Well, every man to his taste, but we do beg you to remember, in the course of your perilous ascents, that we'd hate to have to work with any other producer." (Laughter and applause, in the middle of which Miranda nudged the speaker fiercely and hissed "*His wife, fool!*") "Of course, in—er—in such a case we'd be only too glad to work under Mrs. Lewker, whose talents as producer would amply—ah—I mean—"

"Thank you," smiled the small, pleasant-faced woman in the robes of Ceres, curtsying elaborately beside her husband. "Cut the rest of that bit, Tony. It's getting late."

"Right-ho, Georgie. You know what I mean, and—and anyway, dash it all, here's luck to you, Filthy, and may our next season be more successful than—I mean, *even* more successful—"

At this point his efforts were mercifully drowned by a general outburst of *For He's a Jolly Good Fellow,* during which Mr. Lewker was hoisted on to Prospero's throne and urged to make a speech. Order having been obtained, he proceeded to do so.

"Fellow players," he boomed. " 'I thank you; I am not of many words, but I thank you'—*Much Ado,* Act 1, which we shall be playing next season. I am touched, deeply touched, by Tony's tribute hinging on the possibility of my decease in Cumberland. You appear, however, to be laboring under a misapprehension as to the dangers of the sport of mountaineering. The ignorance of the layman in this matter is astounding. If someone will get me a length of rope"—he stooped with some difficulty and placed his half-empty bottle of beer between his feet—"I will try to demonstrate how devoid of danger, how—in fact—exceedingly safe, is this much-maligned sport. Firstly, the theory of rock climbing—"

"I really don't think you'd better lecture tonight, darling," interrupted his wife. "We're all tired, and some of us are catching the early train tomorrow."

"Very well. At my wife's request I leave you in blighted ignorance. I will merely repeat, and this from the bottom of my heart, thank you. Have some more beer."

He descended from the throne amid loud acclamation, and having drained a fourth bottle of beer was led firmly away by his wife.

"It's a pity Tony can only speak rationally when he's declaiming someone else's lines," she remarked feelingly when they were alone in Lewker's dressing room. "Fancy talking about your getting killed in the Lakes—the idiot! You will be careful, though, won't you, Filthy dear?"

Mr. Lewker set down deliberately the cloth with which he had been swabbing the greasepaint from his heavy jowls.

"Mark me well," he requested. "What do you see? A middle-aged actor of some note, possessed of a fair round belly and a charming wife. Do I look like a man who proposes to risk his life on deeds of derring-do 'mid Cumberland's craggy crests? Observe the alliteration, but make no comment."

Georgina Lewker bent swiftly and imprinted a kiss on his bald head.

"I know, darling. But it's odd how when you and Gideon get together something exciting always seems to crop up. I believe you generate a sort of magnetic attraction for danger between you."

"Then," said her husband, "in Prospero's words, 'this rough magic I here abjure.' In any case, it was Gideon who used to run his red head into tight places. I only acted as extractor." He got up and began to soap his face in the washbasin, talking as he did so. "And Gideon's got a wife, too, with a baby on the way. One imagines that will have quite a demagnetizing effect on this danger attraction you speak of. We shall probably be so careful that only slopes of less than fifteen degrees will be climbed. After all, the main idea of the holiday is to escape from our wives."

"You told the reporter from *Stage and Screen* it was to renew your old acquaintance with the ageless hills."

Filthy waved the remark aside with his face towel.

"What one tells reporters is not evidence," he boomed. "This one had been unearthing the buried treasures of my past and discovered that long years ago I used to climb every season on the Chamonix Aiguilles. He had also been told of my projected climbing holiday in the Lakes. Fearing an article on 'Do Actors Make Daring Mountaineers,' I gave him a cigar and a modest statement which he took down verbatim. If he fails to print it verbatim I shall write to his paper accusing him of taking bribes."

"Well," said Georgie, sitting down and lighting a cigarette, "I sincerely hope no kidnappings or mysterious code-messages or murdered diplomats will turn up at—what's the name of the place?"

"Incredible as it may seem, Bramblethwaite Farm. I am unacquainted with it myself, and would have preferred to stay with my old friend Mrs. Morris of Dol Afon in North Wales, who makes the most satisfactory milk puddings I ever wallowed in. However, Gideon wanted the Lakes, and as you know I am nothing if not unselfish."

"Oh, I wouldn't call you nothing," returned his wife rudely. "But Bramblethwaite Farm does sound rather like something out of an old Aldwych farce—you know, Ralph Lynn chivvying intrusive fowls with an antimacassar while Tom Walls leers at the farmer's daughter."

Filthy threw off the robes of Prospero and began to put on his trousers.

"Our climbing holiday will probably be a bit of a farce if the weather forecast is anything to go by," he remarked. "While you are tramping strenuously over the South Downs with the Todds you can picture to yourself our First Act for a run of seven days. *'Scene: The parlor at Bramblethwaite Farm. Morning. Oak beams and a smell of sour milk and sheep dung. Grandfather clock L.C. strikes eleven and heavy rain is drumming on the window R.C. Enter Gideon Hazel. He crosses to window, looks out, and curses;*

picks up month-old "Farmer's and Stockbreeder's Gazette" from table and collapses into broken rocking chair R . Enter Abercrombie Lewker. He crosses to window, looks out, and curses; goes to horsehair sofa, L., lies down, and composes himself to slumber. Curtain.' "

Georgie laughed.

"I hope it won't be quite as bad as that," she said. "I don't mind your doing some nice easy rock climbs, but for goodness' sake hang a notice on the farm gates—No Murders, No Mysteries."

"My dear," observed Mr. Lewker, patting the top of her head indulgently, "I promise you I shall indulge in no perilous adventures, however tempting. You are all the excitement I need."

"I don't know whether that's really a compliment," smiled Georgie, "but I expect it's meant to be one." She got up from her chair. "Now I'm going to change and pack. You'd better take plenty of warm things with you in case it's cold, and at least two changes if you're going to get wet through every day—"

"My simple needs," interrupted her husband, "will go into one old rucksack, packed many a time and oft with such requisites. The rope, the boots, the tattered breeches smelling of bog myrtle and egg sandwich—ah, the dear dead days beyond recall:

"Bring me my boots, the old ones, heavy-nailed,
Worn with the fierce caresses of the rocks—"

A knock at the dressing-room door cut short his impassioned declamation. Georgie answered it.

"A telegram for you," she announced, returning. "A command to appear before Royalty, perhaps."

"Or before a magistrate for malfeasance," said Filthy, tearing open the envelope. "Or possibly—Georgie, listen to this. *'Sorry must cancel Lakes trip. Doctor says Althea's baby arriving next few days. Have not booked Bramblethwaite. Gideon.'* Great Aesculapius! I had no idea they still made mistakes about these things."

"Don't be absurd, Filthy," said Georgie abstractedly. "It isn't a mistake. It's just a fortnight early—it often happens." She frowned at the middle distance. "This rather alters things. I'd better phone the Todds at once to cancel my visit."

"Why, my dear? Don't tell me you're expecting a baby too."

"No, idiot! But Althea and I arranged months ago that I should stay with her when the time came."

"Oh. Do you think I should come with you to aid, comfort and support the apprehensive father?"

"I don't," said Georgie emphatically. "You'd only be in the way. But you can drive me down to Gideon's cottage, if you will. It's a pity about your holiday," she added.

"We are gratified by this belated sympathy," boomed Filthy coldly. "It is clear that this is yet another case of the young displaying lack of thought for their elders. My long-looked-for and hardly earned week is no more—butchered to make a storkish holiday. I feel—"

"What shall you do?" cut in his wife hurriedly. "Go to Cumberland by yourself?"

Mr. Lewker gazed meditatively at the telegram.

"I feel a providence in this," he declared. "Rough-hew them how I will, my ends are being shaped. Gideon hasn't booked at Bramblethwaite, and Bramblethwaite without his company does not appeal. Moreover, Gideon's cottage, to which I am to drive you tomorrow, is on the direct road to North Wales. My destiny and one of Mrs. Morris's large and creamy milk puddings seem irrevocably linked."

In plain English, you intend to stay at Dol Afon for a week instead. But suppose Mrs. Morris has no room?"

"Unlikely, at this time of year. And if I have to sleep in a barn, what is that, pray, to an old trouper?"

"Fleas and rheumatics," said Georgie succinctly. "But it's a good idea all the same. You won't be able to rock-climb without a partner,"

"Exactly. I shall spend my time, in all probability, either sucking where the bee sucks or walking tiptoe on the misty mountaintops."

"Or more probably," said his wife, " walking hotfoot to the nearest pub. But at least," she added contentedly, "I don't see how you can possibly get involved in any sort of trouble."

Mr. Lewker jabbed a playful finger into her well-covered ribs.

"Content you, dame," he boomed. "I am as a man apart, dedicated to holiday. Send me a telegram when the happy event eventuates, won't you?"

"I will," said Georgie.

CHAPTER TWO

Thou shalt be as free
As mountain winds.
THE TEMPEST

TO HILARY BOURNE, trudging along the London to Holyhead road in the gathering dusk, it seemed that the bliss of her first day of freedom had after all been "utility" material—it was wearing thin before its time.

Her rucksack had performed the usual miracle of doubling its weight between dawn and sunset; she had an incipient blister on her left heel; and the A5 road, where it leaves the tourist-haunted village of Bettws-y-coed to climb to the uplands round Capel Curig, provides a long unyielding hill which she was finding exceedingly trying to her tired leg muscles. She had missed the only bus, and the nine highway miles between Bettws and Ogwen would have to be done on foot. She had already walked fifteen miles.

There still remain a few eccentrics who regard fast travel as waste of time. Hilary was one of these. To flash past sunlit hills and fields in a train was, to her, as irritating as a feast of Tantalus. Her railway ticket would have taken her to Bettws-y-coed, for which she had to change at Llandudno Junction, and for the remainder of the journey she had proposed to catch the bus that runs over the pass of Nant Francon; but by the time she reached the Junction the innumerable brief glimpses of leaping lambs and snowy blackthorn had been too much for her, and she had decided to walk up the Conway valley to Bettws.

It had been a lovely walk, in spite of her untrained muscles and the hard highroad. But she had missed the bus. " Twenty-four miles will be a super training walk," she told herself bravely; and found herself wondering whether Michael would admire her energy or say she was crazy. A cynical small voice inside her remarked wearily that foot-slogging along a road was hardly the best training for mountain climbing and added that Michael would probably be entirely uninterested in her efforts. She would, it continued, be late for supper at the farm and too blistered to do any walking at all tomorrow. Hilary gritted her teeth angrily. This was not the mood for the gay highway. She trampled pessimism under her heavy boots and plodded on, humming a theme from the first movement of the Pastoral Symphony.

The clear sky of the morning had clouded over at sunset, and now it was a still gray evening with only the faintest breeze stirring the trees that hung above the road on their craggy hillsides. On Hilary's right hand the solemn voice of the Llugwy river sounded loudly from the narrow glen below the road. She had walked a little more than a mile from Bettws-y-coed—all uphill—when the higher note of a car engine separated itself from the roar of the stream. It was coming up the hill behind her. Should she try for a lift? No; she'd decided to walk, and walk she would.

But at the last minute, realizing that Michael might ask why she hadn't tried to hitchhike, she changed her mind. Stepping out into the road, she faced the oncoming vehicle and made the approved hitchhiking gesture with her thumb. The car, a large new saloon with every seat empty except the driver's, swept by disdainfully, and Hilary, resolving that to travel doggedly was better than to court further disappointment, renewed her twenty-four-mile decision. A second car, wheezing painfully up the hill in the wake of the first, did not even make her turn her head. It pulled up beside her, a large and very ancient open Wolseley, with a hatless gentleman at the wheel.

"I wonder," boomed the latter, somehow contriving to bow courteously from a sitting position, "whether you would assist me to cool my spleen by accepting a lift."

His massive bald head glimmered palely in the twilight. Hilary goggled incredulously. Those tufts of hair flanking the shining dome, that pouchy, bulbous-nosed face, those jowls worthy of a Roman emperor—it must be he.

"Let me explain," the man at the wheel hastened to add, misinterpreting her silence, "that I use the term 'spleen' in its symbolical or Shakespearean sense as the seat of envy and malice. I chanced to observe your appeal for aid and its ignoring by yon mannerless speed-fiend. The same churlish fellow, but half a minute earlier, passed me on a corner without sounding his horn and nearly took off my front mudwing. Doubtless my language blistered his paintwork, but it would afford me still greater satisfaction to remedy his bad manners. Therefore"—he flourished a massive paw—"allow me to place this automobile at your service."

Hilary found herself laughing and suddenly recollected herself.

"It's very kind of you," she said. "I'm sorry I stared so rudely, but you see it was only last night that I saw you as Prospero. You are Abercrombie Lewker, aren't you?"

"You were there?" exclaimed Mr. Lewker pleasedly. "What were your reactions? Did my conception of the last act satisfy your—but jump in, jump in," he interrupted himself, throwing open the near-side door. "We can converse as we go.

" 'Let us from hence, where we may leisurely
Each one demand, and answer to his part.'

"Dump your rucksack in the back seat."

Hilary obeyed, conscious of a little thrill of excitement. The day was going to end well after all. To ride in the car of a well-known actor, swapping opinions on the theater, was something of an adventure. Conversation proved to be impossible until the old car had been coaxed up through three speeds into the comparative silence of top.

"Pardon me," said Mr. Lewker then, "but are you, in current parlance, hiking?"

"No," said Hilary decisively. "I'm walking, or tramping if you like, but not hiking. I think it's a horrid word."

"I concur entirely. I see we shall get on together. Protagonists of the verb 'to hike' assure us it is a sound English word, but it is not in the standard dictionaries, nor does Shakespeare use it. Moreover, to hike or hoick is a not uncommon colloquialism in the sense of pulling or jerking something out of a tight place. Are you by any chance a schoolteacher?"

"No. I work a machine in a bank."

"Heaven be praised!" said Mr. Lewker fervently. "I hardly think I could have borne that. The world is too full of hearty females goading the young to a lifelong hatred of Shakespeare by forcing them to memorize irrelevant and bowdlerized passages from the plays. By the way, I deduce from your clinker-nailed boats that you are making for the mountains."

"Correct," smiled Hilary. "I'm going up to Ogwen for a week's holiday."

"A happy chance. I am doing exactly the same. Perhaps we shall meet again upon some friendly summit. You have my name—may I enquire yours?"

"I'm Hilary Bourne. I don't expect you've heard of me, but Myfanwy Todd's my cousin, and she's told me quite a lot about your adventures in the Secret Service."

"Has she now?" observed her companion with some disapproval. "Woman, thy name is indiscretion! However," he added, "so long as I am not expected to behave like a secret agent I am delighted to meet a cousin of Myfanwy's."

He disengaged a hand from the wheel and held it out gravely. Hilary shook it and let go hurriedly as a herd of cows appeared out of the dusk, crossing the road in front of the car. The Wolseley came to a standstill with a groan of brakes, and panted impatiently as the slow procession passed in front of its bonnet. A farmhand brought up the rear, to be greeted with a booming "*Nos da!*" from Mr. Lewker.

"Good evening," returned the man briefly, and disappeared into the shadows.

"It is extremely odd," remarked the actor as he let in his clutch, "how they always know I am not a Welshman."

"Do you speak Welsh?" asked Hilary.

"Four phrases—good night, good morning, good ale and thank you. But I am assured that my accent is perfect. Speaking of good ale, by the way, it was my intention to pause for five minutes at the Tyn-y-coed Hotel in Capel Curig for a draught of the same. If you would honor me with your company—but I am forgetting. I do not know how far our ways lie together."

"It's kind of you, but—wouldn't it be rather—well, unladylike?" ventured Hilary, who had been strictly brought up. "The place I'm going to," she went on, "is a farm called Dol Afon, and—what's the matter?"

Mr. Lewker had made a slight noise in his throat. "I have just," he explained, "saved myself from infringing the copyright of the man who said 'the world is a small place.' You see, I'm staying at Dol Afon too, if Mrs. Morris can put me up."

"That's great!" exclaimed Hilary with enthusiasm. "But—haven't you booked with Mrs. Morris?" she added doubtfully.

"No. She often puts ten people up at Dol Afon—I suspect the Morris family hook their toes over the rafters o' nights and sleep upside down like bats—and at this time of year I hardly think she will have all her rooms occupied."

"I don't want to discourage you," Hilary said, but there'll be at least eight people staying at Dol Afon, including me. It's a kind of party, run by Uncle George—the Reverend George Jupp, I mean."

"Your uncle?"

"No, but everybody calls him that. He and Professor Ferriday—I expect you've heard of their climbs years ago, in the Caucasus—make up this party every year between Easter and Whit. Just themselves and four or five younger folk, mostly climbers, and Aunt Mabel—that's the Reverend's wife—to mother the party and mend the socks. I was staying at Dol Afon last year when they turned up and they invited me again this year. The farm'll be pretty full, you see. Oh, I do hope nobody else has joined the party, so that there'll be room for you!"

"I am gratified," boomed Mr. Lewker, swerving violently to avoid a sheep that rose like a wraith from behind a roadside bush. "I feel, however, that a solitary butter-in would spoil your party. Perhaps it would be better if I tried Ogwen Cottage, or—"

"Oh, no!" Hilary was genuinely concerned. "I didn't mean to give you that impression. Of course you'd be welcome. I remember Uncle George mentioning a first ascent of yours to us last year, something frightfully difficult in the Alps, on the Mer de Glace face of the Charmoz I think it was, and he'd just love to yarn about it with you."

Mr. Lewker chuckled and darted a shrewd glance at the girl beside him.

"My dear, that was twenty-five years ago," he said. "I doubt whether Uncle George would really be interested. Are you sure you are not being unduly influenced by the pleasant anticipation of introducing to your party an actor—ahem—of some small fame?"

Hilary felt herself blushing and was thankful for the twilight.

"Well, I was thinking it would make them sit up," she said, a little defiantly, "but it really wasn't only that. I think you're rather nice and I'd got an idea we'd be friends. Of course, if you rather go on to Ogwen

Cottage—and Uncle George's gang are rather a funny lot in some ways—"

"Now don't get angry," said her companion soothingly. " If I have to sleep in the cowshed, still I'll lodge with Mrs. Morris this night, a martyr to my fatal attraction for charming girls with brown eyes and *retroussée* noses. I must warn you, however, that I am married already."

"When I marry," Hilary retorted swiftly, "it'll be somebody honest, a man who can't act."

Mr. Lewker emitted a bass chuckle.

"Bigamy, eh?" said he; and added hurriedly: "Consider my remark unsaid. That will leave you with the last word and we can cease this repartee. I always pause here when I am driving into Wales, to pay my respects to the Doorkeeper."

With this cryptic observation he applied the brakes and the Wolseley groaned to a standstill at the side of the road. Her owner switched off the engine, and he and Hilary sat silently looking up the tall bulk of mountain that loomed over them.

They had reached the sharp corner just before Capel Curig where the softer prettinesses of the Bettws Vale are left behind, and the Holyhead Road enters the precincts of the giants of Snowdonia. A dark shoulder of Hill swooped down on the right of the road; on the left the river flashed palely in the gloaming. In front roared the fine peak of Moel Siabod, heaved against the darkening sky like the head of an alert sentinel peering down at them. A thin cool breeze moved the close airs of the valley, and Hilary, with a little thrill of delight, sniffed the indefinable smell of mountains. Not for the first time she tried to analyze that faint emanation, an aura rather than an aroma, that is the very soul of the hills.

"Peat, sheep, wet rock and a soupcon of bog myrtle, I think," said Lewker, unexpectedly reading her thoughts; "but the main ingredient is the smell of freedom. I once met Jan Masaryk, and his presence carried with it that same mysterious exhalation. It was like being lifted to a mountaintop to talk with him. But this, you will say, piles fancy on whimsy. Or do you concur with my Doorkeeper conceit?"

"Of course I do," said Hilary. "I've always thought Siabod was a sort of outpost of the enchanted lands. Once round the next corner we're over the frontier—we've escaped from—from banks, and pavements, and—"

" 'From the dictatorship of the daily round,' " boomed the actor with enthusiasm, " 'from the Ogpu of Gossip and the concentration camp of Convention—' "

" To 'solace ourselves with the good of these Delectable Mountains,'" finished Hilary, quoting inspiredly.

The two looked at each other with respect.

"You know," said Lewker gravely, "we ought to go on the halls. Lewker and Bourne, in their celebrated poetic patter act. A sob, a smile, and a quotation." He pressed the starter and the old car shook itself into motion. "One thing is certain. We must celebrate briefly in the Tyn-y-coed. It is now twenty minutes past eight. What time is Mrs. Morris's supper?"

"Nine, usually. But—"

"We can spare five minutes, then. And if you still feel the chains of convention restraining you from entering a public bar with a stranger thirty years older than yourself, I'd better adopt you as a niece. Uncle Filthy to you, niece Hilary."

"Thank you," laughed the girl. "But you're not venerable enough for an uncle. I shall call you Filthy, if you won't think it's rude or forward."

"Excellent. And here's our hostelry. Fifteen minutes' drive to Dol Afon." He pulled up opposite a pleasant hotel from whose leaded panes a welcoming light shone through the dusk. " While we quench our thirst, perhaps you will prime me as to the persons I am to meet at supper—that is, assuming Mrs. Morris will take me in."

They crossed the road and entered a cozy little bar whose roughly plastered walls were hung with faded political cartoons. Hilary found it pleasant to have her request for a grapefruit drink translated into an order without comment; most of the young men she knew would have spent some minutes pouring jocular contempt on her choice and urging her, with fearful manliness, to have something stronger. While Lewker was wheedling a pint tankard for his beer out of the pleasant-faced lady behind the bar Hilary glanced at the other three occupants of the little room. Two of them were shepherds, talking in low singsong voices over their pipes of shag in a corner. The third was a very thin young man in spectacles and voluminous shorts, drinking beer without apparent enjoyment; his thin lips, thought Hilary, had a bitter and vindictive twist to them. A tremendous rucksack rested on the floor beside him, and the ends of a sectional bamboo tentpole protruded from one of the pockets.

Her attention returned to her escort, who was now approaching with a tankard in one hand and a glass of grapefruit squash in the other. Either some magic of the stage or his own fine acting must have been responsible for last night's dignified and statuesque Prospero, for the leader of the Abercrombie Lewker Players was certainly not more than five and a half feet in height, and so broad that he looked almost squat, an appearance which an old and baggy tweed suit inclined to emphasize. His odd but genial features relaxed into an extremely wide grin as he set his burdens down unspilled and lowered himself into a chair beside Hilary's.

"With my first sip," he announced, "representing that portion of my money which actually pays for this beer, I propose to drink a toast. The remaining and much larger portion, representing an involuntary but graceful donation to the Exchequer, I shall consume more slowly while you gossip. The toast is to our escape to freedom and better acquaintance."

"Also to a week of fine weather," supplemented Hilary, raising her glass.

They drank ceremoniously. Then, when Hilary had refused one of Filthy's cigarettes and granted his polite request for permission to light up, the actor opened the matter of the party into which it seemed that he, a stranger, was to be catapulted; for at Dol Afon meals are taken in a small dark parlor which barely contains the dining table, and any sort of aloofness is a practical impossibility.

"The Professor Ferriday you mentioned," he said, "is presumably the scientist whose name has been prominent in the newspapers lately. Headline—Weapon To Beat Atomic Bomb, query."

"He is," Hilary nodded. "But if I'm to describe the whole Dol Afon party I'll just have to begin with Uncle George. It's very much his party, you see. He's sixty-something, but still frightfully hearty. Michael—someone I know—once said he's a survival from the Edward Whymper Age. Then there's Aunt Mabel—his wife, you know—who sort of mothers the party. Quiet and always knitting and rather nice. Professor Ferriday looks older than Uncle George, but he's really the same age and still does a bit of climbing. That's all the elders."

"Unto which group I may shortly be added. What about the youngers?"

"Well, there's Mildred Jupp, that's Uncle George's daughter. She's older than me and rather a good rock climber. She develops terrific passions for things, and Aunt Mabel says just now it's foreign missions."

"That would please her father, I suppose," murmured Lewker.

"I don't know. He hates people to talk about religion. Cousin Harold—Mildred's brother—will be there. He's a frightfully keen botanist and often pushes off by himself."

"He is not a rock climber, then?"

"Heavens, yes! All the Jupps have to be mountaineers, by order of the Reverend George. Even Aunt Mabel had to when she was younger, but she's got a gammy leg now. Harold just can't work up any enthusiasm about it, and says rock climbers denude the crags of rare plants, which makes Uncle George wild. I sympathize with Harold rather."

Filthy took his nose out of his tankard and frowned at her. "It sounds as though you disapprove of the climber's sport," he remarked.

"Well, I don't," returned Hilary. " But I haven't done any climbing with the rope yet. I expect I'll do my first climb this week. I want to be an all-round mountaineer, you see, and that means knowing my stuff on rocks as well as on snow and ice, but I don't intend to be fanatical about it like some people. Where was I?"

"*En famille* Jupp. With the professor and yourself, that makes six of the party. Two more to come."

"Oh, yes. Professor Ferriday is bringing two young men who help him in his research laboratory. One of them I haven't met, but he's supposed to be awfully clever—writes books and edits a very advanced magazine, as well as being a brilliant chemist. Aunt Mabel did tell me his name. Caw something. Caulfield—no, Cauthery."

At this point there was a spluttering noise from an adjacent table. Hilary looked round. The spectacled young man appeared to have choked on his beer. His watering eyes met Hilary's over the folds of the handkerchief with which he was stifling his paroxysm, and she had a fleeting impression of some strong but indefinable emotion reflected in them behind those powerful lenses. Then he looked quickly away and continued his mopping-up operations with his back to her.

"Seven," Filthy was saying. "Who is the eighth Jupp protégé?"

Hilary hesitated and was annoyed to feet herself blushing.

"Michael—Michael Rouse," she said hurriedly. "He's Professor Ferriday's assistant, too."

"Young and brilliant, I take it?" Filthy's keen little eyes noted the blush.

"Well, he's quite clever. You have to be, in his job. And he's awfully keen on mountains. He's the one—probably—who'll take me up a rock climb. At least, he said he would."

"A most fortunate young man," observed the actor. He drained his tankard and set it down. "Thank you. You have a natural gift for condensed description. I feel I know the members of your party already. Science and Religion seem to be strongly represented, but you and I will uphold the Arts."

"Not I," laughed Hilary. "I shall represent Finance—the bank, you know."

"Ah—I had forgotten. But I shall expect you to support me at dinner-table discussions nonetheless. Would you like another drink?"

"No, thanks. And if we're going to be in time for supper—"

"You are right, as usual. *Allons.*"

They got up, Mr. Lewker bade the bar a general good night (to which all but the spectacled young man responded) and they went out to the car.

"Did you notice the man in glasses?" asked Hilary as soon as top gear made conversation possible.

"I did. 'The lean and hungry look' well exemplified. What about him?"

"Well, he started to choke just after I mentioned the name of Cauthery, and when I looked at him he had an awfully queer expression."

"The beer of today," murmured Filthy, "would strain the self-control of any but a Stoic philosopher. Our friend had not the face of a philosopher."

"But I'm sure it was the name that upset him."

"Perhaps he was burned when a child and thought you said 'cautery.' "

Hilary laughed and instantly forgot the incident, for away on their left the Capel Curig lakes glimmered faintly under the black hill-slopes, and dark though it was the dim outlines of Lliwedd and Snowdon and Crib Goch, distant but unmistakable, rose beyond at the head of the dusk-filled valley. Another minute and they were past the turn that leads to Beddgelert and the sea and climbing the wild vale of the Llugwy, mounting into a region of treeless moorland between huge dark mountain shapes, where the hill-wind sighed past their ears bearing a peaty fragrance. No other of the great highways of England and Wales runs so close to the heart of the high hills as A5, or can show a sight comparable to the abrupt and triple-peaked Tryfan which towers suddenly ahead. Tonight it was a humped black silhouette, but no less exciting to the two mountain-lovers in the ancient Wolseley.

Tryfan loomed almost overhead, and the waters of Ogwen lake were not far in front, when Lewker turned off the road on to a bumpy track leading up to the right. Some two hundred yards from the highway a long low farmhouse winked its lit windows at them between the trunks of half a dozen pines: Dol Afon.

Five minutes later Mrs. Morris, bosomy and dishevelled as always, was shrieking her delight at seeing Mr. Lewker again, protesting that she had a "*luff*-ly room" for him, and assuring him that milk puddings would be frequently on her menu. Supper, she added, was due in ten minutes.

In ten minutes, thought Hilary, as she washed and did her hair by oil-lamplight in the little bedroom under the eaves, this lovely first day would be at its loveliest. In ten minutes she would be sitting at the same table as Michael.

CHAPTER THREE

When we were boys
Who would believe that there were mountaineers
Dewlapp'd like bulls . . .

THE TEMPEST

"CHEESE!" roared the Reverend George Jupp from the head of the table. "Anyone say cheese? Yes? No?"

" I think I might manage a little," piped the dry thin voice of Professor Ferriday.

"No 'mite' about this cheese, Ferry," shouted Uncle George as he passed the cheese dish; and the rest of the party, with one exception, laughed spontaneously or dutifully according to their personal reactions to puns. The exception, as Mr. Abercrombie Lewker observed, was the young man who had been introduced to him as Raymond Cauthery.

Roast mutton and unlimited vegetables had been succeeded by a gigantic milk pudding, and now the nine people, crowded round the oval table that all but filled Mrs. Morris's snug lamp-lit parlor, were replete and less inclined to respond to Uncle George's inextinguishable uproariousness than they had been at the beginning of the meal. Cigarettes and pipes were being produced, and while the business of lighting-up was in progress Lewker, from his place at the big clergyman's right hand, sent his amused but unobtrusive glance round the circle of his new acquaintances, their cheerful faces softly lit by the big oil lamp that occupied the center of the table.

Uncle George—everybody called him that, he was so obviously avuncular—was easily the most striking figure in the room, with his great limbs and massive, handsome head. Though his mane of silver-gray hair, and the bristling beard that rose to his red wrinkled apple cheeks proclaimed that he was past the prime of life, his great shoulders were unbowed and he possessed (and perhaps rather cultivated) the high spirits of a schoolboy. He it was who had welcomed Hilary's intruding actor with such boisterous good will that the latter had been conscious of a feeling that Uncle George had somehow become his host; and though the installing of the newcomer at the clergyman's right hand had been done with noisy geniality it was plain that Uncle George considered himself to be according a privilege. His wife on his other side, was a small and compact lady with silvering hair and a firm, humorous mouth. Filthy suspected that Aunt Mabel could curb her husband's rowdy heartiness with a look if she so desired, but had decided to allow him unrestricted fun during his holiday.

On Lewker's right sat Mildred Jupp, large of frame like her father but by no means unattractive. She had talked intelligently enough about mountaineering during the first part of the meal, but had somehow managed to switch the conversation on to drama and its relation to the conversation of the natives of the Solomons, a subject on which she contrived to be extremely boring. Beyond her sat a large and very silent young man with red hair—Michael Rouse—and next to him, at the foot of the table facing his old climbing partner George Jupp, was Professor Ferriday, a small, thin, wrinkled man of a precise manner of speech whose dry twinkling humor was in marked contrast with Uncle George's boyish jests.

Hilary Bourne, on the other side of the table from Lewker, had on one hand the large spectacles and serious mien of Harold Jupp, a round-faced youth of nineteen who bore more resemblance to his mother than to the Reverend George; and, on her right hand, Raymond Cauthery. Unlike Professor Ferriday's other assistant, whose square countenance was somewhat stolid and homely under its fiery thatch, Cauthery looked the part of the brilliant young scientist. Had it not been for the sneer that seemed always to be lurking at the comers of his sensual mouth his dark face would have been almost phenomenally handsome. It needed no very keen observer to see that here was a young man with an exceedingly high opinion of himself which he did not trouble to conceal. Nor did Mr. Lewker fail to notice that Cauthery, ignoring the sallies of Uncle George, devoted his attention throughout the meal to Hilary, who was looking extremely pretty in a yellow woolen sweater. The actor had a vague impression that Mildred Jupp's determined flow of missionary conversation had increased with the obvious ripening of this intimacy. His wandering attention was at this point recalled to Uncle George by a hearty roar from the latter.

"Well, now, everybody! What's the program for tomorrow? Who's for a climb, eh? What about the whole party on Pinnacle Rib?"

"Having regard to the untrained muscles of most of us," observed the professor dryly, "a mild scramble or training walk would, I think, be advisable."

"Oh, nonsense, Ferry," shouted Uncle George. "Didn't you and I get off the train at Chamonix in '37 and climb the Petit Clocher for our first day? What's your idea, Lewker?"

"Speaking for myself," boomed that gentleman, "and with the consciousness of my 'too, too solid flesh' upon me, I cast my vote for a training walk."

"Very sensible, Mr. Lewker," Mrs. Jupp's quiet voice put in. "I'm sure it's much wiser to begin gradually. And Hilary hasn't climbed on the rope before—have you, my dear?"

"No, Aunt Mabel. But of course I want to, some time this week—not the first day, though."

Uncle George wagged his head in humorous despair.

"Well, all I can say is—"

"Rouse and I are in pretty good form," interrupted Raymond Cauthery, his loud and rather affected voice cutting easily across the clergyman's grumbling. "We intend to do Terrace Wall Variant if the rock's dry. Damned nice climb." He turned to Hilary, leaning over her possessively and showing very white teeth. "Will you come on our rope? I'd like you to—very much."

Lewker was suddenly conscious of an unexplained tension in the air. Mildred Jupp, at his side, had gone very red and her father was frowning. Hilary hesitated.

"If you think I'd manage—" she began.

"You wouldn't," said Michael Rouse briefly and unexpectedly. It was the first time he had spoken in five minutes. "Terrace Wall's no place for a novice, Cauthery. Thought Mildred was climbing with us."

Cauthery ignored this last sentence.

"I have a theory," he drawled, speaking to the table at large, "that the beginner on rocks should be taken up a Severe for his or her first climb. In the hands of a sound climber like Rouse or myself she would be perfectly safe, and one might thus discover a natural aptitude for steep rocks—no need to go through the dull old round of Milestone Buttress, North Buttress and all the rest." He flashed a smile at Hilary. "You look as though you'd make a very pretty climber and prove my theory."

"Well"—Harold Jupp's slow and stodgy voice took up the argument—"if you ask me, it's a pretty fat-headed theory. You don't make a kid a good swimmer by chucking him into the deep end for his first effort. I'm jiggered if I'd let you tow me up Terrace Wall. I started on Milestone Buttress, and—"

"And look what an expert you are now," smiled Cauthery.

Harold flushed slightly. "I'll never be as good a climber as you, if that's what you mean," he said stolidly. "My nerves aren't strong enough and I'm keener on other things. But I still say your theory's bunk."

Hilary, who had been listening with a slightly puzzled air, decided to put in her oar.

"I know I'm frightfully ignorant," she said, "but I'm not quite clear what the argument's about. What exactly is a *'Severe'?*"

"Here, Ferry," vociferated Uncle George, who had been silent for longer than usual and felt it was time he took charge again, "you're the feller for putting things in the proverbial nutshell. Explain about climbing standards for the lady."

Professor Ferriday raised a clawlike hand to his mouth and removed his cigarette. His thin angular face with the parchment-like skin drawn tightly over its bones might have been the face of a well-preserved mummy, but his little black eyes were sharp and lively.

"Very well, George," he said in his precise high tones. "Let us take as example, Miss Hilary, the peak nearest to this farm—Tryfan. As you know, rock climbers have pursued their sport on the crags of Tryfan—the rock, by the by, is constituted of three lava flows parted by marine shales—since I was a babe in arms. There is no real need to calculate how long ago that was."

Hilary, taking this to be humorously intended, smiled and said: "I don't calculate on holiday anyway."

"Most wise of you," said the professor gravely, with an odd little bob of his head. "Today," he continued, "there are in the neighborhood of seventy different climbing routes on this one mountain, some very hard and some easy, so that each may choose according to his energy or skill. *Non omnia possumus omnes*"

"Likewise, *medio tutissimus ibis.* Get on, you old pedant," said Uncle George with a guffaw.

"All these routes," the professor resumed unmoved, "have been recorded and described in detail in a series of climbing guidebooks, where you will find the climbs graded into five main standards of difficulty—Moderate, Difficult, Very Difficult, Severe and Very Severe. A climb of Moderate standard, such as the ordinary route up the Milestone Buttress, could, I think, be done by almost any athletic person possessing the normal complement of prehensile members—"

"Steady on, old feller," from Uncle George.

"—whereas routes of Very Difficult standard and above can as a rule only be safely climbed by those who have mastered at least part of the technique of advanced rock climbing."

"I see," said Hilary as he paused; but the professor had not finished.

"I may add," he went on, "that as the chief onus of the climb rests upon the leader, the man who climbs first on the rope, it is possible for a novice to be towed up—I borrow the phrase from my young friend here—to be towed up a hard rock climb, just as an incompetent person is frequently taken up the Matterhorn by a pair of good guides. But you would do better, Miss Hilary, to begin with the Milestone Buttress."

Raymond Cauthery turned to the girl with the possessive air that Filthy found increasingly irritating.

"That," he drawled, "is of course just an opinion. It isn't mine." He flashed his brilliant and not wholly pleasant smile at his chief. "The prof and I have our little differences," he said.

Professor Ferriday quirked his thin lips humorously and made no reply; but it seemed to Lewker that a glance of understanding, or something more potent, passed between them.

"All the same," Hilary was saying a trifle uncomfortably, "I think I shall take the professor's advice and start with Milestone Buttress. And I'd rather like a mountain walk tomorrow. It was nice of you to ask me, though," she added, smiling charmingly at Cauthery.

Michael Rouse struck a match with unnecessary violence and applied it to the large pipe he held between his teeth. Uncle George tapped out the ashes of his pipe (which was, of course, old, blackened and briar) on to a dinner plate and was quietly but effectively reprimanded by his wife.

"Call yourselves climbers!" he jeered playfully when he had obediently tipped the mess into the fireplace. "Rouse and Cauthery seem to be the only two worthy of the name. I suppose you'll go weeding as usual, Harold?"

"Yes, father," said Harold with well-concealed tolerance.

"Hum. Well, I may be a decrepit old buffer, but I'm fit for Pinnacle Rib, if anyone—"

"I'll climb with you, father," Mildred Jupp said quickly. Her large-featured but handsome face had recovered its normal coloring, but the observant Filthy noticed that she avoided looking at Cauthery and Hilary.

"Up, the Jupps!" Cauthery remarked with his flashing smile, and Uncle George looked annoyed.

Aunt Mabel laid hand on the small bell that stood on the table.

"Then *that's* all settled," she said firmly. " Four to climb tomorrow and four to walk, and I shall go out and do some sketching—if it's fine. Now I'm sure Gwennie Morris is waiting to clear away, so if you've all quite finished—" She rang the bell loudly and turned to Lewker. "I expect you remember Gwennie, Mr. Lewker, Mrs. Morris's younger daughter. She was down the valley at Bethesda when we arrived this evening—her young man lives there—but she'll be back by now. A great help to her mother since Sarah, the elder daughter, got married—"

Here the parlor door opened and a pretty Welsh girl, rosy and smiling, stood in the doorway with a tray in her hands. A general chorus of "Good evening, Gwennie!" greeted her from the party, who were engaged in struggling round the cramped space between table and wall; but Gwennie Morris, suddenly rigid, had eyes for only one of them. Her gaze fastened itself on Raymond Cauthery, and a swift wave of color flooded neck and checks to subside, leaving her pale and wide-eyed. She had rather fine eyes, noted Lewker, and further remarked to himself that girls seemed curiously prone to change color when in the vicinity of young Mr. Cauthery. Raymond, however, showed not the slightest sign of perturbation.

"Hello, Gwennie," he drawled, and his cool voice broke what threatened to become an awkward silence. "Nice to see you again."

Composure and the power of movement seemed to return to the girl simultaneously.

" Yes, sir," she said quietly. She picked up a pile of plates which the orderly Mrs. Jupp had stacked ready and placing them on her tray went unhurriedly out of the room.

"Pleasant girl, that," Cauthery remarked carelessly to the company at large. "Intelligent, too. We got quite friendly—when I was staying here last August."

"She seemed surprised to see you," said Mildred expressionlessly.

"Perhaps." The tone was casual, but Lewker saw the self-assured, almost swaggering, glance that dwelt first on Mildred and then, less lightly, on Hilary; and felt his mild distaste for Raymond Cauthery transformed into an earnest desire to kick him.

One by one the guests squeezed between the chairs nearest the door and an immense oak dresser laden with china dogs and tinted photographs in fretwork frames and emerged into the stone-flagged passage at the farther end of which was the farm kitchen. On the right a door opened into the sitting-room—the "parlor" at Dol Afon was used solely for visitors' meals—and halfway along on the left of the passage was the short hallway leading to the front door. From the latter direction came Uncle George's enthusiastic roar informing all and sundry that it was a magnificent night and the moonlight on Tryfan was a jolly fine sight which nobody must miss. Filthy, for whom the firelight glow issuing from the sitting-room door was at the moment a finer and more inviting sight, was about to follow Mrs. Jupp and Harold into that haven when Cauthery's drawl came from just ahead of him.

"Let's go and inspect this so notable moonlight."

It was difficult to see, in the gloom of the passage, who was in front of him, but Lewker had no doubt that the invitation was addressed to Hilary. He decided, somewhat vindictively, to disappoint Mr. Cauthery.

"An excellent plan," he boomed before the girl could reply. "Are you with us, Hilary?"

"I'm going to help Gwennie with the washing-up," she replied, with laughter in her voice. "I haven't seen her since this time last year, and I rather like her. I'll come out later."

She went down the passage towards the kitchen, leaving Cauthery and Lewker to escort each other in silence out of the front door. The night air was cool and fragrant of uplands in spring. Towering over the feathered blackness of the pines that stood along the wall of the farm garden the dark bulk of Tryfan rose, with a star perched upon its topmost peak. The moon, peering between dim layers of cloud above the eastward humps of the Glyder range, edged with faint gold the great crags of the East Face. It was a noble sight, and Uncle George, gesticulating in the meadow just outside the garden gate, was enthusing loudly to an audience consisting of the professor, Mildred and Michael Rouse. The two halted at a safe distance from the orator. Cauthery, evidently making the best of a bad job, opened the conversation.

"I saw your *Lear* last autumn," he announced with a certain condescension. "A very creditable production. In fact, I wrote a favorable notice of it for my review, *Postcript*. Perhaps you saw it?"

"My wife reads all the reviews," returned the actor. "I cannot recall yours. Is it a quarterly?"

"A monthly now." Cauthery's tone indicated mild surprise at his companion's ignorance. "Anti-Socialist and pro-Intelligentsia. I'm an Aristo, you know."

"I'm afraid I don't quite—"

The other's drawl sharpened impatiently.

"The new party. We believe the future of society lies in a recrudescence of Class, in a return to a subservient laboring class with a ruling aristocracy. You don't agree?"

"Isn't it a little—reactionary?" said Filthy cautiously.

"A reactionary is the mob's name for the man with courage enough not to run with them. The decline of this country began with the weakening of the ruling aristocracy, as you can see by looking at even a Socialist history book. We need an aristocracy of birth—those born to lead—and brains—science and the arts. As a protagonist of the dramatic art you ought to be interested."

"Oh, I am," Mr. Lewker assured him. And indeed in spite of being talked to like a public meeting in this moonlit garden he was finding the self-assured Cauthery sufficiently entertaining.

"The more intelligent are not hard to convert," pursued that young man loftily. "One would of course expect that. I was for some time a member of the Communist Party myself, by the way, and it was from the Communist doctrine that my concept of Aristoism first sprang."

He paused, and Filthy made the invited remark that the two seemed hardly compatible.

"They aren't. But the Communists exist by their belief in the reality of the class war which the rest of us deny. They're eternally harping on the battle between the horny-handed morons and the intelligent overmen—they don't put it like that, of course. And they're right. The battle's on and the morons, though not the Communist variety, have gained a measure of power. Hence the present mess. I and the Aristos consider that the hope of civilization lies in the victory of the overmen. That's what the *Postcript* preaches. But perhaps you aren't impressed by all this."

"What impresses me," said Filthy evasively, "is wonder at your managing to find time for these political activities when you are also—as I am told—a scientist working on important experiments in Professor Ferriday's laboratories."

"One must vary one's occupations," returned the other airily. He flung away the stub of his cigarette, a tiny meteor drawing a red parabola across the dark of the garden. "The kind of scientific work I'm doing inevitably leads one to consideration of its political repercussions." He stopped short, as though he had said more than he intended, and abruptly changed the subject. "Have you known Hilary Bourne long?"

Before Filthy could reply Uncle George and his audience came in through the garden gate. Professor Ferriday's piping voice was raised in argument.

"I'm still convinced, George, that it is impossible to see the Gashed Crag from here."

"Now you'll jolly well look again, Ferry. See where my finger's pointing? To the left of that patch of moonlight—"

The group paused by the gate to settle the point. Mildred Jupp detached herself and came up the path to where Lewker and Cauthery were standing.

"That's you, isn't it, Ray?" she said in a curious tone. "I suppose you don't mind my climbing with father tomorrow?"

"Why on earth should I?" he drawled. "If you can stand it, Milly, I can."

It was too dark to see the expression on the girl's face. She seemed to hold herself poised and rigid for a moment; then she turned without a word and hurried into the house.

"A-mazing!" roared Uncle George jocularly, approaching with a hand on the professor's shoulder. "Even our scientist deigns to admire the moonlight. Jolly fine, isn't it, Lewker? In you go, Ferry."

He hustled the slight figure of his friend boisterously in through the front door. The silent Rouse followed, but put his head out a second later to demand where Cauthery had put the Tryfan guidebook.

"I'll get it for you," drawled Cauthery, and strolled in without apology, leaving Lewker to his own devices.

The actor walked to the garden gate and leaned on it meditatively, his eyes on the blank black outlines of the hills. The moon had tucked herself under a blanket of cloud, and the giant shapes that ringed the marshy Ogwen valley had taken on a quality of brooding, of secretiveness. Mr. Lewker reflected rather ruefully that the peaceful solitude he had forecast to his wife was no longer in prospect. Uncle George's "frightfully hearty" invitation to join up with the Dol Afon party could hardly be refused. Not that he disliked the company of his fellows; they seemed a pleasant, ordinary crowd (with the exception of Raymond Cauthery) and the small emotional disturbances he had observed at the supper table all seemed to derive from the annoying Cauthery who also appeared to have made an impression on Hilary.

Filthy was idly wondering whether Science would suffer an irreparable loss if he were to push the self-assured apostle of Aristoism off the top of Tryfan when light footsteps sounded on the path behind him.

"Oh—has everyone gone in?" said Hilary breathlessly.

"Let me draw your attention," boomed Mr. Lewker with dignity, "to the fact that I am still here."

"Of course I didn't mean—you're just being absurd." She leaned beside him on the gate. "Isn't it lovely, being here?"

"Every prospect pleases, certainly. Did you enjoy your chat with Gwennie?"

" Ye-es. She's changed though—I suppose it's being engaged. Derwen Jones, that's her fiance, works on the farm here, and he's studying to be a veterinary surgeon, He lives in Bethesda, but he's going to sleep in one of the barns all this week because of the lambing. I saw him. He's tall, with red hair like—like Michael, but he talks more."

"That would not be difficult," observed Filthy. "Your Mr. Rouse seems remarkably taciturn."

"He's not my Mr. Rouse," said Hilary. She gazed at the dark hills for a little. Then she said: "Mr. Lewker. What d'you think of Raymond Cauthery?"

"I cannot be confidential under that title, Miss Bourne."

"Well, Filthy, then—though it sounds frightfully rude. What do you think of him?"

"He displayed an intelligent appreciation of my production of *King Lear,*" replied Lewker carefully. "What is your own opinion of him?"

Hilary shuffled her feet on the flagstones of the path. "Oh, well, he's awfully confident and sort of sarcastic, of course. But he's frightfully attractive, isn't he?"

"It would appear so. Am I wrong in assuming an attachment between him and Miss Jupp?"

"N—no, I don't think you're wrong. Uncle George expects them to get engaged soon," she added in a rush. "Harold told me."

"Hum," said Filthy noncommittally. "Shall we go in? The night grows cold."

They went towards the house. Lights glowed in three of the upstairs windows.

"Someone's going to bed early," said Hilary, " and so am I. I want to go for a walk before breakfast."

In the sitting room Uncle George and the professor were playing draughts by lamplight at the table while Michael Rouse sat hunched over a book by the embers of the wood fire. Lewker decided to follow the example of the majority, and having exchanged good nights with the three, groped his way up creaking stairs to his small bedroom at the back of the farmhouse.

He had blown out his candle and was composing himself to sleep between stiff clean-smelling sheets when he became aware of a low murmur of voices below his window, which looked out above a small kitchen garden separating the farmhouse from the yard and outbuildings. No words were audible, but one of the voices was unmistakably Cauthery's; the other was a woman's.

Filthy shrugged and pulled the sheets over his ears. Three minutes later he started into broad wakefulness. A new voice had joined the others, and low-pitched as it vas it sounded tense and hoarse with anger—a man's voice. He got out of bed and going to the window cautiously put out his head.

There was nothing to be seen, but words came up to him in a furious whisper which had the singsong intonation that only a Welshman could give it.

"—and if I catch you fooling round Gwennie again, mister, same as you did last harvest—*diawl*, I'll knock the life out of you!"

A short pause. Then Cauthery's laugh, low and scornful. Footsteps moved away in different directions. The kitchen garden was silent once more.

Mr. Lewker drew in his head and climbed thoughtfully into bed again.

CHAPTER FOUR

Thy turfy mountains, where live
nibbling sheep.

THE TEMPEST

THE BARKING of a dog, distant at first and then suddenly close at hand; the broken rhythm of many hooves trampling and the mellow anticipatory lowing of a cow; a man's voice sharp and throaty in a terse Welsh command; the groan and slam of a wooden barn door. To these successive sounds, brought as it were into relief by their background of mountain silence, Mr. Abercrombie Lewker awoke. He lay for a while contentedly regarding his tiny bedroom: the cracks in the plaster of the ceiling, the wallpaper of blue roses, the ewer of cold water in its basin opposite the bed and the framed text "Surely the Lord hath looked upon mine affliction;" most assuring of all, the open window framing the sun-flecked expanse of gray-green mountainside. His watch told him it was ten minutes to eight. He got out of bed and went to the window.

It was a cool and breezy morning with dark yet lucent clouds sailing across the valley from the west to trail bright edges along the higher crags. The summits were hidden, but the morning sun, thrusting through wherever a fast moving gap offered, flung a hurrying brilliance of pale gold on the dark green flanks that swept up behind Dol Afon. These were the slopes of the Carnedds, whose summits are second only to Snowdon in height. Tryfan was out of sight from Lewker's window, but by craning his head he could just see the waters of Llyn Ogwen, a glint of steely blue through the dancing fingers of the sheltering trees. The keen and lively air of a thousand feet above sea level stirred him like a flourish of trumpets; and the mingling scent of fried bacon (for though the visitors' meal was at nine the farm folk were already at breakfast) removed the last of his inclination to get back into bed. He took out his ancient climbing breeches and began to dress.

There is an exhilaration about shaving in cold water that is comparable to the effect of a cold bath. The cold shaver feels the same virtuous contempt for enervating modern comforts, the same sense of having passed the severest ordeal the new day can produce, as the cold bather. It may be bad for the blade but it is good for the self-esteem. Filthy was toweling his tingling cheeks and gazing out of the window when the door of the barn on the far side of the kitchen garden wall opened and a man, a lean redheaded fellow in shirt and breeches, came out with two pails of milk.

"Good morning!" shouted the actor, and added, in the fullness of his spirits: "All hail, sweet milkman, and fair time of day!"

The man looked up slowly, and from beneath bent brows his sullen gaze met Lewker's for an instant. Then he turned without replying and clumped off in the direction of the back door. The man at the window continued his toweling with less vigor and a frown on his face. Derwen Jones, it appeared, was not kindly disposed towards the Dol Afon visitors, no doubt because of Cauthery's attempted philandering last night. Remembering the set of that lean jaw and the smoldering fires in the man's eyes, Lewker considered that young Mr. Cauthery would be a bigger fool than he looked if he disregarded the whispered threat. Still pondering the character of the leader of the Aristos, its relation to the behavior of Mildred Jupp and its possible impact on Hilary Bourne, he went downstairs and out of the open front door. And immediately the trivialities of human conduct fled before the presence of the great hills.

Cloud still rolled along the Carnedd heights behind him, but in front, beyond the flat river meadows, triple-peaked Tryfan rose in one tremendous upsurge of dark rock, two thousand feet from its base on the lake shore to the twin stone monoliths on its central summit. Your true lover of mountains—and Lewker had been one all his life—thrills to such a sight as a bridegroom thrills to the sight of his bride. Filthy stood far a long moment gazing up at that sky-stabbing peak and the sun-tipped crags of the Glyders in the background and then began to walk briskly down the cart track by which he had driven up to the farm the night before.

Disheveled-looking sheep rose hurriedly from the nearer hummocks as he approached and, baa-ing anxiously to their lambs, trotted them away to safer ground. A mountain lark fluttered cunningly sideways from its nest before mounting skyward on its ladder of song. The unfenced track curled round an outcrop of gray rock; and from the other side of the rock came a girl's clear voice singing as wholeheartedly as the lark.

"Early one morning, just as the sun was rising,
I heard a maid sing in the valley below—
O don't deceive me, O never leave me—"

Mr. Lewker, as he came round the corner, joined his somewhat untuneful bass to the refrain:

"How could you treat a poor maiden so!"

Hilary Bourne jumped up from the rock on which she had been sitting.

"It's 'how could you use,' not 'how could you treat,' " she said, "but I'll forgive you because you know the tune."

She was in blue ski trousers and gray wind-jacket this morning, and Filthy noted approvingly that she was one of those rare women who can wear trousers gracefully.

"Naturally I know the tune," he boomed. "It is the only song that may be sung before breakfast without sacrilege. I have even hummed it with impunity on an Alpine snow-slope at three a.m. It is distilled essence of morning."

"I don't know whether you really think that or whether you're just being clever," said Hilary, smiling at him, "but it's just what I've always thought."

"As I have already hinted," said Filthy benignly, "we are twin souls.

I am sorry, however, to have interrupted the concert. Is it a regular matutinal exercise?"

"Goodness, no. It just seemed to be the sort of morning for singing." She glanced at the watch on her wrist. "Were you going for a walk? Because it's nearly breakfast time."

"Then I am not going for a walk. He who is late for breakfast—except, of course, through oversleeping—is antisocial and in peril of damnation. Escort me, if you will, to the feast."

They began to walk back up the track. A patch of sunlight, sliding rapidly down from the craggy heights of the Carnedds, lit the gray farmhouse with momentary glory and passed on. A glint of red by the farm gate caught Lewker's eye.

"Mr. Rouse is up, I see," he remarked. "I take it he is not an addict of the before-breakfast walk?"

"I really don't know," returned the girl with an airy carelessness which plainly implied "and I really don't care." Her companion glanced covertly at her.

"I had an idea he was an old friend of yours," he ventured.

"Oh?" said Hilary coldly. She stubbed her toe against a loose stone and said "Damn!" with unnecessary vehemence. The flare of temper seemed, to melt her sudden frigidity. "If you can call anyone a friend when they scarcely speak to you after not seeing you for months and months, and don't even ask how you are or—or how you got here," she blurted, "then he is."

Mr. Lewker saw he was on delicate ground but decided to make one more step. "From the little I have seen of, or heard from, Mr. Rouse," he murmured pacifically, "I would say he is the type of young man who considers polite conversation unnecessary."

Hilary started to speak but checked herself at once.

"Oh, let's forget it, shall we?" she said with determined cheerfulness. "It spoils the morning. I believe I can smell bacon even at this distance. Why does it always smell better in Wales?"

"My theory is that it is the nose, not the bacon, that smells better. Or isn't that grammatical? I have known a piece of imported and tasteless cheese to acquire quite a strong flavor when eaten on a mountaintop. One's senses wake up in this mountain air. For instance," he added, sniffing powerfully, "I detect the aroma of Dibdin's Cut Plug emanating from the garden."

"Michael always smokes that," said Hilary, and looked annoyed with herself immediately.

"He's not old enough to smoke before breakfast," observed Filthy, pushing open the farm gate and standing aside to let the girl pass through.

As they walked up the flagged path Michael Rouse, sitting on the wooden bench outside the door, took his pipe out of his mouth and said, briefly: "Nice morning."

Before they could reply Raymond Cauthery came out of the house. Like Michael, he was clad in worn breeches well bagged at the knee, windproof jacket and tricouninailed climbing boots. A coil of new rope was slung over his shoulders. Unlike Michael, he contrived to look sleek and trim in his mountain clothes. His flashing smile was all for Hilary.

"Hello, there!" he called. "You look like Aurora and Tithonus—though I'm sure Aurora couldn't have looked so charming in ski trousers."

Hilary returned his smile. "I'm not awfully good at classics," she said, "but I seem to remember that Aurora wasn't a frightfully moral goddess."

"And Tithonus," said Lewker reflectively, "was the only immortal who grew aged and decrepit."

Cauthery laughed, a rather too melodious laugh.

"Then I withdraw all classical allusion," he drawled, his dark eyes still on Hilary. "Though I might add that goddesses should be above our so-called morals. That is a matter—"

"I've got the sandwiches," interrupted Michael Rouse, getting to his feet and picking up a small rucksack. "You fit, Cauthery?"

"Yes, of course." He turned to Hilary again. "Rouse thinks we ought to make an early start. We want to look at a possible new route on Gallt yr Ogof, then round to Tryfan in the afternoon for Terrace Wall. I've a brand-new hundred-and-twenty-foot rope, three-quarter weight, and one feels a first ascent would be a fitting initiation for it."

"You've had breakfast, then?" said the girl.

"Yes. Decided last night to have it early. I fear Uncle George will be annoyed. Will you make my apologies, Hilary? I know the old boy has a weakness for pretty girls, and the way you're looking this morning would—"

"Cheerio," said Michael Rouse loudly from the gate.

Cauthery's handsome face showed a momentary frown.

"It appears that we go," he drawled, settling the rope on his shoulders. "Good-bye, Hilary. I hope you have a grand day." He walked to the gate, paused, and turned. "You're coming climbing with me tomorrow, aren't you? I'll take you up Milestone Buttress if you'd like that."

Hilary hesitated. Her eyes glanced past Cauthery to where Michael was already clumping away down the track.

"All right," she said. "Good luck with the first ascent, Raymond."

"Thanks." His smiling gaze lingered on her for an instant before he closed the gate and strode gracefully after Rouse.

" 'By my soul, a swain!' " murmured Mr. Lewker.

"Don't be absurd," said Hilary. "Let's go and see if breakfast's ready."

As she spoke the reverberations of a gong sounded from inside the farmhouse, and Aunt Mabel, putting her head out of the parlor window, told them to come quickly because the porridge was on the table and wouldn't be so nice if it was allowed to get cold.

Professor Ferriday, Aunt Mabel, Mildred and Harold were already in their places round the table; Mildred in riding breeches and a crimson shirt, Harold in flannels and wind-jacket and the professor in an incredibly ancient knickerbocker suit of greenish tweed. Aunt Mabel, busily passing milk and sugar, wore a smart coat and skirt and looked as usual extremely neat and tidy.

"I know you climbers have to look as tough and ragged as possible," she confided to Lewker. "It's part of the tradition. But as I'm only a hanger-on with nothing more exciting than sketching to dress up for, I prefer to uphold the respectability of the party. Just look at George."

Her husband came into the parlor like an avalanche, rubbing his hands and making a good deal of noise. He had on a threadbare corduroy jacket with ragged sleeves and a gray shirt without a collar.

"I'm late, I'm late—don't tell me," he bellowed, pushing into his place. "Shove up, Ferry, and pass the sugar. Wonder you haven't bagged my porridge. Jolly good morning, everybody! Hallo, where's Raymond? And Rouse?"

"They had breakfast early," said Hilary, looking up rather nervously from her porridge. "They wanted to try and do a new climb. I was to ask you to excuse them."

Uncle George looked annoyed. "They might have told me last night," he grumbled. "Do you know where they've gone? I always make a rule that everyone on my party leaves information as to where they're climbing. In case of accident,"

"I'm afraid I can't remember the name," said Hilary, feeling she had somehow disobeyed orders.

"They were bound for Gallt yr Ogof," Lewker put in. "The crag just down the valley towards Capel. They hoped to make a new climb there and then go on to Tryfan."

Professor Ferriday wagged his skull-like head deprecatingly.

"I recall Gallt yr Ogof as a most unpleasant cliff," he observed. "The rock is friable and vegetation is rife. By no means the place to look for a new and doubtless severe climb on the first day of a climbing holiday."

"Nonsense, Ferry," said Uncle George at once. "Shows keenness. And if young Cauthery grabs a piece of your friable rock and breaks his neck, it'd be a jolly good thing for you. Eh?"

He roared with laughter as the professor pursed his thin lips disapprovingly. "For your cloth, George," he said dryly, "you had always a remarkably ghoulish taste in jokes. I must explain," he added to Lewker, "that a certain sensational newspaper recently printed an article in which it was stated—entirely without foundation—that I had insured the lives of both my assistants for immense sums in view of the dangerous nature of our experiments. The implication was that in the event of death the money would come to me for use in the furtherance of my work."

"Hurry up, dear," said Aunt Mabel to her husband as she collected empty porridge bowls. "Quite rightly," she went on, "the professor demanded that the newspaper should publish a correction. Of course it had to, but it was weeks later and just a tiny paragraph between 'Your Fortune From The Stars' and the serial story."

"The only nonfiction on the page," chuckled Uncle George.

"Since when," the professor's piping voice continued, "I'm continually accused by irresponsible clerics of plotting to make away with an assistant who would be quite irreplaceable."

The entrance of Gwennie with a great dish of bacon and eggs changed the course of the conversation, and Harold, who was clearly of those who find light conversation impossible until hunger has been partly satisfied, demanded whether anyone had decided where the walking-party was to go.

The professor turned to Lewker. "As we are the seniors of this contingent," he said, "the route should properly be left to our decision. There is, however, to be one lady in the party. I suggest we ask Miss Hilary to give us our itinerary."

"Most excellent and punctilious," agreed the actor. "I concur, with the proviso that the walk be limited to a suitable length for those who are fat and scant of breath."

"If we were to walk up the Gribin Ridge," put in Harold's slow voice, "there used to be some *Dryas octopetala* growing—"

"Silence, boy!" thundered his father jocularly. "Let the chosen speak."

"Well," said Hilary, looking round rather shyly, "I expect you know the Ogwen mountains better than I do, but would it be a good scheme to go up to Cwm Idwal, then up the Gribin Ridge as Harold suggests, over Glyder Fach and down the Bristly Ridge, and back over Tryfan?"

"A very fine walk," approved the professor.

"Two summits and a lot of scrambling," Filthy deprecated, "but— 'that danger shall seem sport, and I will go.' "

He noticed with some amusement and concern that Hilary's route would bring them to the top of Tryfan at about the time when Cauthery and Rouse might be expected to reach it.

"Mildred and I will look out for you," said Uncle George. He glanced at his daughter, who seemed subdued this morning. "Feeling all right, Milly? Thought I heard you moving about in the night. Bed not comfortable?"

"Quite all right, thanks, father," said Mildred quickly. Lewker fancied her cheerfulness was a trifle artificial. "I expect I was dreaming about Yellow Slab. It'll be dry enough for rubbers, won't it?"

"It jolly well won't!" vociferated the clergyman. "None of your cheating modern footwear, my girl. We climb in boots, the only orthodox mountaineering method—eh, Ferry?"

"What is the Yellow Slab, Mildred?" asked Hilary curiously.

"Oh, it's just an awkward bit on Pinnacle Rib," Mildred answered; she avoided looking at the other girl, Lewker noticed. "It was hard enough before the Commandos used the climb for training. Now nearly all the holds have been worn away."

"All the same," said Uncle George, "you'll do it in boots. If your old father can, so can you. Remember the slab on the Twiber col, Ferry? You said it wouldn't go in boots, and I proved it would. There was a mere excrescence six feet down on the right—"

Breakfast finished cheerfully enough to the sound of Uncle George's loud reminiscences. Half an hour later the party, with the exception of Aunt Mabel, were gathered outside the front door of Dol Afon, lacing up boots, packing sandwiches into rucksacks and listening to Uncle George expatiating on the merits of his nylon climbing rope.

"It's the only useful thing the moderns have given us," he was saying. "Doesn't kink when it's wet and—"

"I hope it isn't going to rain," interrupted his wife, coming out with a leather case full of sketching materials. "I want to find a good viewpoint for a watercolor of the lake with Y Garn and Foel Goch in the background. Fairly high on the grassy slopes just west of Tryfan, I expect. Where's my folding stool?"

"Here you are, my dear." Uncle George picked up the stool and assisted her to sling it on her back with a couple of straps. "Don't overdo it with that stiff leg of yours. Ready, Milly?"

They all set off together along a faint path which took them across the fields on the right of the cart track and after crossing the little river Dena by a primitive stone bridge emerged on to the Holyhead road a few hundred yards short of the near end of Ogwen Lake. Tryfan's soaring pyramid of rock towered above on the left of the road, with a curious little peak, a miniature edition of its gigantic neighbor, rising beside it beyond some boggy land. Uncle George pointed to the latter.

"We'll do the ridge of Little Tryfan on the way up, Milly," he announced. "Good luck, walking party. We may see you aloft."

He and Mildred climbed over the wire fence and set off across the bog. The others began to walk along the road, following its sinuous way between the long silver lake and the boulder-strewn slopes at the foot of Tryfan. By the milestone that marks ten miles to Bangor Hilary and Lewker paused while the latter pointed out to the girl the route she would follow on her first rock climb the following day.

Above a chaos of immense boulders, many of them as big as a small cottage, a splendid nose of rock two hundred feet high jutted from the main mass of jumbled crags, its top merging into the broken upper steeps of rock wall and heather. It is probable that the Milestone Buttress is climbed more often than any other climb in North Wales, and the line of footholds, scratched and whitened by innumerable boot-nails, that zigzags up its firm gray rock bears witness to its popularity.

"It looks frightfully steep," said Hilary, staring up at it with some misgiving.

"An illusion," Filthy told her. "You will find it broken into large ledges and cozy corners. However, for so easy a climb it has plenty of variety and interest. And, of course, it is possible to fall a long way down. Our friend Cauthery will probably run up it with a scornful laugh and his hands in his pockets."

Hilary frowned at him. "I don't believe you like Raymond," she remarked.

"Perhaps I incline to sympathize with red-haired youths who lose their chances of introducing fair damsels to the joys of rock climbing."

"Michael hasn't said a word about it," said Hilary, with a slightly heightened color. "Probably he's forgotten it was ever suggested. Not that I care tuppence. Come on, the others are miles in front."

As they hastened on they met a party of five sturdy youths from the youth hostel at the western end of the lake, accoutred for rock climbing and singing lustily. They exchanged cheery good mornings, and Filthy turning to look back at the striding boys, grinned to see every head twisted round and five pairs of eyes admiring the slim figure of his companion. The others were climbing over the wall on the left of the road when they came up with them, Harold assisting his mother while the professor, on the other side with his back politely turned, offered a bony shoulder as a handrest for Mrs. Jupp.

"I should leave you now," announced the lady as she landed safely at the foot of the steep grass slope and took her sketching case and folding stool from Harold. "I'm going to find a nice place a little way up the hillside. Off you go—and I hope you'll have a lovely walk."

The four waved farewell and began the steep plod up to the boggy moorland that lies between the western flank of Tryfan and the lower end of Cwm Idwal. The professor and Harold led the way; fragments of breathless botanical conversation floated back at intervals to Hilary and

Lewker, who brought up the rear. The highway dropped below the green hill-shoulders and disappeared. A fresh breeze flowed up from the deep trough of the Nant Francon bearing with it the tang of the sea, and a cloud shadow which had hung over the valley since they left the farm, darkening the vast expanses of lake and crag and cwm, suddenly fled away to eastward and left them bathed in the golden warmth of spring sunshine.

Hilary, striding along a little in front of Lewker, drew a long breath and tossed her fair hair back from her forehead. This was what she had longed for—the pathless hillside of rock and grass and heather swelling up to a jagged skyline, the crisp bilberry plant underfoot, a landscape utterly bare of roads or buildings or any work of man. This was freedom. She caressed with her palm the rough face of a gray boulder as she passed it, and felt something of its peace and strength pass into her; or fancied it.

"Don't you think rocks have a sort of personality?" she said over her shoulder.

Filthy answered, between puffs, with the half serious pomposity that was entirely his own.

"Naturally. They are the oldest things on earth. Fire and ice and wind and water carved them. They have watched the beginnings of man. Any mountaineer will tell you they can be both friendly and inimical by turns. The ancients believed they could mate and produce small stones. As for mountains, which are merely immense rocks, they have great personalities. Consider—I can proceed with this panegyric, but not unless we halt."

Hilary obediently came to a standstill. Mr. Lewker, mopping his brow, waved a hairy paw and proceeded.

"Consider Y Garn, on the far side of the cwm there. He is brooding with folded arms on the imminence of his dissolution. A few hundred centuries, and his rotten rocks will crumble. Tryfan, on the other hand, knows his superior permanence. There is something arrogant about him; you can see it. Something cruel, too. Men have killed themselves on his steeper sides, and he feels the sacrifice was only his due. Are you making notes of this? I think it would make a good article for the *Geological Magazine.*"

Hilary laughed. "I think we ought to push on. Thanks for the paneg—what you said, but Harold and the professor are putting on pace. They're out of sight."

"They are making round the foot of the Bochlwyd Buttress," remarked Lewker. "Let us cut over above it. We ought to be on the Gribin before them."

They struck more steeply up to the left, scrambling over grass and rock and squelching across pockets of bog gay with mosses of red and green. The sun smote them with summer warmth from a sky now almost clear of cloud, and the faint sweet fragrance of the bog myrtle hung in the little marshy hollows. They came in ten minutes over a low shoulder to see just below them the wild upper cwm of Bochlwyd, with its lonely blue lake cradled beneath the huge encircling precipices of the Glyders.

"Look!" said Hilary, pointing. "A tent."

Fifty feet above the lake, on a small patch of level ground between great boulders, was a tiny green tent. Their route led past it, and as they approached they saw that the front flaps were pegged wide open. Nobody was inside, however, nor was there any sign of the owner on the open slopes around.

"One deduces a trusting nature," Filthy observed. "Is that a notice tied to the tentpole?"

Hilary stooped to peer at it and then burst out laughing. "Listen," she said. " '*Mountain Comrade! If you are in need of Food or Shelter, this tent is at your service until I return.*' What do you deduce from *that?*"

"Elementary. A poet, possibly; a Communist, probably; an idealist, certainly, since he ignores the mundane possibilities of wandering sheepdogs, foxes or unrighteous humans and leaves an unwrapped loaf and a bottle of milk in full view." Lewker was peering into the cramped interior, where a sleeping bag occupied all the space between various food supplies and some oddments including a rather battered book. " Yes," he added, squinting at the cover of the latter. " Here is proof of one of my deductions. He reads *Das Kapital* in his solitary tent."

"Perhaps he's a bit cracked," suggested Hilary.

"Because he is capable of wading through the singularly toilsome Marx? I take it you are not yourself a disciple."

"Only of Harpo. Aren't those the other two down by the lake?"

"They are. 'Come, sister, will you go?' "

They left the tent and hurried down to join Harold and the professor.

CHAPTER FIVE

Therefore wast thou
Deservedly confined into this rock.
THE TEMPEST

"NO NEWSPAPERS, no radio, no telephone," murmured Mr. Lewker, "no limelight, no greasepaint, no rehearsals, no—"

His voice died away in a bass grunt. He was lying flat on his back on the summit of Glyder Fach, supported by a twenty-foot-long slab of rock, known as the Cantilever, which bridges a gap between the jumbled monoliths of the oddest mountaintop in Wales as if placed there by Cyclops for a footstool. Professor Ferriday sat hunched up like a skinny gnome at one end of the slab, a small silver-mounted pipe between his thin lips and his eyes screwed up against the strong sunlight. All around them spread the blue still spaces of the mountain world: a low rim of peaks dwarfed by the arching immensity of heaven. So quiet was it on their three-thousand-foot lounging place that the far call of a cuckoo floated up to them from the woods of Gwynant. It was too warm for late April, the kind of afternoon that often augurs rain or mist to follow, and Mrs. Morris's ample sandwiches had induced a tendency to doze in all the walking party except Harold Jupp, who was pottering among the rocky nooks below the summit in search of early plants. Hilary was lying face downward on the warm grass a short distance from the piled blocks, sprawled in contented drowsiness.

Filthy, finding the rugosities of his couch unkind to his spine, rolled over and rested on his more generously padded front. He eyed his silent companion with lazy curiosity, and spoke on impulse.

"Do you, as a man of science, feel as I do—that in the face of all this"—he waved a languid paw at the vast prospect—"our politics and wars and bitter ideological squabbles begin to look futile and unimportant?"

The professor took his pipe out of his mouth and blew a thin stream of smoke.

"I do," he replied in his high, precise tones. "But to me, as a man of science, they never look anything else. Science—natural science—has no concern with the efforts of mankind to avoid exterminating itself."

"Yet you provide it with the means of accomplishing its extermination."

"Admitted. Just as the inventor of knives gave it the means of cutting its throat, or Wilbur Wright and his successors gave it the means of slaughtering its women and children from the air."

Lewker nodded. "*Touché*. But this invention of yours—something to do with the harnessing of the sun's energy, if the papers are to be believed—must have tremendous international repercussions. In the hands of one nation such a weapon—"

"It is not a weapon," snapped the professor quite angrily. "Neither is it an invention. I credited you with more intelligence than to read newspapers, Lewker. The process is still in the experimental stage, in point of fact, and if some lunatic turns it into a weapon instead of a boon it will not be I. As for international repercussions, true science knows nothing of national divisions."

Somewhat taken aback by this mild outburst, Lewker was silent for a moment before he ventured further comment.

"Forgive me, professor," he boomed, "but national divisions exist, just the same. It seems to me that science is turning a blind eye to hard facts."

Professor Ferriday gave vent to a dry chuckle.

"Forgive me, my dear Lewker, but the boot is on the other foot. Your sociologists and economists deal in theories and fashionable whims, and the millions call their erroneous findings and changing premises hard facts. There are only two sets of hard facts that cannot be disputed. One set you will find in the Gospels, the other, still incomplete, is the compilation of science. My work is to add to the latter, and I allow no other consideration to interfere with it."

"Nonetheless," persisted Filthy, who could be argumentative when he chose, "these same blind theorists, acting upon their supposed facts, might conceivably interfere with your work. They might start a war, for instance, and bomb your laboratory. Or cut off your funds, the power of money being one of the current fashionable whims."

The other chuckled again, and tapped out his pipe against the rock.

"That would be beyond my control," he said. "I do not say these possibilities are nonexistent, but that they are the result of ignoring facts. I have to conform to modern tomfooleries, as do we all. For instance, my work is financed by the British Government—a ridiculously inadequate allowance, let me add. But its results will belong to mankind, not to the British Government." His small black eyes lit suddenly with something that might have been fanaticism. "I'm a surgeon, Lewker, delivering Nature of a child that may be the greatest source of power man has ever known. Is it for me to hesitate because man may use that power for evil? Is it for me to refuse if an American or a Russian offers to pay for my surgical instruments?"

Mr. Lewker, who was enjoying himself, would doubtless have replied to this conundrum if he had not at that moment caught sight of Hilary's face, round-eyed, peering over the edge of his perch.

"What on earth are you talking about?" she demanded. "Who's going to use surgical instruments?"

"Just a little matter of sacrificial routine," he told her gravely. "The professor and I intend to take Druidical Orders. This rock is to be our altar. All we need is a knife and a golden-haired maiden to sacrifice, and although you will do for the latter we have nothing to sacrifice you with."

"Then you'd better give up the Druid idea," she laughed. "You've got no mistletoe, anyway, and—do you know what time it is?"

"There is no time on a mountaintop," murmured Lewker, rolling lazily over on his back.

"As a conjecture," piped the professor, "I would say two o'clock."

"It's half-past three," said Hilary severely, "and goodness knows where Harold's got to. I can see two people on the top of Tryfan, who look like Mildred and Uncle George, waiting for us."

Lewker sat up and gazed down to northward. Out of the hazy gulf of the Ogwen valley rose the pyramidal summit of Tryfan, two hundred feet lower than their own height and nearly a mile away. He could just make out the two tiny figures, one of whom showed a point of red that might be Mildred's shirt. As he looked, the figures vanished.

"They are no longer waiting," he sighed contentedly, lying down again. " 'Here is my bed: sleep give thee all his rest!' "

But Hilary was already hallooing to the missing Harold, whose round and somewhat grimy face soon appeared from a heathery gully announcing that he had found an immature *Antennaria dioica* and intended to return in June to inspect the flowers. The professor clambered down from the slab and Filthy reluctantly did likewise. They shouldered rucksacks and, led at a good pace by Hilary, started down across rock-strewn turf towards the precipice from which sprouts the narrow staircase of pinnacles called the Bristly Ridge, a natural if somewhat steep way down to the neck between Glyder Fach and Tryfan.

"I gather," remarked Lewker, who with the professor was a yard or two behind the others, "that one of your assistants does not share your views on the futility of politics."

"You refer to Cauthery? The boy's a fool." The professor's high voice was irritable. "A brilliant chemist, but otherwise a fool. Six months ago, he was a fanatical Communist. Now he edits some wretched review that violently attacks Communism. His politics do not concern me, but I do most heartily wish he would sever his connection with *Postscript*. That sort of thing is unscientific."

"Also expensive, I should think. Presumably he has a fond and moneyed parent who backs him."

"He has no relatives," said the professor, "except an uncle in South Africa who was recently in the bankruptcy courts. Have a care of that loose rock."

Hilary and Harold were already out of sight on the lower crags of the Bristly Ridge, and the others had now left the broad slopes for the out-jutting crest of the arête, which presently dipped steeply towards the gap below. The scrambling was simple and safe enough, but sufficiently steep and broken to interrupt the conversation; the fine views on either hand, moreover, commanded such attention as the continuous hand-and-foot work allowed.

Down on the left the green slopes of Cwm Bochlwyd, looking deceptively flat from this height, fell away to the purple haze of the deeper

Nant Francon with its links of silver river meandering beneath a rank of towering mountains. The heavy blueness of the atmosphere lent a richness to the varied colorings that was like the effect of a tapestry design. On the right hand the air seemed clearer, and seen between the giant pinnacles of the ridge the eastward lands, less mountainous, flowed in gentler curves and levels of gold and green to the far indigo line of the border hills. The sharp peak of Tryfan, rising in front of them as they descended, presented its steep South Ridge—three hundred feet of easy but toilsome rock up which they must clamber before beginning the final descent by the North Ridge to the valley and Dol Afon. Contemplating it as he paused for a moment on a miniature rock spire, Filthy mopped his brow for the fiftieth time and muttered, in Ferdinand's words: "There be some sports are painful."

"You are out of training, as I am," observed the professor, balancing beside him and laying a hand on his arm to preserve his equilibrium. "Your degenerate issues are in process of dissolution. It has just occurred to me," he added, "how admirable a place a ridge like his would be for committing a murder. The merest push—and who is to say your fall was not accidental?"

"The point has been remarked upon before," chuckled Lewker. "As the song says:

> "The slightest inadvertent push
> Upon a peak in Hindu Kush
> Will cause the mountaineer to fall
> Upon a glacier in Nepal."

He lowered himself down from his perch and waited for the other to descend.

"Detective novels, I take it, are not among your mental relaxations, professor."

"They are not. I find myself quite unable to follow them."

"Ah. If they were, you would know that murder is rarely committed without a strong motive. If you were to push me off the next pinnacle by way of experiment you would probably get away with it, because no one could suggest a motive for such an act."

"Unless," murmured the professor, "it be the humane desire to spare you the hot and laborious ascent of yonder ridge."

"Thank you. If, on the other hand, I had just made a will leaving everything to you, someone would be certain to ask the classic question: 'Did He Fall Or Was He Pushed?' I think this is where we take to a chimney. Yes, here it is, dropping us neatly on to the scree."

They scrambled down a narrow cleft in the side of the ridge and descended a slope of loose debris to the col. Their two young companions were well ahead on the rocks above, and their voices echoed clearly down through the warm and windless air. By the time Lewker had toiled halfway up the South Ridge he had no breath left for talk, and reached the little boulder-strewn plateau of Tryfan summit to collapse thankfully on a tuft of bilberry, soaked with perspiration and gasping like a newly landed fish. The professor, though he had said he was out of training, showed no signs of distress. Presumably, thought Filthy enviously, his bony frame was so desiccated that he was as incapable of sweating as a mummy.

Harold Jupp and Hilary were standing on the verge of the grand East Face, which sweeps up in rib and gully of sheer rock to end abruptly on the very top of Tryfan. Adam and Eve, the twin upright blocks which crown the highest point and are often mistaken for people by motorists on the Holyhead Road two thousand feet below, overlook the precipice and some of the popular climbs, and Hilary, with a cautious hand on Adam (or Eve) was peering over the edge to follow the direction of Harold's pointing finger.

"I can see Raymond and Michael," she called over her shoulder to the approaching professor.

"They've just landed on Belle Vue Terrace," supplemented Harold.

Filthy succeeded in pulling his jaded limbs to the viewpoint. Some distance down on the left, on a bracket of rock jutting from the immense cliff, were two antlike figures. One of them waved a hand.

"Don't suppose they'll want to come round to the top," Harold said. "We'd better get down to North Peak—that's where they'll finish."

Lewker's appeal for five minutes' rest being disallowed, the party began the descent. They had gone only a few yards down the uneven backbone of the ridge when a querulous voice, proceeding apparently from under his feet, nearly precipitated the startled Filthy from his holds.

"Ay say," it said, "you maight help me out."

Lewker bent and craned his neck to see over the edge. The others did the same. They were looking into the wide upper reaches of the North Gully, whose deep trough emerges under the summit ridge to splay out in a series of turfy ledges abutting finally against the sheer thirty-foot rock wall over the rim of which they were peering. Directly beneath them, and some fifteen feet down, a face protruded from the wall, a thin and spectacled face surmounted by lank black hair and wearing an expression of mingled shame, annoyance, and appeal. Lewker was reminded of a cockroach peering out of a doorjamb.

"Ay'm stuck," said the face piteously.

"Good gracious!" exclaimed Hilary, checking a giggle. "It's the man we saw in the Tyn-y-coed last night."

The professor was kneeling on the edge of the drop, his sharp little eyes surveying the narrow chimney or cleft in which the spectacled one was clinging.

"There are good holds just above you," he observed to the man below. "Unfortunately we have no rope with us, but you should be able to climb quite easily—"

"Quaite so," retorted the other with a sarcasm that sounded oddly in his bleating tones, "only may boot's jammed in this beastly crack. Ay've been here ten minutes, and Ay can't hold on much longer."

Lewker, who had once spent five most uncomfortable minutes with his boot jammed in the Mummery Crack on the Grépon, realized that the man's position might indeed be precarious. To fall backwards out of his chimney would probably drag his boot clear, and though he would only fall fifteen feet on to a well-cushioned grass ledge he would land on it head first. They would have to climb down to him. He turned to say as much to the professor, but the latter, who had moved a few feet along the ridge to find a route of descent, was already lowering himself over the edge. With remarkable agility he shinned down a narrow chimney to the grass ledge. Filthy followed less gracefully, and the two stood at the foot of the square-cut cleft which the spectacled youth had chosen to ascend. There was a wedged stone halfway up it, and his foot was firmly jammed behind it.

"We shall climb up and unlace your boot," the professor called up to him. "You should then be able to draw out your foot."

"Thet's all very well," he bleated with an unmistakable quiver in his voice, "but if Ay pull may foot at all Ay shall fall out."

The professor and Lewker exchanged glances.

"Lost his nerve," muttered the latter. "One of us will have to hold him in."

Professor Ferriday nodded, frowned for a second at the vertical wall of rock on the right of the cleft, and next moment was mounting it with the smooth motion of the expert climber and nimbleness unusual in a man of his years. Lewker wriggled into the foot of the cleft and puffed and scraped his way upward without much difficulty until, safely wedged, he could get both hands to the unlacing of the jammed boot while the professor, poised on very small holds halfway up the face, steadied the imprisoned man with his one free hand. Five minutes later the three of them were safely on the ridge.

"Thenks a lot," panted the rescuee with more chagrin than gratitude in his tone. "Can Ay have may boot?" Filthy, who had been examining the offending footwear, handed it over with a shake of the head.

" O most rash youth!" he boomed. "You should know better than to climb with unnailed soles."

"Ay'm not a rock climber," muttered the young man sulkily, sitting down and pulling on his boot.

"Well, it's a pretty fat-headed scheme to muck about on the East Face if you're not," Harold Jupp said bluntly. "Which climb have you come up? I've seen you before somewhere, haven't I?" he added suddenly, frowning.

"Ay haven't the least idea," retorted the young man, irritably tugging at a bootlace. "And Ay didn't come up any beastly climb. Ay saw two men climbing down there, thought Ay recognized one of them, climbed down there to try and get a better view with may fieldglass, and got jemmed when Ay was climbing back. Thet's all."

Hilary, whose quick temper was roused by this somewhat bearish behavior, chipped in impulsively.

"I do think you might show a bit more gratitude," she said severely. "After all, Mr. Lewker and Professor Ferriday practically saved your life."

The young man looked up resentfully. Then his thin lips relaxed their bitter curl and his long nose twitched absurdly. To everyone's embarrassment tears started from his watery eyes.

"Ay'm—Ay'm sorry," he quavered. "Ay'm not really ungrateful. It's may unfortunate menner, Ay suppose." He stumbled to his feet, a lank and unprepossessing figure in his voluminous khaki shorts, which had got badly torn in his struggles with the chimney; gulped, and shot out a bony hand, first at the professor and then at Lewker. "Thenks . . . thenks."

"There is really no occasion for gratitude," began the professor, but Hilary, already regretting her reprimand in the face of his emotional amends, interrupted him.

"I'm sorry too," she said with a warmth that made the spectacled young man gulp once more. "I oughtn't to have spoken like that, Mr.—"

"Pyecroft," he stammered. "Wenceslaus Pyecroft."

Filthy remarked the faintly defiant tone in which Mr. Pyecroft gave his name. He was clearly the type of youth who prefers defiance to reticence as a defense for his sensitivity. The tactless Harold, who had inherited his father's taste for simple humor, laughed.

"Wenceslaus, eh?" he said. "Well, you'd better look out a bit next time."

Mr. Pyecroft reddened and looked annoyed. Lewker hurriedly forestalled further comment.

"By the way, did you succeed in recognizing your friend?"

"Ay did," returned Pyecroft briefly.

"It was Raymond Cauthery, wasn't it?" said Hilary. "'You were in the Tyn-y-coed when we came in last night, weren't you?" she added. "I thought you seemed to recognize his name when we were talking about him."

"Ah—yes." Pyecroft sounded reluctant. "Ay scarcely know him, really."

"Well, if you want to meet him you'd better come with us as far as North Peak. He'll be almost up by now, and you can—"

"No, really, thenks. Ay must get back to may tent." He backed away and bared his teeth in a nervous grin. "Thenks again. Good-bye."

He scrambled hastily up the rocks of the ridge and out of sight. The professor clicked his tongue sympathetically.

"Neurotic young man, that," was his comment.

"Hypersensitive, emotional, outsize inferiority complex," Lewker amplified.

"That must have been his tent we passed," said Hilary. "We deduced he must be a Communist," she explained to the professor," from his—"

"Got it!" exclaimed Harold. "I know where I've seen the chap before. He was carrying a banner in a Communist procession in Knightsbridge. The police nipped in and spoiled it."

As he spoke a faint hail sounded from farther down the ridge.

"They're waiting for us," said Hilary. "Come on."

Cauthery and Michael Rouse were sitting on the sun-warmed rocks of the sharp rise in Tryfan's backbone which is called North Peak. As the others came in sight above them Cauthery waved an arm, and somehow managed to convey, even at a distance of some hundreds of feet, that his flashing smile was for Hilary. Michael Rouse, who was squatting several yards away from his companion and coiling up the rope, raised his hand briefly in greeting. As the party approached them Lewker received the impression that the self-styled Aristo's usual complacency was a trifle ruffled. He noted, too, that though Michael's square-cut countenance was calm and expressionless as ever, there was a slight tenseness about his pipe-supporting jaws and small patches of color on his cheekbones.

"Hello," said Hilary. "Did you do the new climb?"

"All except the top pitch," Cauthery told her. His glance flickered to Rouse for an instant. "Our cautious Michael preferred to leave that for another day."

"Rock's rotten," said his companion stolidly. "Have to try it with a rope from above."

"Our Safety First expert," drawled the other with a palpable sneer.

Michael Rouse continued to coil the rope.

"Well, I expect you had a good climb on Terrace Wall," Hilary said comfortingly. "There was a friend of yours watching you. We met him and pulled him out of a chimney he'd got stuck in. An odd chap with an odd name—Wenceslaus Pyecroft."

Some fleeting emotion—Lewker could not identify it—gleamed in

Cauthery's dark eyes. The next moment he was laughing and shaking his head.

"A perfectly delightful name, but you must have mistaken his meaning. I've never heard of him." He took a long and graceful stride to the flat-topped boulder where Hilary was standing and tucked her arm through his. "You must have had an excruciatingly exciting day with the elders and Harold the Harebell. Let's go on in front and you can tell me about it, darling."

Hilary pulled her arm away decisively, but her smile was friendly.

"All right," she said, and the two scrambled on down the ridge, leaving the others to follow more slowly.

"Do you know, Lewker," remarked the professor in his driest tone, "if Master Cauthery were not my right-hand laboratory assistant I should be strongly tempted to use him as a subject for my experiment in mountain murder."

Michael Rouse, who was a few yards in front, dropped his pipe. At the same moment a distant peal of thunder growled ominously beyond the hazy and darkening shoulders of the Carnedds.

CHAPTER SIX

And the thunder,
That deep and dreadful organ-pipe, pronounced
The name.

THE TEMPEST

SUPPER in the Dol Afon parlor was to all outward appearance—for a casual observer—the cheerful evening meal of nine ordinary, healthy people who had spent the day in the open air and developed appetites and sunburn. The yellow lamplight shone benevolently on heads dark, fair, silver and carroty; on vigorous play with knife and fork; on Aunt Mabel's sun-reddened nose and Professor Ferriday's equally erubescent bald dome. Uncle George, his beard wagging almost continuously, was in uproarious form after his ascent of Pinnacle Rib with Mildred ("Yellow Slab went jolly well in boots, Ferry—can't understand why these youngsters think it's hard") and managed in spite of his flow of talk to eat twice as much as anyone else. The professor countered his old friend's outrageous puns with drier and less obvious humor. Lewker himself was in fair conversation fettle, and his spirited account—with apt quotations from the works of Shakespeare—of the rescue of Wenceslaus Pyecroft was greeted with loud laughter.

Nevertheless, with that deep and subtle part of the mind which in some people stretches its invisible and independent feelers to the minds of others, the actor was aware of an underlying tension at Mrs. Morris's well-laden supper table. That there was an interplay of emotion between some of the younger members of the party was obvious enough; such youthful jealousies and heartaches were healthy and normal. It was something other than this, something indefinably ominous, that stirred a faint unrest in the subconscious mind of the onetime secret agent.

The feeling was not strong enough to make him seek a reason for it. If he had, he would have put it down to the oppressiveness of the atmosphere. The thunderstorm had advanced and retreated again without breaking, and the air of the now darkened Ogwen valley was still burdened and breathless with a heaviness quite alien to mountain atmosphere. The windows and door of the parlor were thrown wide, but no freshness entered from the thick night outside.

A milk pudding of Mrs. Morris's best and biggest sort had been disposed of to the last morsel (Uncle George, with heavy playfulness, insisting on scraping out the dish himself) and an immense farm cheese was making the round of the table. Filthy, savoring the creamy taste of the cheese, listened rather sleepily to Aunt Mabel's placid discourse on watercolor sketching and the ideal viewpoint she had found on the western skirts of Tryfan, and allowed part of his attention to wander to the others.

Mildred Jupp seemed to have taken Michael Rouse's place as the most silent member of the party. She had, indeed, taken such part in the general conversation as was required of her with apparent naturalness; but always she returned as soon as possible to a determined preoccupation with her food. Once, when Cauthery asked her some question about their route up Pinnacle Rib, she answered without looking at him. A clear case, thought Filthy, of the jilted maiden. He sympathized with her present distress but was quite unable to regard her as unfortunate; from what little he had seen and deduced about the brilliant Mr. Cauthery—now with his handsome head very close to the ear of a flushed and laughing Hilary—he was inclined to consider that too charming young man unsuitable as the fiancé of a clergyman's daughter. He hoped Hilary Bourne wasn't taking the flirtation too seriously. He had developed an almost paternal interest in Hilary.

Michael Rouse, the taciturn, was engaged in friendly argument with Harold Jupp, mainly monosyllabic on Michael's side but still unusually continuous. Such fragments of their talk as reached Lewker's ears through the dropping barrage of Uncle George's hilarity appeared to be of a chemical and highly technical nature. This didn't surprise him. He had learned from the proud Mrs. Jupp that Harold had lately become assistant chemist in the laboratories of a big firm of safety glass manufacturers.

"We had thought he might go into Professor Ferriday's laboratory," she had added. "He's young, of course, but he took a splendid degree. As it turned out, there were reasons against that and he took this commercial position. Luckily he gets plenty of free time for his hobby—botany, you know."

So it was natural enough that Michael should have common conversational ground with young Jupp. More surprising that he should converse at all. His unusual loquacity seemed to be coupled with a marked determination to avoid speaking to Cauthery or looking at Hilary. Filthy thought it quite likely that Rouse and the self-confident leader of the Aristos had differed, during their day's climbing, on more points than the completion of a new climb; and he happened to know that Michael's relations with Hilary had recently suffered a considerable blow.

It had been just before supper. He had strolled out into the purple twilight of the farm garden to see what was to be seen of the weather portents, and Hilary had come flying in through the gate so fast that she nearly knocked him over. He had greeted her jocosely.

"Hold hard, Atalanta! 'Where runn'st thou so fast?' "

She had stood tense and quivering, breathing fast, with small hands clenched.

" I *hate* peoplc who warn you against other people!" she had said in a voice trembling with rage; and vanished into the house.

Two minutes later the glow of a pipe had come up the track and the square, solid figure of Michael Rouse had passed him silently and followed her in.

Mr. Lewker, dealing meditatively with his last morsel of cheese, smiled at the eternal idiocy of youth. If the red-haired chemist had tried to find a surer way of attaching the girl to the fascinating Cauthery he couldn't have found one. Rouse might see that by merely looking across the table—but of course he wouldn't think of blaming himself.

Filthy became aware of Aunt Mabel's gentle chatter beside him.

"—And of course Tryfan is a romantic mountain in other ways. You know, Mr. Lewker, there's a line of one of the very ancient Welsh bards, Taliesin I think, that says 'The grave of Bedivere is in the ascent of Tryfan.' That was the knight who had three tries at throwing away the sword Excalibur, King Arthur's sword, you know. Do you think Llyn Ogwen could possibly be the mere where King Arthur was taken away in the barge 'dark as a funeral scarf from stem to stem' —Tennyson, you know?"

"Hey?" shouted Uncle George, overhearing this. "Course not, Mabel. Malory says it was the seaside. Even your pal Tennyson calls it 'that long water opening on the deep.' "

"Well, it all sounds like North Wales in Tennyson," said Aunt Mabel.

"Talkin' of Tennyson," said Raymond Cauthery, detaching himself from his absorption in Hilary, "does anyone know that perfectly marvellous parody of dear Alfred about the poet's vision of his reception by God? It finishes:

> "And I shall meet Him face to face
> As gentleman to gentleman.

"Lovely, isn't it—and so Tennysonian."

Uncle George looked extremely disapproving, and was on the point of expressing his disapproval when Aunt Mabel, by way of a tactful *non sequitur,* remarked that she loved the *Idylls of The King* and always had a sneaking sympathy for poor Guinevere.

"Fie on you, Mrs. Jupp!" drawled Cauthery in mock horror. He had not failed to observe the clergyman's frown, and Lewker rightly anticipated a further piece of Uncle George-baiting. "Tennyson's Guinevere is the classic example of the wife who couldn't live up to her spotless husband, a lesson for all naughty Victorian wives. Husbands in those days were all above sexual reproach, like dear Prince Albert. No wonder the old Queen made him Laureate."

"Well, I think some of Tennyson's things are jolly good," said Harold Jupp argumentatively. "That thing about—"

"The Victorians," Cauthery pursued rudely, encouraged—if he needed encouragement—by Hilary's admiring attention, "were good but not jolly. Their goodness consisted in maintaining that all sin was sexual and all sex was sin. It was thus clear to them that only the female of the species could be guilty of sin." His glance round the table invited admiration for his cleverness. "What is sometimes called the Emancipation of Woman," he continued, with a malicious eye on the crimsoning face of Uncle George, "was merely successful female insistence on the removal of this discrimination. The leaders of male thought found a way round this difficulty. They abolished sexual sin altogether—a wise move. Thus the erring wife of today can—"

"Silence, sir!" The Reverend Jupp's intervention was not unexpected, but it surprised Lewker with its vehemence of feeling. "I will not tolerate that kind of loose talk at this table," he thundered, "especially in the presence of my wife and daughter."

Lewker had to conceal a smile at this last remark; it so ingenuously revealed the speaker as a hardy specimen of the type Cauthery had been sneering at a moment earlier. But there was no doubt of Uncle George's intense seriousness. For him, Lewker felt, the Seventh Commandment would be the most important.

Cauthery, with a curl of the lip and an eyebrow raised in humorous scorn for Hilary's benefit, sat back in his chair and said: "Oh, sorry and so forth." There was a small but awkward pause, broken, as usual, by three tactful people attempting to speak at once. Their simultaneous apologies to each other were cut short by the entrance of Gwennie Morris, looking flushed and pretty, with an envelope in her hand.

"Mother's very sorry," she said in her soft Welsh voice, "but she forgot to give this to Mr. Cauthery when he came. The postman brought it yesterday afternoon."

As she handed the letter to Cauthery she glanced quickly at him under her long lashes and he smiled up at her as he pushed it into his pocket. Mr. Lewker watched her go out with a mental shake of his head; redheaded Derwen Jones would need a firm hand with his young woman.

"That's come very quickly, hasn't it?" said Aunt Mabel, obviously making conversation while her still simmering husband cooled down. "But of course you took two days driving up, didn't you? I suppose it was posted in London the day before yesterday."

"One's landlady is surprisingly prompt and efficient," Cauthery drawled, offering Hilary a cigarette and lighting one himself. "She has this address. One imagines she forwarded it."

"Oh, yes, of course." Aunt Mabel drew a sigh of relief as Uncle George began to fill his pipe. " Well, has everyone finished? Let's go into the sitting room, shall we?"

Conversation did not flourish in the sitting room. Either Uncle George's outburst or a general lassitude induced by the day's exertions had brought a disinclination for further talk. Cauthery had gone straight up to his room from the supper table, no doubt to read his letter in private, and Mildred, pleading a "thundery headache," had taken herself off to bed. The rest of the party arranged themselves on the various horsehair sofas and decrepit armchairs of the sitting room, as far away from the unnecessary fire as possible. Uncle George was immersed in some old copies of *Punch,* and his bass chuckles presently announced that his indignation had been smoothed away by that useful journal. His intermittent explosions, the click of his wife's knitting needles, and the occasional scratching of Hilary's fountain-pen from the table, where she was writing a postcard to her aunt, were the only sounds in the room. Lewker alternately dozed and read Conway's *The Alps From End To End,* a copy of which he had discovered on the sitting-room bookshelf. Mountaineers were frequent visitors at Dol Afon, as their relics in the way of literature testified; Harold Jupp and the professor were both glancing idly through some ancient copies of the *Journal* of the Fell and Rock Club.

Filthy, jerking himself awake on the verge of a snore, caught his book just as it was sliding off his plump thigh and surveyed the peaceful domestic scene. He wondered why he had ever fancied anything ominous, however indefinable, in the atmosphere of the Dol Afon party. Perhaps it was Raymond Cauthery, now absent, who had been responsible for his subconscious unrest. A nuisance, that young man. Seemed to irritate even the professor. Not Hilary, though. Hum. Good thing if that letter called him back to London. Well, back to Conway and the Alps. "The mountains were draped with a white vesture proper to the month of March. Ascents which should have been simple thus became dangerous. . . thus became dangerous . . . thus became . . ."

He was nodding again. Might as well nod in a comfortable bed. He got up and bade the room good night, rousing its occupants momentarily to reply, and climbed somewhat stiffly up the narrow stairs to his room. It had been a fairly tiring day for a middle-aged actor whose normal life gave him little opportunity for exercise, and he almost fell into his comfortable bed with a contented grunt. In thirty seconds he was asleep.

. . . Raymond Cauthery, dressed like a French aristocrat of the late eighteenth century, was striking a flamboyant attitude on top of a rock pinnacle on the Bristly Ridge. Unseen by him, Professor Ferriday crept up behind him, his bony hand outstretched for the experimental push which would prove his theory of an undetectable mountain murder. And Lewker, observing the spectacle from somewhere in midair, was paralyzed, powerless to intervene. Then, on an adjacent pinnacle, appeared the Reverend George Jupp, brandishing the sword Excalibur and bellowing a warning. The word thundered among the fantastic crags: "Murder! *Murder!* MURDER!" . . . Mr. Lewker woke with a start to find a huger voice in his ears.

Overhead the thunder crashed and boomed and reverberated, its gigantic clamor rebounding from the encircling heights. As though, thought Filthy, some cosmic hand had beaten in the very vault of heaven and the fragments were tumbling about the chimneypots of the farm. Every few seconds the green glare of the lightning illuminated the tiny bedroom with the effect of an impressionistic stage setting. He lay admiring that splendid fury for a while, until with a rush of cool wind that set his window curtains flapping the rain came swishing down, bringing instant relief from the oppression that had lain upon the valley.

Slowly, threateningly, the thunder retreated, rumbling down towards the Nant Francon like a ponderous celestial pantechnicon. The rain slackened to a normal patter on the windowpanes and the strong sweet smell of wet earth and green things flowed into the room like a living presence. Lewker pulled the blankets round his chin and was on the point of dropping off to sleep when he was once more jerked into full wakefulness by a sound. This time it was an agonized wailing cry.

He sat up in bed, listening. There was no repetition of the cry, but it had been too real for imagination. It had been inside the house—one of the neighboring bedrooms. Someone with nightmare? No; it wasn't that sort of cry. It had been the irrepressible outpouring of utter despair—or physical pain. Into his mind came the half-real terror of the dream from which the thunder had awakened him; that great voice crying "Murder. . ." Silly, of course. Still, it might be as well to see if anything was wrong.

He got out of bed and groped for the small electric torch he always carried and which lay on the dressing table, pushed his feet into slippers and—since he had not brought a dressing gown—slipped on his raincoat. Then he went to the door and opened it.

His bedroom was at the end of a short passage which also gave access to two other and larger rooms, opening out of it on left and right; one was shared by Harold Jupp and Raymond Cauthery, the other by Hilary and Mildred. At the other end of the passage was a landing above the stairs and the door of a small room, corresponding to Lewker's, which was Professor Ferriday's, and farther along the landing Mrs. Morris's best bedroom, in the front of the house, was occupied by the Reverend and Mrs. Jupp. Michael Rouse slept in a little downstairs room that had been converted into a bedroom. As for the Morrises, where they slept was uncertain; but it was understood that a separate flight of stairs communicated with some bedrooms over the big kitchen.

As Filthy now stepped out into the dark passage he automatically directed the beam of his torch to its farther end. It shone on the door of the professor's room, and on a figure in a wine-colored dressing gown who was apparently coming out. The figure started guiltily, as people are apt to do when caught suddenly in the beam of a torch. It was Raymond Cauthery.

"Did you hear it?" came his loud whisper as Lewker padded down the passage towards him. He seemed, thought Filthy, rather flustered and nervous. "I thought it came from the prof's room, but he says it was next door."

The face of Professor Ferriday peered out behind him, eerily detached from its body in the light of Lewker's torch. He looked old and pale in the dim radiance, which accentuated the wrinkled parchment appearance of his skin.

"Is somebody ill?" he inquired.

"Sounded like Mildred," said Harold Jupp's slow voice behind them. He came down the passage, pulling on his dressing gown. "Jolly awful row. Wonder if she's—"

"What's the matter?" Hilary's voice chipped in, her tousled head protruding from her doorway and dimly seen in reflected torchlight.

"Is Mildred in there with you?" demanded Harold.

"No, she's not. I didn't hear her go out, but her bed's empty."

A sudden glow of light from farther along the landing made the four men turn. Aunt Mabel, somehow contriving to look very neat and tidy in a long brown dressing-gown, stood there with a candle in her hand.

"I'm so sorry you were all disturbed," she said in her calm voice. "It's Mildred. She felt very ill and came to our room. A violent pain—indigestion, I expect."

The flickering candle played tricks with her expression. The firm mouth was tightly compressed, there was trouble in those usually placid eyes. Beneath the silvery hair—not a strand out of place—her features showed signs of strain.

"Indigestion!" Harold said wrathfully, "You'd have thought she was being tortured to death."

"It certainly sounded as though she was in considerable pain," said Lewker. "I hope it is not serious, Mrs. Jupp. If you think a doctor would be any help, my car—"

"I don't think a doctor is necessary," said Aunt Mabel. She hesitated a moment, looking at them. "I know she made rather an outcry," she went on, "but you see she had some kind of dreadful nightmare. She .thought at first she'd been poisoned, and that's why she cried out. You know how dreams seem real sometimes."

"Well!" snorted Harold with brotherly disgust. "You tell her from me to stop overeating, Mother. She's always moaning about her weight—"

"Please, Harold dear." Aunt Mabel turned to the others. "She's quite all right now, really. Please go back to bed again and don't worry. You won't be disturbed again. Good night."

She went back into the bedroom and closed the door. Lewker thought it rather strange that no sound had come from Mildred or from Uncle George, who was presumably also in the room, during this conversation. He exchanged desultory parting remarks with the others and went back to his own room.

As he got into bed and pulled the blankets round him once more he found himself frowning at the recollection of Aunt Mabel's set features. She hadn't smiled, which one would have expected Aunt Mabel to do under such circumstances, if only to reassure them. Odd, too, that Mildred should have retained her nightmare all the way from her own room to her parents'. Could the gentle, sensible Aunt Mabel be hiding something? Mildred had "thought at first she'd been poisoned." Poison . . ."th' envenomed cup"—bah! Time he got rid of the melodramatic suspicion that had been a part of his profession as an agent in enemy territory. Imagining things. Like Mildred . . . nightmare . . . indigestion, of course . . . all right in the morning. . .

Mr. Lewker slept.

CHAPTER SEVEN

Blow, till thou burst thy wind,
if room enough!
THE TEMPEST

DIFFERENT landscapes require different weather to bring out their characteristic beauties. The light, gay colorings of the French Riviera, so enchanting to the eye under the blazing sunlight, look intolerably tawdry beneath skies that fail to reproduce their customary picture-postcard blue. In North Wales a cloudless noonday shows the mountains as pale bare masses of earth, mere uplifted commons, remarkable only for their spacious views; it is the cloudy sky, the moist dark air, that brings life and majesty to the giant courtiers of Snowdon. Then they lift their shaggy heads nobly, clad in robes of purple and emerald, wearing the foaming torrents like diamonds on their foreheads.

Such were the thoughts of Mr. Abercrombie Lewker as he picked his way across the puddled farmyard to the byre where the cars were garaged. He found that being up and about before breakfast, a very rare circumstance on his working days and therefore a holiday novelty, conduced to poetic meditation. Above him the mists hurried along the mountainsides and the peaks were hidden, as on the preceding morning. But today there were no speeding flecks of sunlight or promising breaks in the clouds. The craggy slopes swept up on every hand, blue-black and enormous, to lose themselves in a slow-drifting blanket of gray mist that showed no sign of lifting; its hem trailed above the slaty gleam of wet slabs and the tiny white threads that were streams born of the thunderstorm. The rain had stopped, but the air was laden with that cool invigorating wetness which is the very breath of the Welsh mountains. On such a day the rock climber prepares for a soaking.

Filthy opened the big wooden door of the byre and went inside. It was a huge old place, built of massive unhewn rocks piled cunningly and uncemented. A partition of rotting wood divided the portion set aside for the accommodation of the visitors' cars from the jumble of farm implements, rusty harrows, harness and wooden sledges at the other end of the building. The garage part was just big enough to take Filthy's ancient Wolseley, a battered saloon in which the Jupp family and Professor Ferriday had journeyed from London and a very smart sports two-seater in robin's egg blue which belonged to Raymond Cauthery. Lewker groped behind the back seat of the Wolseley and pulled out what he had come for—a serviceable oilskin hat. He was replacing the seat when a scuffling sound from the other side of the partition made him pause and listen. Gwennie Morris's voice, between a gasp and a giggle, came to his ears.

"No—no, please, Raymond!"

A little shriek followed, and then light steps running towards the farmhouse. A low and not very pleasant laugh from the girl's companion brought a frown to Lewker's forehead, and the whistled tilt of *La donna e mobile* fading as the other moved out of earshot did not remove it.

"Blasted young fool!" he said severely to his oilskin hat. He went out of the byre and closed the door behind him. As he turned a lean figure came striding round the comer of a small outhouse that abutted against the byre. It was Derwen Jones. His face was away from Lewker as he stalked across the yard to the kitchen door but his back looked purposeful. Lewker, following more slowly, wondered whether the man had seen or overheard anything.

As he passed under the low lintel into the kitchen a torrent of angry Welsh smote his ears. Mrs. Morris, red-faced from cooking on the big range, had interposed her buxom form between Derwen and a frightened Gwennie and her plump arm was extended dramatically towards the door. The red-haired farm hand swung on his heel as Lewker came in, pushed past him without a word, and stamped away across the yard. His angular features were twisted with rage.

Mrs. Morris flung a jet of wrathful vowels at Gwennie, who shrank away and busied herself with the porridge, and beamed at the intruding actor as though she had been waiting to welcome him.

"Good morning, sir," she said. "It iss not a ferry good morning, indeed."

"But not unpleasant after the rain, Mrs. Morris. I fear I am interrupting your most important work—"

"Indeed, no!" put in the good lady, with polite emphasis.

"—but Mrs. Jupp asked me to tell you that her husband and daughter will neither of them require sandwiches today. If it isn't too much trouble they would prefer to lunch indoors. The rest of us will be going out—to get wet, I'm afraid."

"Well now," said Mrs. Morris, wrapping her arms round each other, "that will be all right, sir. It wass a surprise, like, when Mr. Jupp came in my kitchen an hour ago and asked me for bread and cheese. Going for a walk, he says, and won't be back for breakfast. There's funny, on a morning like this, indeed!"

Lewker, to whom Aunt Mabel had already explained this eccentricity, hastened to explain it to Mrs. Morris.

"Mr. Jupp slept very badly last night, and his idea is to tire himself out with a good walk and make up his lost slumber this afternoon." As she plainly still thought this proceeding odd he changed the subject quickly. "How is the lambing going, Mrs. Morris?"

"Ferry well, mostly, sir," she told him; paused to jabber angrily at Gwennie; and returned with beaming composure to her conversation with the *saesneg* gentleman. "There's some of them ewes has strayed nearly up to Cwm Bochlwyd, Mr. Morris wass telling me," she went on. "Derwen will be fetching them down this morning. Nine o'clock, Gwennie!"

"*Ie, Mam,*" said her daughter sulkily. She began to spoon porridge out of the big pot into seven bowls on a tray.

"I hear Miss Bourne iss to go for her first climbing today," resumed Mrs. Morris, glad of the chance to chatter with one of her visitors. "On the Milestone Buttress, she wass telling us last night, with young Mr. Cauthery to pull her up, like. A ferry pretty young lady—and such a handsome young man!"

"A pity it isn't a better day for her first attempt," said Filthy, disregarding this invitation to gossip. "The rocks will be wet and slimy after all that rain."

Gwennie took the tray of steaming bowls and went into the passage leading to the parlor, administering a thump to the gong that hung there as she passed it.

"Well," said the actor cheerfully, "I mustn't allow your excellent porridge to cool, Mrs. Morris:

> "But that a joy past joy calls out on me
> It were a grief, so brief to part with thee;
> Farewell."

"The same to you, sir, indeed," returned Mrs. Morris politely as he made his exit.

Aunt Mabel, Hilary, Michael Rouse and Harold were already at the breakfast table busily passing each other milk and sugar. Lewker greeted them and sat down by Mrs. Jupp.

"I'm jiggered if I know what's come over Father," Harold was saying. "Never knew him miss breakfast before."

"You know he sometimes takes queer ideas into his head, dear," said his mother placidly. "Pass the sugar to Mr. Lewker."

"Thank you," said that gentleman, helping himself liberally. "How is Miss Jupp this morning?"

"Her pain's gone," Hilary answered, looking up. "She says she thinks she'll get up later on and go for a walk."

"What she wants to do," said Harold, digging into his porridge, "is to eat less. I bet a double dose of salts would—"

This brotherly prescription, perhaps fortunately, was interrupted by the entrance of Professor Ferriday, who said good morning in his piping tones, sat down opposite Michael Rouse, and cocked an eye at him.

"It appears," he remarked, "that the legendary *tylwyth teg* or Fairy Folk are still active in this part of North Wales. I found my climbing-boots very efficiently cleaned and greased outside my door this morning. Or have I to thank you, Michael?"

Michael, surprisingly, went very red and mumbled briefly that it was better than leaving them to the farm folks. Lewker perceived what he had already suspected; the taciturn Rouse entertained an affection amounting to hero worship for his chief.

"It was a kindly thought," said the professor with a twinkle. "Last year Mrs. Morris, no doubt with the best intentions, baked my wet boots in her oven, together with George's. It was the only occasion on which I have heard George swear. He said 'confound it!' " He turned to Mrs. Jupp. "I hear he is indisposed. Will he not be climbing today?"

"Oh, I don't think so. He didn't sleep at all after Mildred disturbed us, you know, and he thought a good walk before breakfast would—"

She stopped abruptly. Raymond Cauthery, radiating conscious charm and laughing apologies for his lateness, had come in. Lewker felt Aunt Mabel's knee tense and trembling against his thigh. Glancing at her he saw that she was quite unconscious of this; her eyes were lowered and her mouth was tightly compressed as though she were bracing herself for an ordeal. Merely the reaction of a fond mother towards the young man in process of "cooling off" from her daughter? Once again he had the feeling that stronger currents than these ran below the surface. However, when she spoke it was with perfect naturalness.

"You won't mind if I ring for the bacon, Raymond?"

"Oh, please don't wait for me. I was writing a letter, and one doesn't notice the time." He turned to Hilary. "Ready for the great adventure? We'll find the rocks wet, but who cares?"

"Not I," said Hilary happily. She was careful not to look at Michael Rouse, who was cutting a big farm loaf into enormous slices with marked concentration. "It's going to be great fun."

"I've got a job to do before we tackle the Milestone," said Cauthery. "Must get my letter off by the first post. Business before even the most delightful of pleasures. I shall run down to Capel Curig post office in Cynara—my car, you know. You'll come with me, won't you?"

"Of course. I'd love to."

Gwennie came in with a big dish of bacon and eggs and went out again without looking at anyone. Mrs. Jupp began to serve it out.

"What are the rest of you going to do?" she inquired. "If the rain keeps off I shall go to my viewpoint and finish my sketch. Are you going to climb, Harold?"

"Harold will take his little tin box and go hunting for Maiden's Bedstraw as usual," Cauthery sneered.

"Lady's Bedstraw," corrected Harold, not to be drawn.

"Oh, sorry. Not at all the same thing."'

"And as it happens I'd like a climb, providing I don't have to lead. I'm a jolly slow climber, but if anyone feels like leading up Grooved Arête—"

He paused hopefully. Lewker took up the invitation.

"Deliberation was ever my motto," he boomed, "even before I became more fat and scant of breath than Hamlet. What is more, Grooved Arête used to be one of my favorite climbs, and I think I could still lead it if I am given time to consider which ledges to rest my paunch on."

He fancied Harold had named Grooved Arête more from a desire to counter Cauthery's sneer than from any other cause; the climb was a well-known and somewhat strenuous one of Very Difficult standard on the East Face of Tryfan, quite as hard a route as Lewker in his present condition cared to lead. However, a certain sympathy for Harold had egged him on, and Harold seemed grateful.

"Fine," he said. "You and I, then, Mr. Lewker—and you to lead."

"We shall be a slow rope," Filthy said, with a glance at Rouse and the professor, "but if anyone else cares to tack on—'come thy ways; we'll go along together.' "

"Do you quote exclusively from the Comedies?" Cauthery put in, with his air of being cleverly rude.

"Yes, when I am on holiday. An irritating habit, I fear," he added blandly, "but the most unlikely people recognize my quotations sometimes."

"I think," said the professor, who had exchanged a word or two with Rouse, "four on a rope is too many. Furthermore, I would prefer something a little easier for my old bones. Michael and I will do Gashed Crag."

"Good," said Harold. "We can all go up to the Heather Terrace together."

Michael Rouse made the throaty noise which usually preceded his rare utterances. He was understood to say that he had no tobacco left and wished to try and buy some at Ogwen Cottage before starting for the climb.

"I doubt whether you'll get any there," Lewker told him. "I have a spare ounce if you would care to have that."

"Thanks. Rather try Ogwen. Want to phone from there."

He looked apologetically at the professor. The latter nodded briskly.

"Then I will wait for you on the Heather Terrace, Michael. A pity George cannot join us, Mrs. Jupp, but he will no doubt be delighted to hear there are three ropes on the mountain."

"Perhaps you'll meet him," said Aunt Mabel. "I think he was going to walk up the North Ridge. Now, if everyone has finished—?"

The party got up from the breakfast- able and scattered to prepare itself for the day's climbing. A fine mist, accompanied by a rather cold wind, prevented the flagged path in front of the farm from being used for that communal donning of boots, adjusting of ropes and packing of rucksacks which begins every climbing day, and Filthy, coming downstairs with his boots in his hand, found the gloomy passage which served as a hall filled with bodies thrusting themselves into windproof jackets or crouched over the tying of laces.

"I trust, Miss Bourne," said the professor's dry voice from a corner, "that you have with you the proper emergency equipment—spare rations, map, compass and whistle?"

Hilary looked up from stowing sandwiches in a small rucksack.

"I've got all those except the whistle," she responded. "Do I have to take that?"

"Of course," laughed Cauthery from farther down the passage. "One blows it to signal to the leader one's intention of falling off."

"It should be carried in case of accident," said the professor severely, "to give the Mountain Distress Signal—six blasts in a minute. Do you carry one, Raymond?"

"Good lord, no. I have no ear for music. You don't imagine we're going to fall off the Milestone, do you?"

The professor disregarded this flippancy.

"You should certainly have one with you," he told Hilary. "Don't you agree, Lewker?"

"Quite right," Filthy boomed. "I keep one permanently in the pocket of my climbing jacket."

"I've got one," said Harold Jupp, groping in his pockets. He handed a large police whistle to Hilary.

"No good," remarked Cauthery, looking over his shoulder. "It hasn't got a pea in it."

"Well, what of it?"

"Oh, must have a pea. Then you can eat it for an emergency ration."

"I'll put it in with the sandwiches, anyhow," laughed Hilary. "Thank you, Harold."

Cauthery came up to her and flung an arm carelessly across her shoulders.

"Ready, darling? Come and help me get the car out."

"All right."

They went out of the front door. Aunt Mabel, encased in a long oilskin coat and carrying her sketching materials, came downstairs.

"Mildred's getting dressed," she announced. "I think a short walk will do her good. But oh dear, I do hope this mist won't last all day. So disappointing if I can't finish my sketch,"

"Rain's stopped," said Michael Rouse from the doorway.

There was a general move outside. The gray clouds still hung on the summits, but their drooping edges were a little higher on the dark slopes. The moist air moved briskly about their ears, suggesting that it would be cold on the crags. The five of them, crossing the squelching fields by the path to the main road, cried a greeting to Derwen Jones, who, bareheaded and with two dogs at his heels, was trudging with his long slow stride in the direction of Ogwen Lake. At the road they separated, Rouse and Aunt Mabel going along the road westward to gain their destinations and the others climbing over the wall to begin the long slog up to the Heather Terrace.

Tryfan, the most abrupt mountain in Wales, in shape resembles a lean dragon with a very humped back; a dragon couchant, with its massive hindquarters turned towards Ogwen Lake and its head nosing into the transverse range of the Glyders. Where the adamantine monster's tail should be is the Milestone Buttress, overlooking the road that twists its way between lake and mountain. Straight and steep above this minor buttress soars the rocky spine of the North Ridge, a moderately easy route to the summit, deeply notched in its higher reaches. The flanks on either side fall very steeply from the backbone, the left flank—known as the East Face—being a six-hundred-foot precipice of bare rock seamed by deep gullies. Contouring along this flank, at the base of the precipice but still high above the boggy valley at the foot of the mountainside, runs a natural ledge or terrace from which the East Face rock climbs start. It was for this Heather Terrace that Lewker, Harold and the professor were making.

The professor led the way up the sheep-nibbled turf of the lower slopes, setting the steady pace of an alpine guide; the deliberate placing of the foot on the spot most suited for it, an automatic and almost unconscious selection derived from innumerable ascents over broken ground. Harold followed him and Lewker brought up the rear, carrying his hundred-foot rope. Nobody spoke. All three were accustomed to mountains and knew that the uninterrupted rhythm of breath and muscle can take a man up a grueling slope with only a small percentage of the effort employed by the chatter-and-dash enthusiast. Filthy, who had not had a climbing holiday in North Wales since before the war, allowed his thoughts to wander among memories of bygone climbs and companions. There is no stronger stimulant to memory than scent, and the evocative odors of wet mountain grass, crushed wild thyme and sheep sent him back a dozen years to the days when, younger and slimmer and still struggling for small parts in Shakespearean drama, he had come to Wales for snatched weekends of climbing on Tryfan with Gideon Hazel the poet. Now he had as much fame and wealth as he could wish for and Gideon had a best-seller on the bookstalls; but Tryfan had not changed. Gideon might have sons (perhaps had one, by now) and grandsons and great-grandsons, who would wear peculiar garments and speak a language even more unlike Shakespeare's English than was our present speech; but Tryfan would not change. Perhaps in this lay the strange fascination of mountains—that they were never the same for two days of a climbing week together, yet remained changeless in their mutability above the years and the centuries. They were as nearly eternal as any material thing could be.

A crescendo growl and a melodious blast on twin horns came from the road below. They saw Cauthery's little blue car nose out of the Dol Afon track on to the main road and slide fleetly in the direction of Capel Curig, four miles away. The professor led relentlessly on, zigzagging now to surmount a glacis of little crags thickly clad with heather. Filthy began to feel the ache in his leg muscles and sighed for his youthful tirelessness. Then he remembered that this was his second day out and was comforted; the second day of a mountain, holiday is always the most trying. The steep heathery barriers discharged their load of pendant drops upon him as he scrambled at Harold's heels, and he felt that delightful release from care that comes with the act of getting wet through. But in ten minutes the heather gave place to a steep and loose scree gully much trodden by nailed boats; by the time they had stumbled and grabbed their way up its purgatorial length to a ledge running across the craggy face above it he was convinced that the heat he had generated must have dried his clothes completely. The professor called a halt here and sat down on a wet rock.

"The worst part of the day's work is over," he announced. "We have reached the beginning of the Heather Terrace."

Lewker threw the coiled rope on a flat boulder and invited Harold to sit on it. He himself produced his oilskin hat and sat down on its protective surface.

"Beshrew me, but I am spent already," he gasped. " 'As the most forward bud is eaten by the canker ere it blow.' "

"Well, I hope you won't be too far gone to burst into flower on the top pitches of Grooved Arête," Harold grinned. He produced a small tin from his pocket. "Have a glucose tablet. So called because it's made of dextrose. That'll kill your canker."

The others accepted his offering, and having rested for a further five minutes began the ascending trudge along the Heather Terrace.

On their left precipitous slopes fell away to the green hollow of Cwm Tryfan. On the right the great gray bastions of the East Face reared themselves into the mists that curled and wavered among the upper crags. The mouths of lesser gullies opened between the pedestal rocks, noisy with little waterfalls. Harold jerked a thumb at a broken buttress that jutted into the Terrace.

"Nor' Nor' Buttress," he remarked. "Next buttress is ours, Mr. Lewker."

They passed the deep groove of Nor' Nor' Gully and a shallower trough known as Green Gully and reached a steep rib cleft by a groove. The white nail-scratches on the tiny knobs and ledges of the rib told of the passage of many climbers. At the foot of the rib, which formed the left wall of Green Gully, the three halted and Lewker unslung his rope.

"Here we are," he boomed, staring up at the dark spine of rock that soared into obscurity as though it reached to some country of the giants like Jack's beanstalk. "As Juliet observes, 'the orchard walls are high and hard to climb.' "

As he spoke the melodious elfin fluting of Cauthery's twin horns came to their ears. More loudly sounded the snarl of his badly silenced engine, driven at top speed. Far below on the thin ribbon of road the blue sports car came hurtling towards the foot of Tryfan, a small shining beetle travelling at most un-beetle-like speed. It shot past the Dol Afon turn and then passed out of sight under the nearer crags.

"Going to park on the road under the Milestone," grunted Harold, tying a bowline knot round his waist. "That is if he can stop at that speed."

"I imagine," Lewker said, "that Mr. Cauthery's velocity varies directly as the beauty of his feminine passengers."

He tucked the end of the rope in an extra half-hitch round his waist-loop and buttoned the neck of his climbing jacket. There was a chill little wind blowing down the Heather Terrace. The professor shivered. He was still staring at the spot where they had last seen Cauthery's car.

" Yes," he said slowly. " Yes. Raymond is careless. I am worried about that young man."

Something in his tone made Lewker glance at him sharply; but the professor seemed unaware that he had spoken aloud. He was looking at his watch.

"Michael cannot very well get here for another half-hour," he continued. " And this is an unsheltered spot indeed. I had better find a cave and become a Troglodyte for the nonce."

"If Michael's got to buy tobacco and make a phone call and then come up over the North Ridge," said Harold, "he'll not be much less than an hour. Why not tie on our rope?"

"I thank you—no. Grooved Arête will take you considerably more than an hour and I must not desert my partner. I will stamp up and down the Terrace to preserve my circulation. Off you go, Lewker."

Filthy slid his waist-knot round to the small of his back, grasped the first handhold, and began to climb.

As always when he felt the good rough rock under his fingers, and the grit of his bootnails on small firm holds, a part of him seemed to flow upward with the great upsurge of the mountain; his spirits lifted with the joyful mounting, foot by foot, of his body. He did the first thirty-foot pitch with ease. Harold, climbing slowly but quite steadily, joined him on the small ledge above.

Below on the Terrace the professor was watching them, a small hunched figure with his hands tucked into the sleeves of his jacket. He looked cold.

"On second thoughts," he called up to them as they paused on the stance, " I shall scramble up and down Green Gully. If Michael arrives I can easily curtail my scramble."

With that he began to climb energetically in the bed of the gully beneath them. Lewker and Harold continued their slow ascent of the rib. The professor's easier line took him much more quickly up the mountain, and he was already well above Lewker when the latter pulled himself on to the stance at the top of the second pitch. By the time Harold had gained the stance the thin solitary figure was almost out of sight in the mists that drooped lower and lower down the upper crags. As they watched him he waved an arm and disappeared into the grayness.

"Gosh!" commented Harold, with feeling. "The old prof could give a mountain goat points and lick him."

They turned to their own climb, and forgot all else but the successive problems presented by the steep facets of the rock.

On a difficult rock climb life is beautifully simplified. To hang on, to get up—those are its sole aims and ambitions. The myriad complications of life at lower levels, the vanities and doubts and divided loyalties, are sloughed like a withered skin; life is revealed to the climber as the antithesis of death instead of the process of existing in the world of his fellows. When he has conquered his mountain he must return to that huddle of petty cares and jealousies wherein we contrive to forget that our flesh is as grass. But for the time being he knows himself alive, and life is the more sweet for the knowledge that he holds it firmly between foothold and handhold, that if his own confident skill fails or his will ceases for one second to guide his fingers and toes life for him may be over.

Time, too, take new values to itself on a rock climb. Lewker had lost all sense of passing minutes when Harold, arriving breathless beside him on a grassy ledge something over two hundred feet above the Heather Terrace, gripped his arm and bade him listen. Very faintly to their cars, more a high pulsation on the damp breeze than a sound, came the distant and repeated shrilling of a whistle.

Harold's grip tightened. "Whistle," he said unnecessarily. "But—if it's on the Milestone, would it carry this far?"

"The wind might carry it," Lewker began, frowning; and was interrupted by a thin high screech from the invisible crags overhead. The professor was hailing them from the ridge above.

"Below there . . . distress signal . . . Milestone Buttress . . . hurry!"

CHAPTER EIGHT

What shall I do ? Say what;
what shall I do?
THE TEMPEST

HILARY had been conscious of a faint surprise, not unmingled with disappointment, as she sped down the long hill to Capel Curig in Cauthery's shiny little car. He had seemed so anxious to get her to himself that she had half expected him to make love to her as soon as they were sitting, or rather reclining, in "Cynara's" cramped cockpit. Not that she had any intention of responding; she found flirting with Raymond exciting, but it must remain a game—and besides, Michael wasn't there to be scarified. All the same, the clever and good-looking Raymond was obviously attracted, and she wouldn't have been human if she hadn't felt a trifle piqued by his unexpected silence and preoccupation. He wasn't even driving very fast, and Hilary liked being driven fast on a clear road.

She glanced covertly at her companion as he frowned over the wheel, his dark curls dancing in the wind of their passage. Yes, he was awfully good-looking, something like Rupert Brooke only dark instead of "a young Apollo golden-haired," and there was a kind of animal warmth about him that she found strangely attractive; something Michael hadn't got. But then Michael was quite different, and— She checked herself as she remembered his attempt to warn her against Raymond. Such utter cheek—as though he'd any right to talk to her like that when he'd scarcely noticed her since she arrived! What on earth did it matter if Raymond *had* had a lot of affairs? Master Michael should have a good chance of seeing just how much she cared for his warnings. Angrily she thrust him out of her mind.

At the little post office on the Capel Curig crossroads they stopped and Hilary went in with Cauthery to marvel at the miscellaneous groceries, tobaccos and oddments while he explained to the grave Welshman behind the counter that he wanted his letter sent Express. This did not take long, and as soon as they were on the road again and heading back towards Ogwen, Cauthery's spirits seemed to rise with a bound. He wriggled his shoulder against hers with that taken-for-granted intimacy which pleased her as part of what she imagined to be his frank friendliness and flashed his gay smile at her.

"Hold on to your hair, darling," he said. "I'm going to let Cynara have her desire."

He sent the little car flying like a scalded cat along the perfect surface of A5, calling Hilary's attention to the speedometer as its needle quivered round to touch the figure 80. That this was fast by ten miles an hour he did not think it necessary to mention. He did not slacken speed until the dark and topless cliffs of Tryfan rose close above them. Cynara swept round a wide bend and came to a halt on the grass verge opposite a milestone marking ten miles to Bangor. On their right beyond the wall of the road Llyn Ogwen lapped ceaselessly on its stones; on the left a steep glacis of gigantic boulders rose to where the Milestone Buttress, smooth and gray and apparently vertical, awaited them. It looked no less steep than when she had looked at it yesterday, and considerably more forbidding in the somber light of a dark morning.

"We shall have Milestone to ourselves, as I expected," drawled Cauthery with satisfaction as he dragged his hundred-and-twenty-foot rope, its white newness scarcely impaired by yesterday's climbing, from the boot of the car. "The weekend rabble have dispersed and one's cars will not be insulted by the patois of Brummagem and Manchester."

"I come from Manchester myself," returned Hilary with spirit. "We can't get our tongues round the slovenly accent of London, you know."

He laughed rather patronizingly, and put his arm round her shoulders in the gesture he had used earlier that morning.

"Your voice, darling, would make Patagonian sound musical. I only meant that on very special occasions like this one doesn't want *hoi polloi* swarming round one. Got the rucksack? Then the adventure begins."

He led the way over the wall and wire fence at the roadside, crossing it by a wooden double ladder at the side of the milestone. They began to climb laboriously upward over the jumbled boulders, following a trail of nail-scratches so white and well-marked that it was as though it had been marked out with whitewash. Pausing while Cauthery negotiated a smooth boulder Hilary noticed for the first time that he was wearing black gym shoes.

"I say," she said, "oughtn't you to have boots on?"

"The Milestone," Cauthery explained as she scrambled up to him, "has various more sporting routes only a few feet away from the easiest line. I want to diverge from the Ordinary here and there—you can follow me, of course, if you like—and one is more comfortable for such divergences in rubbers."

"But I thought rubbers were supposed to slip badly on wet rock."

"So they do. If it's wet I can always climb in stockinged feet, but it won't be. This wind has dried it by now, and the mist's well above the top of the Buttress."

He might have condescended to wear heavy boots, like me, Hilary caught herself thinking; but knowing little of climbing custom she decided that her faint resentment was unjustified and scrambled on in the wake of her leader.

They came up under a little wall of rock, just below the main buttress and crowned by a rowan tree, which Cauthery said was a kind of initiation pitch or preliminary canter. He stood watching while Hilary climbed its sloping ledges, smoothed and polished by the bootnails of generations of aspiring climbers. She took it slowly and steadily, found it quite easy, and made a neat finish without using the tempting trunk of the rowan tree.

"Very nice," applauded Cauthery. He climbed nimbly up to her. "I said you had the figure of a pretty climber and a very pretty figure it is, darling," be added, standing unnecessarily close to her.

He was getting just a little too fond, thought Hilary, of putting his arm round her. She stepped away from the attempted caress and looked up at the great nose of bare rock. They were right under it and she had to tilt her head far back. It still looked steep, but she could see now that what had appeared from the road to be a smooth and vertical precipice was in fact a much broken ridge with projecting ledges and pinnacles at frequent intervals. They scrambled up a few feet of scree to a sloping shelf on the very toes of the Buttress and Cauthery uncoiled his rope.

"Can you tie a bowline?" he inquired.

"I think so—I'll try, anyway."

"Better let me do it." He moved round behind her and passed the end of the rope round her waist. "I get it wrong myself if I tie it from any unusual angle," he laughed.

His hands, coming between Hilary's arms and her body, skilfully knotted the rope just below her breasts; and then, confidently and without hesitation, moved upward. She felt herself drawn against his body and suddenly twisted herself free.

"We're supposed to be doing a climb," she said sharply but a trifle breathlessly.

His ready laugh had a complacent ring.

"So we are. With you so close, darling, I almost forgot. Well, first one finds a belay." He took the rope leading from her waist, made a loop in it, and dropped it over a convenient spike of rock. "There. One does that at the top of every pitch—at least, on these easy climbs. You're tied on to the mountain all the time, so even if I do fall off you won't be pulled down."

"But if you should fall—"

"The leader doesn't fall, darling. But if he does he still has quite a good chance, with the aid of his second. We're at the bottom here, so one couldn't fall farther than one climbs up. Higher up, of course, one would drop a good deal farther, right past one's second until one brought up with a jerk, dangling on the end of the rope. That is, if the rope held."

"*Would* it hold?" asked Hilary, trying not to feel discouraged by these dark hypotheses.

"*Ça dépend.* This three-quarter-weight rope has a breaking strain of a ton." Cauthery was enjoying his little lecture; he also rather enjoyed the apprehensive look in his companion's gray eyes. "A jerk like that—my twelve stone failing a hundred feet or more—might snap it. On the other hand it might snap me. But the stuff has elasticity, and so has one's second man. This is where you come in, darling. You pay out the rope over one shoulder as I climb—like this, holding it in both hands. Got it?"

"Yes."

"Good. Now, if I fall and go sliding past you, you stand firm and brace yourself. The jerk may pull you off your balance, but you're tied to your belay. The mountain holds you, and you hold me. That's the theory."

"I see," said Hilary. Cauthery laughed at her grave expression.

"Unwrinkle that pretty brow, darling. People never fall on the Milestone. That's the Ordinary way up."

He pointed to a wide and shallow trough running up on the left of the steep nose, so well provided with ledges and bucket-like footholds that it made a natural staircase up the rock. A little to its right a line of whitened scratches, leading very steeply up the hundred-foot bulge of bare rock, showed where a more difficult route had been made. Cauthery stepped to the beginning of this.

"The Superdirect route," he drawled. " I shall take this way. You can try it if you like—but in any case all these routes finish on the same ledges."

"I shall do the Ordinary way," Hilary said with decision; and watched somewhat apprehensively as he began to climb.

Mountaineering is a sport that has no spectators. Its venue is too remote, its tempo too slow, the opportunities for betting on results practically nonexistent. It is, and will remain, the most pure and individual of sports, with no side issues to detract from the issue between man and mountain. Yet it has charm of spectacle, and, when an expert rock-climber is at work, charm of movement. Cauthery was a neat climber on rocks. His natural grace, allied to an acquired balance and rhythm, made his climbing a thing akin to the other human movements that stir the thrill of delight in the onlooker: the ballet, ice skating, the perfect harmony of a three-quarter line sweeping in to attack on the rugby field. He was showing off for her benefit, she knew, but the ease and smoothness of his upward movement commanded her admiration. He gained a small ledge fifty feet above her head and paused to smile down at her.

"The rock's quite dry, you see," he called. "You'd manage this easily, darling."

"It looks frightfully airy," she replied. "I shall stick to my Ordinary, thanks."

He began to climb again, passing now out of sight above the bulging rock. Hilary knew of his progress only by the steady movement of the rope through her hands. On the hitherto deserted road two hundred feet below a green bus rumbled into sight; Hilary knew it for the bus that ran over the pass each morning to Llanrwst. It passed and left solitude again. Away at the far end of the lake she saw the tall djinns of the mist marching up from the sea, blotting out the mountains as they came. A faint hail from overhead invited her to take off her belay and come on. She untied the loop from the rock spike, the slack was hauled in, and she began to scramble up the shallow trough.

It was so easy that she found herself regretting that she had not followed Cauthery's route. It would have been a nice tickler-up for Michael if she could have announced nonchalantly in his hearing that Raymond had taken her up the Superdirect. When she was halfway up the pitch Cauthery's voice shouted something, but the words were inaudible and she continued to climb, emerging by a heathery exit to find him standing on a broad ledge, above which the Buttress swept up more formidably steep.

"That was too simple," she panted, making an overhand knot in the rope and dropping it over the small pinnacle from which Cauthery had just removed his own belay. "What did you say? I couldn't hear properly."

"I saw someone scrambling up the screes over to the right, about our own level." He pointed round the steep right-hand edge of the Buttress to where the western slope of Tryfan swept up in a rubble of loose rocks to disappear behind the wall of rock against which they stood. "He's gone out of sight now, but I think it was Rouse. He had red hair, anyway."

"It might have been Derwen Jones," said Hilary. "Mrs. Morris told me he was going up on this side of the mountain to look for some sheep. I wonder if Mrs. Jupp's in sight."

She gazed downward, letting her glance rove across the chaos of boulders below, already looking far away and deceptively flat. There was no sign of Aunt Mabel; she was probably ensconced under a rock busily putting the finishing touches to her sketch. There was Cynara on the gray ribbon of the road, shrunk now to a little blue toy. The ruffled surface of the lake, just beyond, made her feel like Tennyson's eagle—"the wrinkled sea beneath him crawls." A fresh damp breeze, blowing up the dark trough of the valley from the Nant Francon mountains, added to the sense of being high and remote above the lower world of everyday things. Hilary felt a little thrill of excitement.

"Things get a little more interesting here," Cauthery was drawling. "One could take the next two pitches in one run-out, but we'll be very orthodox. It makes the climb last longer." He smiled at her possessively. "It's lovely to have you to myself, with no Jupps and Rouses about. You're rather fond of Rouse, aren't you?"

The question surprised and annoyed Hilary.

"I think he's rather nice," she said defiantly, to her own astonishment.

"Oh, quite. Definitely nice. Safe, silent and stainless—that's our Michael. Well, here we go."

He started up the next pitch. Here the Buttress rose above them in a steep rectangular slab which ended thirty feet higher against a vertical wall. Cauthery mounted easily and perched himself on a narrow shelf with his back against the wall. Hilary followed less swiftly. There were plenty of small but good holds for hands and feet but she felt that now she was really climbing; a careless use of the holds and she would slip and dangle on the rope over the depths below. She had her first faint inkling of the exhilaration the rock climber knows, the peculiar delight of defeating height, gravity and the fear of falling by the mere confident grip, of fingers and toes.

There was not much room on the narrow ledge. She was relieved that Cauthery didn't take advantage of their necessary proximity to put his arm round her, and surprised at herself for feeling relieved.

"How do we get up this wall?" she asked as he looped her rope over a rock spillikin.

"We don't. There are various ways, but we'll take the crack." He pointed, and she saw that just above his shoulder a sloping crack ran up on the right. "One jams the left leg in that and writhes. Milly once got her thigh stuck, but you won't. You've got lovely slim legs, darling."

Without waiting for comment he swung up the corner and into the crack, wriggling swiftly upward and out of sight. As Hilary paid out the rope she was aware of a sudden darkening of the air about her. A damp finger of mist brushed across her cheek, and looking outward from her ledge she saw gray tendrils of vapor curling down from a ceiling of cloud that was only a few feet above her head. There was something eerie in the slow writhings of those mist specters. She felt chilled and half-afraid—but only for an instant. Cauthery's voice from some invisible niche overhead bade her take off her belay and come on, and the absorbing business of getting up that short but awkward little pitch banished all other thoughts.

The crack, she found, was not easy to climb into and still less easy to get up. It was formed by the splitting away of a huge flake from the right flank of the main buttress, so that while her left leg strove to wedge itself between the smooth walls of the cleft her right boot was scraping in search of nonexistent footholds on a steep wall that dropped over into space. Looking down on this side she saw immediately beyond her nailshod toe the dwarfed boulders of the scree two hundred feet below. A glance behind her as she straddled this rearing spine of rock showed the gray slabs sweeping sheerly down to the spot where they had begun the climb. It seemed almost as though a strong outward leap would land her on the road where the tiny blue globule of Cynara gleamed. As she looked, the mist slid across below her and everything—mountains, lake, road and scree—was gone; as though this great mass of rock beneath her had soared off into empty space like a meteorite.

Her head swam for a second and then steadied. She was exhilarated, filled with the heady wine of a new experience. This was living, this was crowding into your flying minutes their fullest measure of splendid life. And if the easy Milestone could bring such sensations, what of the numberless harder climbs that waited to lift her on their soaring shoulders?

"You don't need a pull, surely?" said Cauthery derisively above her.

"No. I was thinking. Here I come."

It was easy enough when you got a bootnail on a tiny hold, almost scraped away by previous novices. One steady reach upward and her hand was round a large and solid spike, a spike that was the sill of a delightful little cubbyhole cloven in the steepest part of the Buttress. She drew herself over the edge and got to her feet, flushed and with shining eyes. Cauthery was there, close to her.

"That was lovely, Raymond," she began; and then, catching her toe in a coil of the rope, stumbled forward.

His arms caught her tightly. She threw her head back to protest, but before she could speak his lips were hard against hers, his tongue thrusting forward in a fashion of kissing which Hilary, who was not without experience, had always thought disgusting. She dragged her head away and pushed violently against him.

"Let me go—you're spoiling everything," she gasped angrily.

He grinned down into her eyes.

"Don't be silly, darling, This is our moment, away out of time, alone up here. Be your age and let's enjoy ourselves."

"I'm not enjoying myself!" she almost shouted at him, losing her temper and dodging another kiss. "Stop being an idiot, Raymond—we might fall off."

"That would be your fault," he drawled, holding her close in spite of her struggles. "Look, my lovely one. Here's a charming nook. And just the two of us. Why shouldn't we—"

Hilary, sick with disgust and fury, adopted a plan which had served her once before in similar circumstances. She drew back her head as far as she could, turned it sideways, and butted it into his face as hard as she could. Cauthery swore and let her go. With a fierce delight she saw that his nose was beginning to bleed copiously.

"There!" she said, her wrath evaporating a little. "Now you'll bleed all over your nice new rope."

He dragged a handkerchief from his breeches pocket and applied it to the injured and Grecian feature without speaking. His eyes were watering freely and he looked distinctly ridiculous. Hilary began to feel almost sorry for him, but she decided that a little rubbing in wouldn't do any harm.

"I'm sorry," she remarked, "if I didn't give you the right impression. I suppose I ought to have said 'I'm not that sort of girl' or something before we started. I'd no idea rock-climbing involved such amorous passages."

"I thought you had modern ideas," Cauthery muttered sullenly into his handkerchief.

"Thanks. I must be frightfully old-fashioned, of course. I thought we were climbing, not going on a petting party."

Cauthery snuffled behind his handkerchief. His nose was certainly bleeding with remarkable freedom. She relented a little.

"Look here, Raymond," she said more gently, "I'm sorry this happened. I was so enjoying the climb. Let's forget it and get on with the Buttress."

She looked round her, taking in their position for the first time.

They had been climbing, she saw, on the right-hand side of the giant nose of rock. The niche—quite a big one and not easy to fall out of—was right up against the bridge of the nose, which sloped very steeply above and below and was so narrow at this point that she could see right through a thin vertical crack to its other side. Above her head the rock overhung. The mist swirled dank and chill about them.

"Where on earth do we go next?" she demanded, smitten by a sudden dread that Cauthery had brought her to a place from which there was no exit.

He turned away, holding the handkerchief to his nose with one hand and gathering the rope into coils with the other. His voice, when he answered, was sulky and hardly audible.

"Over the nose. It's called 'Over the Garden Wall' by some fools. There's a narrow ledge on the other side. It leads up to a cave."

"Sounds exciting," said Hilary, trying to bring things back to a comfortable level.

Cauthery said nothing. Still with his back to her, and without waiting for her to take hold of the rope from his waist, he hurled his crimsoned handkerchief into the void and climbed up the corner on to the crest of the sharply angled ridge. The thin crack that split through the nose made a good handhold at its top. Bestriding the narrow rib Cauthery swung right over on to the far side with his hands round this convenient spike. Hilary, who by this time had placed the rope across her shoulder and was paying it out correctly, noticed that as he made this step his rubber shoe slipped on the damp rock. However, he was out of sight now and presumably edging along the ledge towards the cave above it.

The rope moved steadily out. It had dropped into the nick at the top of the thin crack, but it ran quite easily without jamming. About twenty feet of it had run out when the unexpected happened.

From the other side of the nose Cauthery's voice rose in an agonized yell. At once the rope seemed to slacken, but only for a second. Then it jerked savagely at her shoulders, pulling her forward on to her knees. She hung on grimly, aware of a heavy thud on the far side of the rock. The rope ceased to drag at her, and looking up she saw that it had jammed itself into the top of the crack.

"Raymond!" she called as loudly as she could. "What's happened?"

There was no reply. A flurry of wind drove the mist across the ridge, making a faintly derisive noise as it whistled through the crack. Hilary called again, and a third time, her voice rising to a shrill note with a break in it.

That wouldn't do. She forced herself to think calmly. Raymond had fallen. He was hanging on the end of the rope, unconscious, perhaps badly hurt. She must first try to see what had happened, then call for help. Tentatively she eased her grip of the rope. The crack held it, tightly jammed by the weight on its other end. She made a loop and put it over a rock spike in case it slipped. Then, shaking a little but with tight-set lips, she clambered very cautiously to the crest and holding on with every nerve and sinew tense peered over the edge.

She was looking down a vertical wall. A narrow ledge ran up it to the right. Beneath the ledge was a sloping earthy gully falling at its lower end into space. The rope, vibrating slightly, led down and over the edge of the gully; but Cauthery was suspended only just below that edge. She could see his head, but not his face. And what she could see of his head was a ball of wet crimson: the color of the handkerchief he had flung away.

Sick and shaken, she lowered herself back again into the safety of the niche. Her fingers trembled so that she had difficulty in taking off the rucksack and getting out the whistle. What had the professor said?—"Six blasts in a minute."

She put the whistle to her lips.

CHAPTER NINE

A mark so bloody on the business.
THE TEMPEST

"AS FAST, as you like, laddie," urged Lewker from his post at the top of a steep pitch. "I can hold you on the rope if you slip."

Harold's round face, worried and rather pale, looked up at him from twenty feet below.

"I know I'm jolly slow," he said apologetically. "But it's the best I can do."

Haste on a difficult climb is unwise and only possible within a narrow limit. The majority of climbers are slower in descending steep rocks than in ascent, and Harold was no exception. Filthy, who as leader descended last on the rope, chafed inwardly at his companion's cautious progress but knew better than to drive him too hard.

The decision to climb down again to the Heather Terrace had been Lewker's. The distress signal had caught the two in an awkward place, for they were halfway up Grooved Arête at a spot where descent into Green Gully, itself not without short pitches of Difficult standard, was not possible without making an *abseil;* and the art of roping down was not one of Harold's accomplishments. Movement up or down would have to be slow in any case, and Lewker had decided to go down the climb because the top of Milestone Buttress was well below their present level, but the cautious slowness of Harold's descent was making him wonder if it would not have been quicker to finish the climb and run down the North Ridge. Professor Ferriday must have taken that way down immediately after his shout. They had heard nothing more from him, and Lewker felt some comfort in the fact that a reliable man would be quickly on the scene of the accident, if accident it was. For all his years the elderly scientist would, he thought, deal very ably with whatever emergency had arisen down there on the butt-end of Tryfan.

To chasten his impatience and anxiety as he played Harold down the sheer bastions of dark rock he began to conjecture what sort of accident could have happened to Hilary and Cauthery. To a climber of the latter's skill the Milestone Buttress was what five-finger exercises would be to a concert pianist. Had the young fool egged Hilary on to lead, and had she fallen? If so, she must be badly hurt, for only the most serious accident would have made Cauthery blow that whistle after his sneers of this morning.

Lewker's heavy brows drew downward and his bald forehead wrinkled. He had grown fond of the girl, with her straightforward manner and steady gray eyes, and he disliked extremely the picture that forced itself into his imagination; the slim young body twisted and broken, the fair hair puddled with blood

He interrupted himself with an exceedingly heartfelt oath spoken aloud. Harold ceased his snaillike descent and looked up inquiringly.

"Nothing!" Filthy snapped at him with unaccustomed sharpness. "Get on, laddie, get on!"

They were almost down to the Terrace now. The last fifty feet. . . . Lord, how the lad dawdled! The rope would have to be coiled, they might need it. . . .

Harold was down. Lewker came down the pitch so quickly that he jumped the last six feet.

"Quickly, now," he told Harold as his fingers flew to untie his waist-loop. "You should be faster on the flat than I am. Coil the rope and bring it; Make for the top of the Milestone. You know the path?"

"Yes. Right," said Harold, who was ashamed of his slowness on the climb and anxious to make up for it.

"Good."

Lewker set off down the Heather Terrace, running where the projecting boulders and reefs of rock allowed, swinging himself over obstacles like an anthropoid ape; to which creature he was often likened by envious members of his profession. On this northern end of Tryfan there are three main foot routes, hardly to be called paths, for they are merely the easiest ways on a steep and chaotic mountainside, made visible by bootnail scratches. One, the Heather Terrace track, down which Lewker was racing, keeps on the eastern flank for its descent to the road; another comes down from summit to road on the spine of the North Ridge. A third and fainter track, used by climbers who have done the Milestone on their way to the longer climbs on the East Face, runs from the top of the Milestone Buttress round the rump of the Tryfan-dragon, crossing the North Ridge track on the way, and joins the Heather Terrace at its lower end. Filthy made such good speed that he reached the divergence of this transverse track before Harold caught him up, panting like a donkey-engine.

"On you go!" Lewker gasped at him as the other's footsteps pounded behind him.

"Can't—go—faster than you," Harold told him.

They stumbled on in single file. Mist swirled about them now; it must have come up the valley and swathed the Milestone Buttress earlier, Lewker thought. Still, Hilary's clinker-nailed boots should be all right on wet rock. He tried, as he clattered and skidded across a scree of large rocks, to calculate times. It must have taken Harold and himself little less than half an hour to get down to the Terrace after hearing the professor's shout; they had taken another ten or fifteen minutes to reach their present position. Three-quarters of an hour gone! Of course, the professor would have been on the spot fairly quickly. The top of Green Gully was well below Tryfan summit on the way down the North Ridge, and the track was an easy one. Remembering the scientist's agility and fitness Filthy thought it possible that he had reached the heathery ledges above the Milestone fifteen or twenty minutes after hearing the distress signal. There was the possibility of other helpers hearing it, too. Michael Rouse should be somewhere about on his way over from Ogwen Cottage. And what about Uncle George, who had gone for his curative stroll in the neighborhood of Tryfan? Then there was Aunt Mabel, water-coloring on the grass slopes half a mile or so away; the wind—now quite a strong one—would probably have carried the sound of the whistle away from her, and in any case her arthritic leg would prevent her lending much assistance

His anxious ponderings were rudely interrupted by a gaunt figure that rose up before him on the path like a specter of the mist. He recognized the spectacled youth they had rescued on the previous afternoon.

"Ay say," he was beginning, when Lewker cut him short.

"Someone's in trouble on Milestone Buttress. Come along, will you? You may be able to lend a hand."

Wenceslaus Pyecroft blinked and joined the party, falling in behind Harold.

"You seem to haunt this bally mountain," Lewker heard Harold say with the forced jocularity that reveals nervous strain.

Pyecroft seemed oddly annoyed.

"Ay suppose Ay've got a perfect raight to remble where Ay please, haven't Ay?" he retorted.

"All right, all right," Harold muttered hastily.

The three clattered on without further speech. The mist prevented any view of the track for more than twenty yards ahead, but Lewker, recognizing an outjutting crag beside the now descending route, knew that they were almost at their destination. Tall heather, laden with diamond drops from the mist, drenched them as they slid between its twisted roots from ledge to ledge. A few seconds more and they scrambled down to a bald platform of rock whose rounded edge plunged over into an emptiness of swirling gray—the top of Milestone Buttress.

They peered over into the obscurity. Voices, just below, were audible. Lewker called down to them.

"Ferriday! Lewker here! Shall we come down?"

"No. We are almost up," came the reply in the professor's high precise voice.

Almost at once he came into sight a dozen feet below, climbing swiftly upward out of the mist. He drew himself over the stab at the top and stood up, the rope from his waist dangling like a tail behind him. His wizened face was drawn and rather pale as he met Lewker's eyes and replied to the question in them.

"Cauthery. Dead," he said briefly, and turned to take in the rope.

"Miss Bourne?" Filthy said quickly.

"Unhurt. Slight reaction from shock," jerked the professor over his shoulder. He pulled tightly on the rope as Hilary climbed up, white-faced but apparently composed. She stumbled slightly as she stood up on the platform, and Lewker, grasping her arm, felt her trembling uncontrollably. Close behind her came Michael Rouse, his square face grimly set and expressionless.

"I'm all right, thanks," Hilary said with an effort.

"How did it happen?" asked Harold, recovering from the shock of the professor's announcement.

"That can wait," Rouse's gruff voice broke in. He shouldered past and took hold of Hilary's arm. "First thing, get her down."

"Quite right," boomed Filthy cheerfully, pulling his spare sweater out of the rucksack Harold was carrying.

"Put this on," he added, handing it to Hilary, "and concentrate on getting down. Harold will go with you.

"You had better get on to the North Ridge track," advised the professor. "See that she has a hot drink and goes to bed as soon as you get to Dol Afon, Harold. Michael, we shall want you with us."

Rouse, who was untying Hilary's waist-knot, nodded.

"Can Ay do anything?" put in Wenceslaus Pyecroft timidly from the background.

"In one moment," Filthy told him. He waited until Harold and Hilary, the latter very quiet and obviously holding herself rigidly, had passed out of sight in the mist. "Now. What is the position, Ferriday?"

Curtly the professor outlined the events of the last half-hour. He had reached the top of the Buttress and his shouts had drawn a reply from Hilary, though her words, from a hundred feet below and muffled by the intervening rock, had been inaudible. He had just started to climb down to her when Michael Rouse, who had been crossing the mountain higher up on his way over to the Heather Terrace, had come scrambling down out of the mists above.

"I was only two or three hundred feet up," put in Rouse. "Heard the whistle very faintly at first. It must have been sounding a bit before I heard it, otherwise I'd have been down before the professor got there."

Lewker, rather surprised by this unusual loquacity, threw a quick glance at the young man. Rouse's face was curiously pale, and there was a kind of defiance in the way his eyes flickered from one to another of the three who stood round him.

"Well, the wind plays odd tricks," said Filthy. " You had a rope with you, I see?"

The professor took up the story again. He had waited for Rouse to climb down to him and the two had descended quickly to where Hilary crouched in her niche. They had found her shaken but unhurt, and had at once proceeded to reach Cauthery. The professor, as the lighter of the two men, had been lowered on the rope to where Cauthery was hanging and had made a brief examination.

"He was dead," said Professor Ferriday in dry unemotional tones. "I make no claim to medical knowledge, but judging from the nature of his injury death was instantaneous. His skull was badly fractured. Clearly he had slipped while traversing the ledge above, pitched head first on to a rock in the gully beneath, and slid down to where he was suspended when we found him."

Pyecroft gulped loudly, breaking the short silence.

"Anything one can say," the professor continued abruptly, "seems inadequate. We had better proceed with the recovery of the—the body."

"You didn't get him—it—up, then?"

"It was not possible to pull it up from above. It was held by the lip of the gully. We therefore left it with the rope belayed, to be lowered. Three of us should be able to manage that, I think, Michael?"

"Yes, with the extra length of rope," Rouse muttered. He appeared to be still very shaken—more so than might have been expected from his usual imperturbability. Lewker was frowning heavily.

"How the dickens," he wondered aloud, "did a good climber like Cauthery come to fall of an easy place like that?"

"Wearing rubbers," Rouse said briefly. "Handholds poor."

"And the mist has made the rock slimy," nodded Lewker. "It must have happened like that. Well, it seems we shall have to lower the body and—"

"Ay say," bleated Pyecroft suddenly, "Ay'm afraid Ay shan't be any use. Ay faint at the saight of blood."

He was looking green already. Filthy clapped him on the shoulder reassuringly.

"We want a messenger, Mr. Pyecroft. You know the youth hostel at the end of the take? There is a stretcher there, also a telephone. The warden will know what to do. Tell him what has happened and that we are getting the body down to the foot of the Milestone. Bring the stretcher and what helpers you can collect from the hostel up to us. The warden will ring for an ambulance and it should come straight to the tenth milestone from Bangor."

He glanced inquiringly at the professor, who nodded.

"That is quite adequate," he approved. "You had better make all speed, Mr. Pyecroft. The nearest way is down the traverse on this side, but it is rather steep and—if I remember correctly—you are unused to even easy rock-climbing."

"Oh, Ay can menage thet, thenks."

Pyecroft was clearly anxious to get away from the neighborhood of the corpse and the possibility of having to see or touch it. He scrambled off in the opposite direction to that taken by Harold and the girl and vanished into the mist.

"Seems nervy," commented Michael, who seemed to have himself in hand again. "Think he'll get the message right?"

"We will hope so." Lewker picked up the rope Rouse had been coiling. "A hundred-foot length? That gives us two hundred and twenty, with Cauthery's. Will that be enough?"

"Think so. Ledge under the gully where we can break the lowering."

"Good. Then we will go down. Ready, professor?"

Professor Ferriday seemed not to hear. He had gone to the edge of the platform and was gazing down into the blankness with his shoulders hunched and his clawlike hands folded in front of him. He looked suddenly old and worn.

When Lewker repeated his question he started and looked up in a dazed way. His high voice, which had not faltered before, now trembled slightly.

"He—he was my right hand," he said simply. "I hardly know what I shall do without him."

Michael Rouse took a step forward and laid his big fingers awkwardly on his employer's shoulder.

"There are—compensations," he said gruffly in a low voice.

Lewker thought this rather an odd comment; he was to remember it later. The professor made no reply, but he seemed to recover his normal, controlled, stiff manner. The three of them set about the unpleasant business in hand without further discussion.

To reach the "Garden Wall" they had first to climb down beside a deep chimney to an easy slab pitch whose lower edge overhung the Cave. This was in fact a deep and roomy cleft cutting right across the Buttress above the bridge of its steep nose. One end of it opened like a square-cut door in the vertical flank of the Buttress, and from the sill of this door the narrow ledge ran steeply down along the smooth rock to the point at which the step over the Garden Wall could be made. One by one they climbed down into the Cave and stepped round the vertical corner on the ledge. Beneath them the rocky funnel of the little gully fell away to plunge over into perpendicularity. As he edged across, spread-eagled against the rock, Lewker could see the taut rope coming over from the niche where Hilary had been when the accident occurred. It was dragged sideways by the weight of Cauthery's body below the end of the gully; he could also see the top of the dark head, with an ugly crimson mass set jauntily upon it like a cap. The length of rope seemed to indicate that the dead man had almost reached the mouth of the Cave when he slipped. He must have fallen very awkwardly to land headfirst in the steep bed of the gully, Lewker thought.

When they were all gathered in the comfortable haven of the niche it was decided that Rouse should go on down the Buttress and climb up to the ledge below the gully. Meanwhile Lewker and the professor freed Cauthery's rope, which was tightly jammed in the crack at the back of the niche, and made their arrangements for lowering. The mist still swirled clammily round the great nose, and except for a few feet of rock wall above and below there was nothing to be seen but gray emptiness. They were like men perched on a shelf at the world's edge.

Presently Rouse's hail came up to them from the depths and they lowered away until a second hail told them he had secured the body. They threw the rope's end down and descended the route by which Hilary and Cauthery had mounted little more than an hour before. When they reached the foot of the Buttress and had clambered round beneath Rouse's ledge he shouted down to tell them he could lower the body by himself. Five minutes later the stiff ungainly thing that had been Raymond Cauthery lay in the wet heather under the gray crags, its empty eyes staring up at the mist whose light touch brushed across the dead face.

The professor, his thin fingers working to untie the waist-knot, kept his eyes averted; but Lewker, who in more adventurous times had had much acquaintance with sudden death, made a quick examination. The frontal bone above the right temple had been smashed in, evidently by a sharp edge of rock. There were one or two rock splinters protruding from the wound. The face wore a fixed expression of terror that was not pleasant to see.

Professor Ferriday, having removed the rope from the body, took off his windproof jacket and laid it gently over the dead man. Rouse came scrambling down to join them.

"The professor and I will stay here," Lewker told him. "It might be as well for you to go down to the road and guide the stretcher party up to us."

Rouse nodded, but he did not at once leave them. He stood looking down at the body almost absentmindedly, ramming tobacco into his pipe with large steady fingers.

"He'd have hated to know he'd fallen off an easy climb," he said at last, as if to himself.

Filthy glanced up at him quickly. The words sounded like a sneer, but it was plain that Michael didn't intend them as such. He had merely spoken his thought aloud; and if the business of an epitaph is to record something of the character of the deceased (thought Filthy), Rouse's comment might do for Cauthery's epitaph. He watched Rouse walk a few yards away, pause to light his pipe, and go on down the mountainside towards the road. The strong, homely odor of the tobacco came to his nostrils on the moisture-laden breeze—Dibdin's Cut Plug; he remembered joking about it with Hilary yesterday morning. Michael must have succeeded in getting some at Ogwen Cottage, after all.

The professor, squatting beside him, began to discuss in a low tone the procedure they would have to follow when the ambulance arrived, and after. There would be an inquest, of course. Cauthery, he said, had no relatives in England. There was only the uncle in South Africa who would have to be advised. He and Rouse would look after things in London.

Lewker listened with half an ear. He could hear someone scrambling down the scree on the other side of the Buttress. They were below the mist level now, and the slopes spreading down to the road, the lake, and the lower flanks of the mountains were darkly clear under the cloud-pall. The scrambler came into sight rounding the foot of the Buttress. It was Mildred Jupp. She saw them, stopped and waved, and then made up the heathery glacis towards them. With a word of warning to the professor Lewker rose to his feet and went down to meet her. The girl must have guessed from his face that something was badly amiss, for she halted when he was still some yards away and stood tensely awaiting him. She was very white.

"Is it—Raymond?" she asked before he could speak.

He nodded slowly, watching her. Uncle George, according to Hilary, had expected Cauthery and Mildred to announce their engagement shortly. Mildred, if Lewker's brief observation of her behavior were to be trusted, had been in love with the dead man. He expected an hysterical outburst.

"Dead," whispered Mildred; and the word was not a question but a statement. She made as if to continue up the hillside to the body, and Lewker put an arresting hand on her arm.

"He is not a pleasant sight," he said gently.

"Let me pass, please," she said tonelessly.

He followed her up the slope. Ignoring the professor's outstretched hand she reached down and pulled back the coat from the dead face, looked at it long and steadily, and covered it again.

"He was killed instantly," said the professor, giving the one possible crumb of comfort, but the girl seemed not to hear him.

"Is there anything I can do to help you?" she asked, still in that same toneless voice.

They told her there was nothing.

"I suppose Hilary's at the farm. I'll go there," she said, and turned away.

They watched her go down, picking her way between the boulders without hesitation or stumbling. As she reached the road a party of four or five men came round a corner fifty yards away, from the direction of the youth hostel. They were carrying a stretcher. Mildred did not stop or even look at them. She turned and walked steadily, a small erect figure, towards Dol Afon.

CHAPTER TEN

O, the cry did knock
Against my very heart!
THE TEMPEST

"THERE now," said Mrs. Morris, bustling across the kitchen with a large cup of very strong tea, " here's good for you, *anwyl.* "

"But I've just had two cups at breakfast," Hilary protested.

"Ach, that poor thin drink the English make!" Mrs. Morris dismissed it with a wave of her large red hand. "Indeed, it will not color the sides of the cups. This iss *Welsh* tea, now. You drink it up, like a good girl."

Hilary took it meekly and sipped it as she sat in the rocking chair by the fire. Mrs. Morris chivvied Gwennie into the little scullery to do the washing-up while she busied herself with the mixing of a pudding on the kitchen table. In a corner near the window Derwen Jones was eating his breakfast of bread and cold bacon and tea, having been out at daybreak on some matter connected with sheep. Derwen was as chary of speech as Michael, thought Hilary; and at once that secret dread of hers came back with redoubled force, stabbing at her heart with a physical pain. She gulped hastily at her tea and tried to forget it in the homely atmosphere of Dol Afon kitchen.

It was the morning after the death of Raymond Cauthery, and she had escaped from the breakfast table, with its uncomfortable silences which Uncle George tried to relieve with heavy-handed platitudes, to the kitchen. Somehow Mrs. Morris, who could not forbear to ask questions about the tragedy, was better company than the Jupps with their obvious avoidance of the unpleasant topic. Even Mr. Lewker's presence was disturbing, for his quick little eyes seemed to hold a suspicion of what she was concealing. Michael had shown a desire for her company, but she couldn't bring herself to talk to him while that dreadful thought rattled its bones in the locked cupboard of her mind.

As to the fatal accident itself, Hilary was surprised and a little shocked to find how quickly she had recovered from its impact. The untimely death of a brilliant young man whom she had scarcely known; that was how it presented itself to her now, in spite of the passing attraction—she recognized its true nature now —which the dead man had exercised over her. Ashamed she might be of this impersonal attitude, but she was too honest to conceal it from herself. It was not so easy to tell how the others felt, but it seemed almost as though the professor was the only one of them who honestly regretted Cauthery's death. Mildred Jupp, who might have been expected to show at least some grief at the violent passing of a man with whom she had presumably been in love, presented a façade of calm resignation to the world that was strangely like her mother's settled matter-of-factness. Harold Jupp was merely glum. Michael, as usual, was silent, though he seemed more restless than was his habit.

"Poor Mr. Jupp! " Mrs. Morris's voice interrupted the girl's thoughts. "He will be ferry upset, like, him being in charge of the party. Fancy now, he came into my kitchen yesterday, just before lunchtime it wass, not knowing anything had happened. 'Oh, sir, young Mr. Cauthery's been killed,' says Gwennie when she sees him come in, foolish girl. Mr. Jupp, he stands quite still staring at her, like. 'I've just come back from walking up Cwm Tryfan,' he says like a man talking in a dream, 'and I heard nothin'.' Poor, poor young fellow!' he says, and goes out ferry quick. Will he be at the inquest, miss?"

He would, Hilary told her. The inquest was to be held that morning at a quarter past ten, in the little town of Bethesda six miles away down the Nant Francon valley. Hilary had driven there with Professor Ferriday, Michael and Lewker the previous afternoon to make her statement to the police, and they would all four be required to give evidence at the inquest. Uncle George was to accompany them. The body of Raymond Cauthery had been taken by a Red Cross ambulance to the mortuary in the same town.

"Well now," said Mrs. Morris, kneading dough with energy, "it will be Dwyfor Evans for the corona. A ferry nice corona iss Dwyfor, miss, and ferry well liked. He will make it all ferry easy for you, I'm sure. Another cup, now?"

"No, thank you," said Hilary, getting up from the rocking chair. "I must get ready now."

Mrs. Morris, who had not nearly satisfied her desire for gossip, detained her hurriedly.

"You will be back for lunch, I'm sure," she said. "Will Mrs. Jupp be going to the inquest, now?"

"No. There's nothing for her to tell the coroner, you see. She didn't know anything had happened until she met Harold and me coming down on to the road and came back to the farm with us."

"Just fancy, now!" Mrs. Morris folded her floury hands on the bosom of her red-checked apron. "There wass her, doing the likeness of Llyn Ogwen with her paints, only just round the corner of the road, like, and never heard you whistling."

"She couldn't have helped much," said Hilary. "She's got a bad leg, you know. And it was the wind blowing the wrong way that prevented her from hearing the whistle."

"What a pity Derwen didn't hear you! " Mrs. Morris pursued. "He could have climbed up to help you. He goes climbing on the crags sometimes. You wass up by Tryfan, Derwen, wasn't you?"

"I was a mile away in Cwm Bochlwyd," said Derwen Jones, so sharply that he startled Hilary, who had forgotten he was in the kitchen. He got up abruptly and stalked out, leaving his cup of tea half full.

"Derwen and Gwennie has quarreled," said Mrs. Morris to Hilary confidentially. "Derwen saw Gwennie crying and got out of her that it wass because of poor Mr. Cauthery. Derwen iss ferry quick-tempered. He said it wass a good thing Mr. Cauthery wass dead. There's wicked he talks sometimes! Now they aren't speaking, the two of them."

"I really must go," Hilary said. As she turned towards the door Mr.

Lewker came briskly into the kitchen.

"We are all ready for the road," he announced. "And I, my dear, am appointed to drive you to Bethesda."

He explained as they went out to the waiting car that Mrs. Jupp had decided to take Mildred to see a doctor in the little town. The Jupp car would thus be full, and had indeed already started.

"This inquest should not take long," he boomed as they rattled and splashed down the Dol Afon track to the main road. " You will have to describe what happened all over again for the benefit of the coroner. Do you feel equal to that?"

"Of course I do," replied Hilary rather irritably. Then she repented her sharp tone and added less peevishly: "But thanks, all the same, for being sympathetic."

Filthy swung the big Wolseley to the right on to the main road.

"It has appeared to my doubtless inaccurate observation," he said, without taking his eyes from the road, "that there is something lying heavily on your mind, my dear. This most unhappy occurrence has of course upset you. But I do not think it is that alone. If you would care to confide in me—"

"There's nothing," said Hilary shortly.

He shot a quick glance at her, opened his mouth as if to speak, and closed it again. They drove on in silence, passing between the ruffled waters of the lake and the somber mass of the Milestone Buttress.

The morning was cloudy but yesterday's trailing mists had lifted from the peaks, and patches of pale sunshine ran up the greening hill-side like golden dishes skimming before the west wind. The great shapes of Y Garn and Foel Goch heaved themselves darkly above the trees at the end of the lake, and Hilary, frowning ahead at their scarred and weather-worn faces, wondered whether she would ever again think mountains beautiful.

During those long minutes when she had crouched lonely in the niche on the Milestone, tied to a man who might be either dead or dying, the gray rocks she had once loved as the symbols of freedom and holiday had turned dreadful faces upon her, like the rocks in Belloc's poem; she had known then that her fancy, expressed to Lewker, about rocks possessing human qualities was false. For here was exemplified the utter apathy of Nature towards a human tragedy. She would never climb again, she told herself—never look at a crag without a shudder.

The car flew past the roadside buildings of Ogwen Cottage under their sheltering fringe of greening birches. Telford's great Holyhead Road twisted over the bridge that crossed the top of the three-hundred-foot cataract of Ogwen Falls and the wide green strath of the Nant Francon opened out below. Just past the bridge, where the ground fell steeply away from the roadside on the left to plunge down to the foot of the Falls, some yards of the flanking wall had been broken and smashed. Hilary, noticing it, remembered Mrs. Morris describing with gusto how a heavy lorry had crashed through and gone over the edge a few days earlier. The driver and a man with him had been killed outright. Hilary shivered and felt sick. Under these huge inimical peaks of Ogwen tragedy seemed to lurk as by right. She looked eagerly and with relief before them and the long bar of blue sky that told of sunnier weather on the coast beyond.

They came winding down through tall woods, above whose budding branches rose the ugly symmetry of mounds of slate quarry debris, into the narrow main street of Bethesda. A gleam of sunshine lent a certain dingy homeliness to its little shops and gaunt chapels. Uncle George's car was standing before a tall red-brick chapel on the right; its passengers had already disappeared. As Lewker pulled up behind it a police constable stepped forward from the shop-front where he had been chatting with the shopkeeper and whispered confidentially that they were to go in behind the chapel. The small old gentleman, he added, had just gone off to do the formal identification. Lewker and Hilary mounted some steps and entered a door at the rear of the chapel.

Hilary's ideas of a coroner's court were based on descriptions she had read in books. Somewhat to her relief she found all her notions upset. She had pictured a big dark-paneled room filled with grave people and buzzing with legal talk. Large numbers of helmetless policemen would be standing round the walls and there would be a sort of high pulpit for the coroner to sit in majesty. The coroner of fiction she was quite familiar with; he was invariably an irritable little man with glasses and the manners of a Fascist dictator. Her imagination had clothed him in a black robe and an aura of omnipotence.

She found herself now in a tiny room smelling of chalk and musty books, into which a cheap yellow table and four iron-framed benches crowded to fill it completely. It was obviously used as a Sunday school classroom, and a picture of Christ among children hung on one of the walls. With fatherly words and reassuring smiles a large sergeant of police arranged them on the foremost of two benches in front of the table, with Uncle George, Harold and Michael sitting behind them. Less sympathetically, he edged two nondescript men who later turned out to be reporters into the benches at the side, and shooed out a big tabby cat who had strolled in after them. The little room seemed tightly packed with eight people in it.

"Wherever will the jury sit?" she whispered to Lewker.

"There will be no jury," he whispered back. "There is no doubt as to the cause of death, you see, and no blame to apportion."

Hilary bit her lip and watched the sergeant arranging papers on the table.

There was a short pause, and then a stout gentleman with a walrus mustache and a watch-chain came in accompanied by a harassed looking bald-headed man who was greeted as "Doctor Williams" by the sergeant. The stout gentleman sat down at the table and glanced through the papers. An inspector of police arrived, exchanged a few sentences of rapid Welsh with the doctor, and sat down a little to one side of the coroner.

"I think we might take your evidence right away, doctor," said the latter in a husky voice, resting his paunch against the edge of the table so that his watch-chain rasped against it every time he breathed.

The sergeant produced a small Bible and the doctor repeated the oath after him. Hilary felt the hackneyed phrases like iron fists beating on the doors of her conscience: ". . . *the evidence I shall give . . . the whole truth* . . ." She closed her ears resolutely to the words. Sleepless hours had decided the course she was to take and it would not be the whole truth when her turn came. But she had forgotten, when she came to that difficult resolution, that she would have to say "I swear by Almighty God . . ." The crime of perjury, legal or moral, was one which Hilary Bourne had never considered in any of its aspects. She did not consider it now. Her dilemma was concerned with her own strict code of ethics, which accounted it not playing the game to promise a thing, whether Bible in hand or not, and fail to perform it. Against that was set another loyalty and perhaps something stronger than loyalty, and she knew that she must keep silence on a matter which would bring the inquest to an abrupt and startled adjournment. All the same, that was a very terrible oath to break when you set out to do so. . . .

"—and extending to the parietal," concluded the doctor. He glanced surreptitiously at his watch.

"Which, for us laymen," said Mr. Dwyfor Evans, glancing at his little audience with a toothy smile, "means that this unfortunate young man died almost instantly from a fractured skull. Thank you, doctor."

Doctor Williams grabbed his hat and was out of the room in two seconds. The coroner had scarcely time to cough and rustle his papers before a constable ushered in Professor Ferriday, looking grave but not unduly discomposed after his identification of the body. He seated himself beside Lewker, but was called to his feet again to take the oath.

"Well, now—James Morpeth Ferriday," muttered the coroner, peering at his papers. "Professor Ferriday, I believe?" he added, looking up and stroking his mustache.

The professor inclined his head.

"Ah," said Mr. Dwyfor Evans, nodding profoundly. "I am given to understand, professor, that this unfortunate young man was your chief assistant in your highly important work. I may say, I think, that—hum—in the absence of any relatives, the sympathy of this court goes out to you in your loss."

"Thank you, sir," said the professor simply.

The coroner coughed and rustled his papers.

"You have identified the remains as those of Raymond Francis Cauthery, professor?"

"I have."

"Aged twenty-five, of 3 Winton Crescent, London, West 7?"

"Yes."

The coroner wrote, coughed, and rustled.

"Well, now, professor," he said when he had blotted his writing, "you can tell me, I daresay, whether this unfortunate young man would be considered an experienced rock climber."

"I would consider him as such, certainly. He had climbed in North Wales to my knowledge for five years at holiday times."

"Ah. He was capable of—hum—leading, I believe is the term, quite difficult climbs?"

"Perfectly capable."

"Yet the accident occurred on the Milestone Buttress. That, I am informed, is one of the easier climbs, in high favor with novices of the sport."

"Yes. The rock, however, was—"

Mr. Evans raised a large white hand in gentle protest and smiled toothily.

"Pardon me, professor. We will leave that point, if you please. One last question. Had Mr. Cauthery, as far as you know, any heart trouble or similar disability?"

"I think not. I had occasion recently to witness an application for life insurance made by him, on which his medical examiner certified him to be perfectly free from any such defect."

The coroner looked disappointed.

"Ah. Hum. Well, now, professor, be good enough to sign this statement, please. Thank you."

Professor Ferriday returned to his seat. Mr. Dwyfor Evans conferred in whispers with the police inspector, who (Hilary thought) seemed rather surprised at being conferred with. She suspected that Mr. Evans, who had doubtless seen Professor Ferriday's name in the papers, was putting on an extra show in honor of the occasion. She hoped that was it.

The coroner's watch-chain rasped on the table as he leaned forward to take up another sheet of paper.

"Yes. Well, now," he said as he peered at it. "Miss Hil—hum—Hilary Bourne, please."

Hilary stood up and took the Bible handed to her by the sergeant. She repeated the oath steadily and faced the coroner with an inward prayer that he would not say "this unfortunate young man" again. If he did, she felt, she would scream.

"Now, Miss Bourne," Mr. Dwyfor Evans said with a very toothy grin and a fatherly nod, "I know this is not a tiny bit pleasant for you and we'll make it quite short, quite short. You were climbing the Milestone Buttress with—ah—this unfortunate young man—"

Hilary managed to control an incipient hysterical giggle at the cost of missing the rest of the question. She got out a rather squeaky "yes."

"Ah. You are not yourself an expert rock-climber?"

"No. It was my first climb."

"Hum. Most upsetting for you, Miss Bourne, I am sure. You were second on the rope and Mr. Cauthery was leading, I understand—just the two of you."

"Yes."

"Now, if you will just cast your mind back, Miss Bourne—I would not ask you this if it were not important—just cast your mind back to the period immediately before the accident." Mr. Evans's expression was a valiant effort at combining fatherly sympathy with devastating penetration. "Did you notice, at any time, any sign that Mr. Cauthery was unwell?"

Hilary had a fleeting vision of Raymond mopping his nose with a bloodstained handkerchief. She had wondered, for a short time in the small hours of last night, whether her active rebuttal of his advances could have contributed to his fall. Common sense had told her then that it could not.

"No," she said positively.

"Nothing at all? No sudden shortness of breath, no paleness or complaint of pain?"

"Nothing like that. He seemed—he seemed very fit, physically."

" Hum." The coroner seemed disappointed again. He looked round his audience of ten with a rather aggrieved air. "You see what I am trying to get at, gentlemen. This unfortunate"—he appeared to observe his own repetition this time—"this experienced climber falls from an easy rock climb. Why? Might not an attack of heart failure be the root cause?"

"The rock was slimy and he was wearing rubber shoes," Hilary put in rather impatiently.

Mr. Dwyfor Evans looked annoyed, coughed, rustled, and whispered to the inspector before turning his attention to Hilary once more.

"Well, now, Miss Bourne. Please tell me, quite shortly, quite briefly, just what happened. In your own words, if you please."

Hilary found herself wondering what other words she could have used. She pulled herself together. This was the part she had been dreading. Careful, now.

"We had reached the pitch called 'Over the Garden Wall.' The leader has to step over an edge and go out of sight. Mr. Cauthery did so, and I paid out the rope. He continued to climb for several seconds after he had stepped over. Then I heard him shout and just afterwards the rope jerked at me violently. It jammed in a crack then and I was able to climb up and look over the edge. I could see Mr. Cauthery hanging below on the rope. There was a—a wound on his head. I didn't know whether he was alive or dead but he made no answer when I called. I couldn't get to him, so I gave the Mountain Distress Signal with a whistle. A long time afterwards—it seemed a long time—Professor Ferriday and Mr. Rouse climbed down to me and took me up to the top."

The coroner nodded as he finished writing.

"Yes. Very clear, Miss Bourne, that is very clear. I won't keep you much longer. You say this unf—hum—Mr. Cauthery was wearing rubber shoes?"

" Yes. He insisted on doing so."

"The rock, however, was wet, and therefore slippery?"

"Yes."

Mr. Evans made one last effort.

"You say you heard him call out just before he fell. Was there anything in that cry to indicate its cause—did it sound as though Mr. Cauthery had experienced a sudden pain?"

Hilary braced herself and spoke through clenched teeth.

"It was just a yell," she said. "As though he felt himself slipping."

Mr. Evans, glancing at her expression, decided that this pretty girl was on the point of breaking down. He gave a final rustle to his papers.

"That is all, Miss Bourne. Thank you very much. Be good enough to sign here, please. Thank you. Thank you."

Hilary sat down again hurriedly. She felt Lewker's eyes upon her and realized that she was trembling.

"I hardly think," said the coroner, looking up from another conference with the police inspector, "that we need to hear any further evidence. The two gentlemen who first examined the body, and who later very laudably assisted in bringing it down from the crag, could testify that the unfortunate young man was then dead, but Doctor Williams has given it as his opinion that death was instantaneous and due to the fracture of the skull by violent impact against a rock, doubtless in falling. We have no actual witness of the fall, but it is clear that Raymond Cauthery met his death by misadventure in slipping from the wet rocks."

He cocked an eye at the reporters to make certain they were attending to him and delivered the short peroration he had written out beforehand. "There are many who will deplore this mountain tragedy as yet another proof of the dangerous nature of the increasingly popular sport of mountaineering. But let us not forget that all sports that appeal to our young people—"

Hilary ceased to listen to him. She was feeling quite ill. She closed her eyes, and did not open them again until Lewker's hand was under her elbow and he was hurrying her out into the open.

"What, shall we forth?" he boomed cheerfully. "Twenty minutes in an atmosphere of must and sympathy has given me, like you, a surfeit of inquest. However, it is over now and we forget it."

He helped her into the car, started the engine and let in the clutch.

"The professor will be some little time," he explained as they drove out of the winding street and began the ascent of the long hill back to Ogwen. "There are sundry arrangements to be made. There is no need for us to linger."

Hilary laid a hand on his arm.

"Please stop," she said hurriedly. "I think I'm going to be sick."

Lewker pulled up quickly and she jumped out. It was fortunately a houseless and deserted stretch of road, for her presentiment was amply fulfilled. When she got into the car again, white and shaky, Lewker was measuring liquid into the cap of a small silver flask.

"Courvoisier—don't gulp it," he said. "I keep it for emergencies only."

Hilary sipped the neat brandy and felt a little better.

"Thank you," she said apologetically. "I'm afraid you'll think I'm awfully weak."

"No." Filthy frowned as he put away his flask. "I think you are foolish, my dear."

"Why?"

"That little reaction of yours was due to a heavy nervous strain. I should say you had no sleep last night. I do not believe you had any affection for the late Cauthery or that the events of yesterday morning have shaken you so badly as to account for all this. You are hugging some painful secret to yourself, are you not?"

Hilary hesitated only a moment. Then:

"Yes," she said in a small voice.

Lewker said nothing. He sat looking in front of him and waited.

"Of course you're right," the girl broke out suddenly. "It's no good, my trying to stand it alone. I'll have to tell someone, if only to get some sleep at night."

She spoke with a hardy bravado that failed to conceal her distress.

Her companion made no comment.

"If I tell you," Hilary went on, "I want your solemn promise that you won't tell anyone else—anyone at all."

Filthy turned his head and looked steadily at her.

"You must realize, my dear," he said gently, "that that is rather a tall order."

"I don't care. I want to tell you because I think you'll be able to help me. But I won't, I won't—unless you'll promise."

He considered her in silence for a moment. Her gray eyes met his, and the depth of misery in them troubled him.

"I promise," he said slowly, "that I will not divulge what you tell me without your permission."

Hilary drew a long breath.

"It's that shout that Raymond gave before he fell," she said rapidly. "I lied about it to the coroner."

She glanced at Lewker, but he merely nodded with bent brows.

"I said it was just a yell," she went on, "as though he realized he was slipping. Well, it was more than that. It was a word he shouted—just one word, in a sort of dreadful terrified voice."

She paused and swallowed hard.

"And this one word?" said Lewker quietly,

"It was— '*Don't!*' "said Hilary.

CHAPTER ELEVEN

There is in this business more than Nature
Was ever conduct of.

THE TEMPEST

AFTER Hilary's disclosure there was quite a long silence. She and Lewker sat in the motionless Wolseley gazing in front of them at the distant peaks that towered above the green hillsides and the climbing toad. The girl had expected an exclamation of surprise or incredulity, followed perhaps by a severe comment on her folly in suppressing important evidence. Instead her companion took a leather case from his pocket and offered her a cigarette.

"I know you do not usually indulge," he observed when she started to refuse, "but the soothing effect will be all the greater on that account. I have often thought that Hamlet would have found tobacco a useful remedy for 'the heartache, and the thousand natural shocks that flesh is heir to.' " He flicked his lighter and lit Hilary's cigarette and his own. "A sad reflection, that a pack of Player's might have calmed the Prince of Denmark and saved Ophelia and Laertes and all the rest of the stabbings and poisonings. I take it, my dear, you are certain that the word was 'Don't'?"

"Absolutely certain."

"You infer that Cauthery was speaking to, or imploring, some third person out of sight who was threatening him in some way. Why should he not have been speaking to you?"

"To me?" Hilary was startled.

"Yes. Suppose the rope had caught in that crack. I know from experience that it often feels as though one's second were pulling on it. Cauthery might have thought you were pulling and called to you, or started to call, 'don't pull.' "

Hilary shook her head with decision.

"No. I'm sure the rope was running freely for one thing, and for another it wasn't that sort of voice he used. It was—well, a sort of agonized shriek."

She found herself able to speak quite calmly and steadily now. Lewker puffed at his cigarette and tapped off the ash against the edge of the windscreen.

"Very well," he boomed. "You think, then, that there was someone else on the Milestone Buttress, someone who was the cause of Cauthery's fall. Will you tell me why you concealed this at the inquest?"

Hilary had known she would have to explain, and she had dreaded it. But it didn't seem hard to tell Filthy.

"It was something that happened when we were lower down the climb," she said. "Raymond thought he saw Michael scrambling up the scree at the side of the Buttress. It was somebody with red hair, he said, and I told him it might be Derwen Jones—he was going up to Bochlwyd that morning, you know. Whoever it was, he was out of sight when I got up to where Raymond was standing. But afterwards, when I was waiting for help, I began to think, and—and—"

"You remembered," Filthy said gravely, "that you had been making Michael jealous, and rather enjoying it. You remembered that there were signs that he and Cauthery had quarrelled. You thought Michael might have climbed up from the scree, descended the top pitches of the Buttress, and pushed Cauthery off that ledge. In short, that Michael was a murderer."

"No!" Hilary's denial was vehement. "I didn't think that at all. But don't you see, if I'd told about that shout there'd have been a lot of questions and all the rest would have to come out and people might *think* Michael had—had—"

"Exactly," said Filthy. "You were afraid for Michael."

"Yes. But I know he couldn't do a thing like that. *I know.*" She looked at him anxiously. "You aren't forgetting your promise, are you?"

"I am not forgetting. But you realize, of course, that if the third person on the Buttress was not Michael, and if your suspicions are correct, then someone else is a murderer."

Hilary shivered. She threw away her half-smoked cigarette and clenched her small fists.

"All the same," she said, "you'll not persuade me to tell the police."

"I shall not try to, my dear. It seems to me that you may be making too much of this matter. A shout from behind a massive wall of rock can easily be mistaken."

He refrained from mentioning what an awkward position the girl would be in if she now revealed to the police the fact she had hidden and lied about at the inquest. It was part of the Abercrombie Lewker philosophy that spilt milk was better left where it lay. He knew, however, that to leave unresolved the doubt that was working like poison in Hilary's mind was impossible.

"Well," he said cheerfully, "we can but put the business to the test. All things are capable of proof, as somebody or other said. This afternoon you and I will go for a walk, alone, taking a rope. And you shall do a second ascent of Milestone Buttress."

Hilary twisted round in her seat and stared at him in dismay.

"But I can't possibly," she declared. "You don't understand. I hate climbing and mountains and everything to do with them now. I never want to *see* the Buttress again. I'll never—"

"Wait," said Lewker. He laid a hairy paw over her hand on the seat beside him. "Listen. Yesterday was one day out of the twenty thousand days to come. Tomorrow or the day after it will be behind you for ever. You are not the girl I take you for if you intend to let it spoil all the enjoyment of the hills that lies before you—the richest heritage, some of us think, that this world holds for the recreation of human beings. Your remedy is the remedy of the rider who falls at his first fence—mount and at it again." He released her hand with an odd chuckle. "Bless me," he added, "but I grow as eloquent as a tourist pamphlet. 'Wonderful Wales for Weary Workers!' By the way, have you had any experience of detective work?"

"No."

"Neither have I. This shall be my first case, *you* shall be my Watson, and we shall probably find that there is nothing to detect. But I must have my Watson on the Milestone Buttress."

"All right," said Hilary suddenly, "I'll come. It's better to know, isn't it?"

"Even," said Filthy, watching her gravely, "if it should turn out to be—Michael?"

Hilary faced him, lips firmly set and gray eyes blazing.

"Yes—even if it was Michael. But of course," she added, "it wasn't."

"Well done," Filthy said. He started the car and drove on up the pass. Beside him Hilary sat silent, her eyes on the lofty crags of the Glyders. Sunshine was chasing the somber colors from the summits and sparkling from tumbling waters high up among the rocks. There was, she reflected, no reason for her to feel any less troubled now than she had felt on the journey down to Bethesda; things were really just as dark and uncertain as they had been then. But somehow her spirits had lifted, perhaps because the burden that had weighed so heavily upon her had Lewker's broad shoulders beneath it now.

She looked sideways at her companion. The tufts of black hair on either side of his massive bald head were flicked upward by a back-draught of air so that they had the shape of a laurel wreath. He looked like a Nero with a bulbous nose. Yet for all his odd appearance there was a comforting solidity about Mr. Lewker. Hilary, remembering her cousin's stories of the many tight wartime corners from which Filthy's quick wit had extracted him, felt glad she had confided in him. Whatever was to come she had an ally who would not fail her.

She sat back with a little sigh, and a genial warmth filled her as the car ran into a pool of spring sunshine.

The depressing atmosphere that had hung over the Dol Afon breakfast table seemed to have cleared away when the party met at lunch-time; rather, thought Hilary, as though getting the inquest smoothly over had been a relief to everyone. She refused to follow this impression down the dark avenues of speculation, however, and tried to forget her fears and suspicions in the conversation going on around her .

With the exception of Mildred Jupp the party seemed to have decided that the time for hushed voices and avoidance of all mention of the accident had gone. Mildred, who had been vaguely affirmative when Hilary asked her if her visit to the doctor had been helpful, kept her eyes on her plate and did not speak at all. Michael Rouse was taciturn as always, but Professor Ferriday, though his wrinkled face looked graver than usual, was discussing in a matter-of-fact way with Uncle George the disposal of the dead man's belongings. Aunt Mabel was being very practical about the funeral.

"None of us will feel like climbing any more this holiday, of course," she was saying to Harold, "but I do think we all ought to go to the funeral. The poor boy had no relatives, you know. It's on Friday, so we'll have to stay here two more days. I've told Mrs. Morris we shall leave immediately after the funeral and she quite understands. I hope, dear," she added to Hilary, that you'll feel you can stay till then."

"I will, of course," said Hilary.

"Splendid. That will be so nice." Mrs. Jupp's voice sounded as though she were arranging a vicarage tennis party. "Have you thought how you'll get home to Manchester? "

Uncle George interrupted his conversation with the professor to break in; his jovial roar was almost back to normal.

"Look here, Hilary, Ferry and I were just talking about how we're going to get Raymond's car back. Ferry says he can drive it. I daresay he wouldn't mind running you to a railway station somewhere on the line for Manchester."

"I would certainly do that," the professor agreed.

Hilary hesitated. Lewker spoke before she could say anything.

"That would be out of your way, professor. I suggest you and Rouse drive back together. I will see that Miss Bourne gets to wherever she wants to go."

Hilary flashed a grateful glance at him.

"Then that settles that," said Aunt Mabel with great satisfaction. "Now the only thing that's bothering me is what we are all to wear at the funeral."

She tried without success to enlist her daughter's attention to this vital matter, and Hilary had to act as consultant and committee. The girl found it hard to concentrate on a business that seemed to her both trivial and distasteful; and when the sartorial resources of the party had been duly discussed and allocated, Mrs. Jupp frowned at her in some concern.

"You look pale and ill, dear," she said gently. "It has been a very trying time for you, of course." She glanced out of the parlor window. "The sun is shining, and I think you should go for a nice walk to get some fresh air into your lungs, and then early to bed."

"An excellent prescription," boomed Lewker approvingly. "If Miss Bourne will accept my escort for the first part of the program, I offer it gladly."

Michael Rouse looked as though he was about to volunteer to join the walking party. Hilary forestalled him hastily.

"I do accept, Mr. Lewker—if it's just you and I. I don't feel like a crowd, somehow."

"Naturally, naturally," nodded Uncle George with noisy sympathy. "A little gentle exercise and then a good night's steep—do you all the good in the world. For my part—and I daresay you feel the same, Ferry—I shall take a nap this afternoon."

They rose from the table and dispersed to the sitting room or their bedrooms. Ten minutes later Hilary and Lewker were walking away from Dol Afon across the fields in the direction of the Milestone Buttress. A few fleecy clouds high above the sharp peak of Tryfan hurried over the blue, and a fresh wind tempered the warmth of the sunshine. There was every sign of a spell of fine weather, but Filthy wore his stained windproof jacket buttoned about him. Hilary had changed into trousers and windproof.

"You haven't brought a rope," she remarked as they climbed over the wall on to the road.

Filthy tapped the bulge round his middle.

"My spare fifty feet of Alpine line is here," he replied, "and confoundedly uncomfortable it is. I shall remove it as soon as we are out of sight of Dol Afon. I feel like Macbeth—'cabin'd, cribb'd, confin'd, bound in.' "

"Are you going to quote only from the Tragedies now?" asked Hilary with a faint smile.

He nodded a benevolent head at her.

"That is the spirit. A long face will not help us in this business."

They tramped along the road in silence for a little while. As they rounded a corner under the crags of Tryfan the gray nose of Milestone Buttress came into sight above on their left. Hilary raised her eyes to it with a little shudder. Lewker was gazing upward under a shading palm.

"It appears to be deserted," he observed. "Excellent. We do not want an audience for our investigations."

"What—what do you expect to find?" she asked him half-fearfully.

"I expect nothing, neither do I conjecture—yet. We are looking for facts. Facts are the—er—grist for the investigator's mill." He grinned at her. "Bear with me, I beg. The part of Great Detective is one I haven't played before. I shall study to improve."

They reached the tenth milestone from Bangor and clambered over the fence. The afternoon sun beat down with summer heat as they mounted slowly over the jumbled boulders to the little rock wall, crowned by its rowan tree. Hilary seemed to hear Cauthery's drawling voice, as she had heard it less than thirty hours before, saying: "It's a sort of preliminary canter, darling." She thrust the memory quickly from her and followed Lewker past the rock wall to the foot of the Buttress proper. He had already taken the coil of line from his waist, and now made a bowline loop in each end and handed one to Hilary.

"We will be thorough," he announced, covertly watching her face for any sign of strain. "I want you to tell me everything that happened or was said on this climb. Also I want you to let me know at once if you find the task too trying."

"All right," Hilary said, slipping the loop over her shoulders. She was quite calm now. First of all we did that rock wall below."

She went on to repeat what she could remember of their conversation, and ended by pointing out the steep Superdirect route by which Cauthery had climbed the first pitch.

"He called down that the rock was quite dry, and then climbed out of sight. Let me see—nothing else down here, I think. Oh—except that a green bus, the eleven o'clock to Llanrwst it'd be, went past on the road while I was waiting."

"Very well. We commence. I shall refrain from doing the Superdirect." He scrambled up the first few feet of the Ordinary route and then paused, looking down at her. "By the way, did Cauthery make rather intense love to you that morning?"

The girl's pale cheeks colored.

"Yes," she said briefly.

"I thought he might. *De mortuis* apart, he was that sort of young man."

The shortness of the rope necessitated the first easy trough being taken in two pitches. They reached the broad ledge under the steeper part, and Hilary told how Cauthery had here spoken of seeing a red-headed man on the screes high up to westward of the Buttress. Lewker nodded thoughtfully.

"He was not certain that it was Rouse?"

"No."

"When we saw Derwen Jones starting off across the fields that morning he had two dogs with him. Neither of you saw any dogs on the scree?"

"I didn't. Raymond said nothing about them, so I suppose he didn't."

They began the next pitch—the steep little slab. Lewker was almost at the top when he diverged from the route to make a long step over to the left. He reached down to a narrow crack in the slab and pulled something out. As he drew himself up to the ledge above Hilary saw that he was holding a bloodstained handkerchief.

"I can explain that!" she called up to him.

"You can do it better when you are on this ledge, then."

He took in the rope as she climbed and belayed her securely to a spike of rock before allowing her to describe her active repulse of Cauthery's advances. When she had finished Lewker chuckled.

"You may call me callous if you will," be said, "but I cannot bring myself to regret that Master Cauthery was taken down a peg in this world before he so prematurely left it for the next."

"You don't think—it might have—caused his fall?"

"I certainly do not. The idea is absurd."

He spoke quite sharply, and Hilary knew he was concerned that she should have thought herself responsible. She felt grateful as she paid out the rope while Lewker hauled himself up the sloping crack of the next pitch.

Hilary had dreaded the moment of arrival in the niche where she had spent those interminable minutes of suspense. But to her surprise she found her apprehension fading as the great gray slabs of the Buttress fell steadily below under her nailed boots. Nothing of tragedy had lingered here after all. The sunlit spaces of lake and mountain smiled all around and the rock was warm and rough and friendly under her fingers. Almost she was enjoying herself. She managed the narrow crack more neatly than she had done the first time, and its conquest occupied her mind to the exclusion of distasteful memories.

"I forgot," she panted as she pulled herself into the niche. "The mist came down while we were climbing this pitch—a drizzly sort of mist that wet the rock quickly."

Lewker grunted and slipped a loop of rope over the small pinnacle of rock that Cauthery had used in the same way. He was peering at the sloping floor of the niche, where a brownish spot or two had escaped being washed away by rain.

"The remains of nose-bleeding, I presume," he muttered. "You can face the next pitch?" he added, eyeing her keenly.

"Of course, I'm all right now. The rocks aren't so dreadful, after all."

"Good girl," he boomed. "Now for the Garden Wall. If I dawdle a little over this pitch do not be surprised."

He stepped up on the edge of the niche, threw a leg over the thin flake of the arête, and lowered himself out of sight on the other side. For a moment, as the rope crept slowly out round the rock, Hilary experienced again the numbing shock of Cauthery's fall and the sick empty feeling that had followed it. It passed swiftly and she was herself again. The rope stopped moving. There was a pause, and then a muffled shout made her jump. It was only Lewker, however, announcing that he proposed to climb down into the gully. For five minutes she heard nothing more. She was beginning to wonder whether she ought to call out to ask if he was all right when the slack of the rope was hauled in and his booming voice told her to come along. She climbed up and swung herself over the ridge, out of the sunlight into the chill shade of the eastern flank of the precipice.

She had been too dazed and shaken, when Michael and the professor had brought her up the upper pitches of the Buttress on the previous morning, to take much notice of the situations. She found herself now pressed face inwards against a vertical wall of rock, her boots on a smooth ledge that ran steeply across and up to the left. The rope from her waist curved in a long scallop across the wall and appeared to disappear into its surface fifteen feet away. There was no sign of Lewker. Without looking down into the gully where Cauthery had fallen she sidled cautiously up the ledge. It was broad enough for her boots, but there was very little for her fingers to hold on to; it would, after all be quite easy to fall off if one's foot slipped. She did the last part rather hastily and suddenly found herself peering round a sharp corner into the deep cleft of the Cave. It was dank and dim inside and smelt of recently struck match. Filthy was there, squatting like a bald-headed gnome in the gloom among the rock fragments that formed the floor of the place.

"I felt a bit out of balance on that ledge," Hilary said breathlessly as she drew herself in beside him. " If his feet slipped, you know, perhaps it was—"

"It was not an accident," said Filthy.

His deep voice sounded ominous in that hollow chamber of the rock. He groped behind him and picked up what appeared in the obscurity to be a splinter of rock about two feet long.

"There is no need for you to look at this," he went on as Hilary craned her neck to inspect it. "I found it pushed under that flat boulder at the inner end of the cave. On the sharp edge at one end of it there is some dried blood and a few dark hairs."

CHAPTER TWELVE

An undergoing stomach, to bear up
Against what should ensue.
THE TEMPEST

FROM time to time those who climb mountains have recorded their opinion that if the momentous councils of the world were held on mountaintops the business of mankind could be transacted without rancor or bloodshed. "No one," wrote C.E. Montague, "could be utterly mean on the very tip of the Weisshorn." For the less earth-shaking decisions of individuals a Welsh peak, or even the top of a rock climb when one has just done the climb, has a similar virtue. There is nothing like taking one's life in one's hands, even with every precaution against accident, for stripping away the accumulated layers of false value from one's eyes. From the top of a climb the doubts and fears and problems of a human life can be viewed like the patchwork fields and farms of the valley below; they have not disappeared, but they have shrunk into their true relation with the landscape.

Mr. Abercrombie Lewker, seated comfortably at the summit of Milestone Buttress with the afternoon sunshine warming his paunch and his back against a convenient boulder, knew this well enough. He had had it in mind when he persuaded Hilary Bourne to climb the Buttress with him. Cauthery's death a few feet away from her, and her suspicion—now confirmed—that he had been murdered, were not minor troubles, and they would have to be faced. But he had brought her to a spot whence she might see them, not as gigantic walls cutting her off from all happiness and peace of mind, but as two isolated if highly unpleasant facts in a world that was still full of pleasant things. He hoped he had been successful in this, not only for Hilary's sake but also because he foresaw difficulties ahead wherein he would need her as an ally.

Hilary had taken off her wind-jacket and was lying upon it among the heather, gazing down at the sunlit lake below. The breeze stirred her straight fair hair and there was a little color in her cheeks.

"It's funny," she said without turning her head, "but all this dreadful business—Raymond's death, and someone having murdered him and all that—doesn't seem quite so horrible up here. I ought to feel all worked up, and sick, and afraid. So I do, a bit. It's just as terrible as ever, but somehow—oh, I can't explain."

"You can look it in the face," Lewker nodded. " You are afraid, but you're going to fight."

"That's it, exactly."

"I am glad of that."

He leaned forward and offered her a cigarette. She shook her head and sat up, facing him.

"Because," he went on, lighting up himself and blowing a long stream of smoke, "we are going to face some ugly possibilities together. First of all, we have discovered beyond any possible doubt that Raymond Cauthery was murdered, almost certainly by someone who waited in the Milestone Cave and struck him with that splinter of rock as his head appeared round the corner."

The girl, her eyes steady on his face, waited.

"Our plain duty, yours and mine," Lewker continued, "is to take that information to the police at once."

Hilary shook her head violently.

"No. You promised—"

"I know. But a respectable citizen would consider that promise untenable. However, I am not a respectable citizen, nor am I a policeman. I will take the responsibility of compounding a felony by suggesting a compromise. We have two days before the Dol Afon party disperses. If at the end of that time we have not discovered the murderer, I shall, with or without your permission, my dear, go to the police and tell them everything we know."

"I see," said Hilary in a small voice. She looked up suddenly. " Why," she whispered, "shouldn't we leave things as they are? The thing can't be undone—and no one but ourselves thinks it was anything but an accident."

Lewker wagged his head at her sorrowfully.

"You know quite well you are talking nonsense, my dear. You have said yourself 'it's better to know.' For my part I am of the opinion that some murders may be justifiable—but to let the murderer get away with it is quite unjustifiable. You are thinking, of course, that if Michael Rouse did not kill Cauthery it is quite likely that some other member of the Dol Afon party did."

"I won't think that—I can't," cried the girl quickly. "They're all nice, ordinary people. Besides, none of them had any reason to do a thing like that. Derwen Jones is much more—"

"Wait." Lewker held up a hand. "How long have you known them?"

"Well, I met them all—except Raymond Cauthery—at Dol Afon this time last year."

"For the first time. Have you seen any of them between then and now?"

Hilary reddened. "Only Michael Rouse. He came to Manchester on business last December and we went to the theater together."

Lewker drew at his cigarette and frowned at the cloud of smoke.

"You know next to nothing about them. People who had known Charles Peace for years swore that he was incapable of murder. Tell me," he added suddenly, "are you in love with Michael Rouse?"

Hilary turned away and looked out over the sun-flecked landscape of crag and valley.

"I don't know," she said in a low voice. "I don't know. But I do know he didn't kill Raymond Cauthery."

"Pardon me, but you know nothing of the kind. It is time that we came to the meat and marrow of the matter. Vague intuitions and half-baked predilections—overboard with the lot! Facts, facts, facts, my dear, from this time forth, if we are to find our murderer—and find him I will, though his name should be Abercrombie Lewker!"

The combination of his ancient garments and lounging attitude with this dramatic utterance was so odd that Hilary, who had bristled with anger at his first sentence, ended by laughing in spite of herself.

"I am happy," said Mr. Lewker stiffly, "if my earnest resolve affords you amusement. Let me assure you—"

"I'm sorry," she said hurriedly. "Of course we must start work in earnest. I warn you, though, I'm not going to be much good at it. I haven't got a scientific mind."

"Neither have I. Between us we must cultivate one. However, all we require at the moment is a calm detachment, an impersonal and callous consideration. I think you are able to produce that now?"

"I'll try," said Hilary. "There's one thing," she went on. "You talk about the murderer as 'him.' Couldn't it have been a 'her'?"

"Very well," said Filthy. "Let us consider that." He squashed the stub of his cigarette against a rock and folded his arms with an air of getting to business. "The weapon, a two-foot rock splinter used as a club, could have been used by a man or a woman. With such a weapon it would not need any abnormal strength to batter in a man's skull."

"Why did you leave it in the cave? Couldn't there be fingerprints on it? And why didn't the murderer throw it away?"

"To take your last question first, because he—shall we use the masculine for convenience?—because he had nowhere to throw it. If he had hurled it down to the screes, might not some passing scrambler have found it and reported the blood and those black hairs? No, it was safer hidden in the floor of the cave, where he had found it. The odds were against anyone looking for such a thing."

"But he knew the—the murderee shouted 'Don't,'" objected Hilary. "Wouldn't he think his game was given away by that?"

"I do not think so. No doubt he had hoped to get in his blow before Cauthery had time to shout. But the wind was blowing and you were on the other side of the ridge. You might not have heard it at all. And as it was, you probably would not have attached so much meaning to the word if Cauthery had failed to mention the red-haired man he saw on the screes."

"No," Hilary admitted.

"As to fingerprints, even if we had the requisite apparatus we should get no results from the rough surface of that piece of rock." He removed a sharp stone from beneath him and settled himself more comfortably. "'There, then, we have the means of murder. Simple, but ingenious, because a skull smashed on a rock is a very likely happening when a climber falls. Now, speaking broadly, who could have used that means?"

"Almost anyone," ventured the girt. "It might have been somebody we don't know at all."

"Someone who wanted Cauthery dead and who happened to be climbing down the Buttress as he climbed up? Come, come—the bounds of possibility cannot be strained so far. We must surely say that the murderer was someone who knew that you and Cauthery were to climb the Buttress yesterday morning. Did anyone know that except the members of the Dol Afon party?"

Hilary was silent. Then she leaned forward eagerly.

"Derwen Jones did. He was in the kitchen when I was telling Mrs. Morris. And I think he was—well, Raymond and Gwennie—"

" 'Hold, or cut bowstrings'!" Filthy raised a stubby forefinger. "You are encroaching upon Motive. Remember your detective novels. Means,

Opportunity, Motive—the Three Weird Sisters to whose oracular cave the hopeful sleuth drags his dark suspicions. A metaphor," he added thoughtfully, "that needs polishing somewhat. But we are not yet finished with Means. Did Derwen Jones know of the Milestone Cave and its peculiar opportunities for murder?"

"He might have done. He sometimes goes climbing—Mrs. Morris told me so. And he seemed quite annoyed when Mrs. Morris said it was a pity he didn't hear me blowing that whistle."

"Hum. We must find out if he has ever climbed Milestone Buttress. Now, we have nine people who on the score of Means alone could have killed Raymond Cauthery—the eight visitors at Dol Afon and Derwen Jones. I could include Mrs. Morris and Gwennie, who both knew where you were going to climb and when, if you think it necessary,"

"Well," said Hilary, with a faint smile at the thought of their buxom landlady climbing down the Buttress to commit a murder, "Mrs. Morris told me she and Gwennie were together in the kitchen all that morning, so unless they're in cahoots—"

"They can be eliminated, I think. Now let us turn our joint scientific mind to the next considerations. Here we shall find ourselves short of facts, but at least we shall discover what facts we need to establish."

A cloud shadow passed over Tryfan and for a few minutes their eyrie of rock and heather was darkened and somber. Hilary shivered involuntarily, and Filthy glanced quickly at her and away again.

"You play Watson as though you'd rehearsed the part," he remarked cheerfully, rummaging in his pockets. "Keep it up. You will need the undergoing stomach that Prospero talked about, for we are about to pick holes in the characters of people we have walked and supped with."

He took out a pencil and a red-covered notebook and set the latter on his ample thigh. The girl was frowning at a sprig of bilberry she held between her fingers.

"It's hateful," she said slowly, "to work against them secretly like this. Couldn't we tell them frankly what we're doing?"

"And have someone insist on calling in the police at once? Well, we may come to that if it becomes necessary to ask questions which would give our game away. But we are only working against one of them—the murderer. Remember that."

He had been writing down a list of names as he talked. Hilary scrambled to her feet, put on her wind-jacket, and sat down beside Filthy so that she could look over his shoulder.

"Why," she exclaimed, "you've got my name down first!"

Filthy chuckled. "Why not? Haven't you ever read a detective story where the Watson character turned out to be the murderer? Perhaps you fail to realize that there are no witnesses to your story. You had

Opportunity, and I could find you a Motive."

"But how on earth could I—"

"You admit yourself that you had a violent quarrel with Cauthery. The cause of that quarrel may have been something other than you stated it to be." He closed his eyes and went on in a monotonous booming voice. "Cauthery climbed into the cave and you joined him there. The quarrel was renewed. When his back was turned you picked up the rock splinter from the floor and hit him with it, killing him. Aghast at what you had done, you sought a means of making it look like an accident. You pushed the body into the gully, where it slid down over the edge and hung on the rope. Then, with some ingenious arrangement of belays, you climbed back again over the ridge below and into the niche, jammed the rope into the crack, and blew your whistle." He opened his eyes suddenly. "Presto! The illusion is complete."

Hilary's laugh was a trifle forced.

"I think that theory falls down on the 'ingenious arrangement of belays,' " she said. "I admit the rest is possible, but I don't see how I could have got back down that ledge and at the same time held the body on the rope."

"Right!" approved Lewker swiftly. "Consider the cases of the others as impersonally as you considered your own and the task will be easier. We pass on to the next name on our list. Abercrombie Lewker."

"Motive—didn't like the deceased," said Hilary. "And thought he was getting—" she stumbled a little—"getting too fresh with me. Opportunity—"

"I fear Opportunity rules me out. Professor Ferriday and Harold Jupp can both testify that I was climbing up Grooved Arête on the other flank of Tryfan when the murder took place. What is the verdict?"

"Eliminated, I should think."

"That is two of us eliminated. Next, Harold Jupp. Any motive?"

"Well," Hilary said slowly, "I know he was expecting to get a job in Professor Ferriday's laboratory until Raymond came along and got in first. He told me that when we were walking that first day—and he said if Raymond or Michael should leave, the professor had promised him the place."

"Hum. There have been less plausible motives than that for murder. On Opportunity, however, we again fall down. Harold was on the other end of my rope at the time of the murder. I can give him a complete alibi from the time we left Dol Afon to the time you were brought up to the top of the Buttress. By the way, we must try and establish these various times."

"Why?"

"It is invariably done. The Great Detective's timetable frequently reveals the one flaw in an otherwise perfect alibi. Even so, I cannot see any timetable revealing a flaw in Harold's. I admit I was climbing slowly on Grooved Arête, but not so slowly that Harold could have untied himself from the rope, dashed round to the Milestone and done the deed, and tied on again before I had reached the top of the pitch."

Hilary laughed and then became suddenly grave.

"Have you thought," she said, "that someone might have rigged a booby trap in the Milestone Cave? Could that rock have been arranged so as to fall when Raymond started to climb in?"

"This is ingenious," boomed Lewker with enthusiasm. "No, that had not occurred to me. You propose, I see, to upset all our alibis. However, it would be a difficult trap to arrange and exceedingly hit-or-miss. Furthermore, there was the cry of 'Don't' and the lethal weapon tucked neatly away in the back of the cave where it could not possibly have fallen after hitting Cauthery."

"All right—I withdraw the suggestion."

"Not at all. We shall pigeonhole that idea along with Harold's motive. Small though that motive appears at present, Harold benefits by Cauthery's death. On our present data, though, we shall have to eliminate him on the score of Opportunity." He consulted his notebook. "Professor Ferriday. Motive?"

"I shouldn't think he can have one," Hilary objected. "Raymond was his senior assistant, you know. He'll be stuck without him, because even if Harold takes his place it'll take months to get up to date with the sort of work they've been doing. I know that from what Raymond told me."

Lewker rubbed his chin thoughtfully.

"There are two things we must chalk up against the professor," he said. "There was that rather odd matter Mr. Jupp was joking about. The newspaper story about his insuring the lives of his assistants. It seems to have been unfounded, but we may have to go into it."

"How can you do that without explaining everything to him?"

"Forgive me if I quote from a writer other than Shakespeare—'I have my methods.' The second suspicious circumstance is that during our first day's walk the professor put forward a theory that it would be easy to push someone off a crag without being detected as a murderer."

Hilary knitted her brows. "Doesn't that rather tell in his favor? He surely wouldn't talk about it before doing it."

"That might be intended to put possible trusting investigators off the scent. I believe it is known as the Double Bluff. And it is at least certain that the idea of making a murder look like a climbing accident was in his head. Let us look at Opportunity. Alas, the professor is given an alibi by Harold and myself. When we heard your whistle he was out of sight, it is true, but I will swear till all's blue that it was his voice we heard five seconds later coming down from the mist—no more than two hundred feet above us."

"Suppose," said Hilary rather bitterly, "suppose he had a gramophone already hidden up there, with a record of his voice."

"I will not believe that you read that sort of detective fiction, sweet coz. Who would have set the record going, if such a recording were possible? No, I cannot but admit that unless the professor has been using Welsh wizardry or practicing long-distance ventriloquism he is joined with myself and Harold Jupp in a tripartite alibi—a pretty expression, which I hereby copyright. However, we note down Professor Ferriday with Harold for investigation on the score of Motive, bearing in mind your suggestion of some ingenious form of booby trap."

He scribbled in his notebook busily. From the valley below came the faint excited barking of sheepdogs at work. Hilary saw a close-packed flock of sheep moving swiftly across the green of a lakeside field with the smooth motion of a drifting cloud. She became aware that her companion was making a longer pause than usual; and even as she noticed this he began speaking in the same judicial boom.

"Michael Rouse. Motive—had some sort of disagreement with Cauthery on the previous day. And you will agree we must add jealousy."

Hilary forced herself to maintain an impersonal attitude, but it wasn't easy.

"Opportunity, full marks," she said with rather strained casualness. "He told you himself he was only two or three hundred feet above the top of the Milestone when he heard the whistle. And there was the red-haired man Raymond saw on the scree—I suppose that would be ten or fifteen minutes before the murder. Michael could have done it."

"Bravo," whispered Filthy, pausing in his notebook entry to pat her shoulder. "Motive could be adequate. Opportunity, as you say, full marks. That finishes the people whose movements we know something about."

He snapped open his cigarette-case and passed it to her. This time she accepted a cigarette and for some moments they smoked in silence. The westering sun was warming the heathery ledge again and the blues and greens of the distant mountains had the smooth clarity of hill scenery on a railway poster. The faint high voices of the sheep floated up to them on the light breeze, an irregular *obbligato* to the murmurous whispering of a thousand faraway streams.

"Now for the others." Filthy's booming voice made Hilary jump. "The Reverend George Jupp. Motive—none that I know of, unless we read some deeper meaning into that little tiff he had with Cauthery at supper the night before last. Opportunity—he was out on the hills all morning until well after the murder. He will have to go down as full marks for that. Mrs. Jupp. Motive—again none that we know of. Opportunity, I think, good."

"She can't climb, you know. There's that gammy leg of hers."

"Arthritis is a variable trouble, and gammy legs can be counterfeited. Mrs. Jupp, so far as we know, was within a mile of the scene of the crime from the time Rouse left her to go and get his tobacco from Ogwen Cottage to the time she met you and Harold on the road below the Buttress. She has been a climber in her time and doubtless knows the Cave on the Milestone. We must grant a possible opportunity to Mrs. Jupp, unless she has an alibi, which I doubt."

"All right," said Hilary, " but it's pretty farfetched."

"Perhaps. Now we come to Mildred Jupp. We do not know what time Mildred left Dol Afon to go for a walk that morning, but that can be ascertained. She came round the bottom of the Milestone about ten minutes after we had brought the body down. Without being too positive about it, we may say that there is probable Opportunity in her case. As to Motive—well, there is the fact, reported to me by you, that Uncle George expected her engagement to Cauthery shortly, to set against my own impression that Cauthery had ceased to be interested in her. A woman scorned, if you'll forgive the cliché."

Hilary tore viciously at a root of heather.

"That's beastly," she burst out suddenly.

"So is murder," said Lewker mildly.

"I know. I'm sorry. The scientific mind slipped up for a second. Please go on considering Mildred."

Lewker scratched his head with his pencil and glanced sideways at her.

"I rather thought you might do that," he said.

"Why me?"

"Mildred may tell you what I want to know. There was something odd about that night when she woke us all up, with a scream variously described as being the result of acute indigestion, nightmare and an illusion that she had been poisoned. Both her parents behaved oddly next morning. Why did she not scream in the room where she was sleeping with you, if it was any of these things? Why wait until she was in her parents' bedroom? Why did Uncle George go off before breakfast? Why did Aunt Mabel stiffen like a swearing cat when Cauthery came into the room next morning?"

"I don't see what all this can possibly have to do with the murder," Hilary said rather wearily.

"No more do I. But it is an oddness, and all oddnesses affecting the people in this notebook may have a vital bearing on that last monstrous oddness of murder. Will you see what you can find out? I have a considerable program of investigation laid out for myself already."

"All right—if I must." She sat upright quickly, her head on one side. "I can hear voices."

Filthy pulled himself to his feet and going to the edge of the top slab peered over down the Buttress.

"A party of climbers coming up," he announced. "Also it is after four o'clock, and time we were returning from our walk. There is, however, one more name on our list. Derwen Jones. We have time for him, I think. On the hypothesis that he has climbed Milestone Buttress, he had Means and Opportunity. You, I believe, suspect, and I know, that he had Motive."

He told her briefly of the conversation he had over heard from his window three nights before, and the incident in the barn-garage later.

"So you see," he concluded, "that with Cauthery's tale of the red-headed man on the scree we have a prime suspect in Derwen Jones."

"I suppose," Hilary said with a cynicism that was unlike her, "that makes it quite impossible that he should really be the murderer."

"These things, I fear, do not always conform to the customs of fiction."

Cheery shouts from below indicated that the climbers on the Buttress were nearing the top. Lewker and Hilary left their sunny ledge and scrambled away in the direction of the path leading down from the North Ridge. On the way back to Dol Afon Lewker set himself to entertain his companion, who was inclined to be gloomily meditative, with anecdotes of theatrical personalities. He succeeded so well that by the time they were walking up the track to the farm Hilary was asking eager questions about the stage and the odd, warmhearted folk whose life was in the glare of limelight.

Mrs. Morris was taking in some clothes from a line slung at the side of the farmhouse as they approached the gate. She waved to them and called out something inaudible. With a word of apology to Hilary, who went on into the house, Filthy walked across to her.

"I wass not wishing to trouble you, sir," said Mrs. Morris, puffing a clothespeg neatly out of her mouth into a basket, her arms being full of newly dried linen. "It wass only that there iss a thing I forgot. Gwennie reminded me about it just now, and I did think I ought to tell some one of the gentlemen or ladies, but they wass all up in their rooms, like, and when I saw you and Miss Bourne coming now, I remembered it again, and—"

"And what is this most important matter, Mrs. Morris?" Filthy cut short the flow.

"Oh, it iss not important, indeed. It wass only a young man that called asking after poor Mr. Cauthery, the morning he wass killed. It wass just a few minutes after Miss Bourne and poor Mr. Cauthery had drove away in the car. I told the young man they wass off to climb up the Milestone Buttress, and he went away. I didn't ask his name, being busy, like."

"What was this young man like in appearance?"

Mrs. Morris picked up her basket of pegs and straightened herself with a grunt.

"Oh, ferry thin he wass, sir. Glasses he had, and a voice like them lambs you hear crying for their mams."

"Thank you, Mrs. Morris," said Lewker abstractedly.

"Thank you, sir, indeed," said Mrs. Morris, turning to walk away with her burden of garments, sheets and pillowcases. "His short pants," she called over her shoulder as she went, "wass too long."

Lewker went thoughtfully into the house and up to his room. For five minutes he stood gazing at the floor. Then he took out his red-covered notebook and added another name to the pencilled list.

CHAPTER THIRTEEN

The strongest oaths are straw
To the fire i' the blood.
THE TEMPEST

"IF YOU'D really like to see it, I'll get it," said Aunt Mabel. She glanced rather dubiously at her husband. "I suppose it's all right—after all, it's really two days ago—"

"Of course it's all right, Mabel," interrupted Uncle George, his roar almost back to normal. "Our sincere reverence for the dead need not prevent us from admiring your watercolor."

"But if you would rather not, please ignore my request, Mrs. Jupp," put in Lewker hypocritically.

"I'll pop up and get it," said Aunt Mabel, who like most amateur artists was averse to exhibiting her efforts unasked but delighted and resolute when anyone asked to see them. She got up from the table and went out.

Supper was just finished. It had been a perfectly normal sort of meal. Hilary felt, indeed, that the only persons round the table who had anything to conceal were herself and Filthy. She alone guessed that Filthy's request to see the sketch was a move in the game of detection; and the knowledge added to her sense of isolation from the rest of the party. She was not suspected of murder. All these others were. Yet the thought did not make her feel sick and angry as it would have done a short time before.

She was conscious of a new hardiness in herself, an ability to consider each of them—even Aunt Mabel—as the possible perpetrator of a murder for which Michael Rouse was in danger of being suspected.

And even Michael . . . Shudderingly her mind admitted what her heart denied. He could have done it. And after all, what did she really know about him? Little indeed beyond her liking for him. Watching him covertly now as he listened expressionlessly to Uncle George arguing with Professor Ferriday about the date of some first ascent in the Alps, she found new ambiguities in that square red-thatched countenance that had seemed so open and honest. Wouldn't some people consider that rather heavy jaw a mark of brutality? And wasn't red hair supposed to show a violent temper? He was glancing at the professor now—something strange and furtive in that look. His eyes were a pale blue color; surely she'd read somewhere that murderers often had pale blue eyes. . . .

Aunt Mabel came in with her sketch and gave it to Lewker with a smile. It was a study of lake and mountains in dark weather, quite competently executed in dark greens and blues. The others craned their necks politely and made congratulatory noises.

"You have indeed caught the atmosphere admirably, Mrs. Jupp," boomed Filthy with sincerity. "I like your composition, too. You have a good eye for a viewpoint."

"I'm glad you think so," responded Aunt Mabel, pleased by this intelligent criticism. "My spot was just below that big boulder on the grassy knoll, the rather boggy hillock between Tryfan and Ogwen Cottage, you know."

"Yes, A fine belvedere. And well away from passersby who want to look over your shoulder." He handed the sketch back to her. "You had no visitors while you were up there, I suppose?"

"Not a soul—unless you count the two sheepdogs from Dol Afon. They came up to me, but they didn't stay long. Derwen Jones whistled them away."

"Oh—you saw Derwen, then?"

"I didn't *see* him, but I know his whistle. He was somewhere on the mountainside above the knoll, I think. Yes, it was a good place to work uninterrupted, Mr. Lewker. Even the road below was very free from traffic. I only remember seeing the green bus go along."

"Jolly good effort, this, Mabel," roared Uncle George, who was examining the watercolor. "Think we might hang it in the guest room at home?"

Aunt Mabel demurred, Harold chipped in and Hilary released her pent breath. Lewker had made his questions seem casual, but to Hilary it had appeared certain that the others must see what he was getting at. She knew that he had been trying to obtain some further news of the red-haired man Raymond had seen on the scree below the Milestone Buttress, and so far as she could see he had got only indefinite results. But Mr. Lewker had not yet finished.

"Odd thing about Derwen's dogs," he remarked to Mrs. Jupp under cover of a noisy argument between Harold and Uncle George. "I thought I saw them with their master going up Cwm Tryfan when we were on the Heather Terrace. What time was it when they came to interrupt your laboring?"

"Oh, it couldn't have been them you saw," said Aunt Mabel. "It was only a little while after I got settled down—about half-past ten, I suppose—and the whistling went away in the direction of Llyn Idwal. Derwen was going up to Cwm Bochlwyd, I believe."

"So he was. And of course we saw him starting off in that direction earlier, didn't we? I fear all sheepdogs look alike to a mere Saxon."

And even then, thought Hilary, he's got nothing definite. Derwen could still have doubled back out of sight of Aunt Mabel and been the man on the scree. And the dogs? Well, sheepdogs were trained to stay put where their master wanted them. . . .

Gwennie came in to clear away and the party got up from the table. Mrs. Jupp averred that Mildred looked tired and ought to go early to bed, and her daughter meekly acquiesced. The others made their way to the sitting room, but in the passage Lewker linked his arm in Hilary's and bore her off for a stroll down the Dol Afon track. It was a very still night, dark but windless, and the cool air was moist on their cheeks. Hilary was the first to speak.

"You didn't get very far with that business about Aunt Mabel's sketch," she said rather unkindly.

Filthy chuckled ruefully. "No. I can see that without direct questioning we cannot do much in that aspect of our inquiry. But it was a very good sketch. I chanced to catch a glimpse of it after Mrs. Jupp's first day's work, and most of the work was done yesterday. A small thing, perhaps, but I find myself unable to think of an amateur artist working so delicately in the intervals of committing a murder."

"Aren't you carrying this open mind business a bit too far? She has got a gammy leg, you know."

"Perhaps you are right, my dear. At least we may shelve Aunt Mabel for the moment, along with Harold and the professor. And we have now an additional suspect."

He told her of Mrs. Morris's account of the visit of Wenceslaus Pyecroft on the morning of the murder.

"We can fit him in for Motive," he continued, remembering that Cauthery edited a review that was attacking Communism. "Pyecroft seems to be an ardent Communist."

"A bit thin," commented the girl. "Besides, you're forgetting what he told us when you rescued him on Tryfan. He isn't a rock climber."

"Yet he made no bones about scrambling down a rather exposed little traverse from the top of the Milestone when we sent him off to get help after the 'accident.' Also, a very moderate scrambler, with so important a thing as a murder in mind, would manage to get down those upper pitches into the Milestone Cave without much trouble. But I will admit the slenderness of the motive. We must have speech with Wenceslaus tomorrow."

"If he's still in Wales. And if he is the murderer, won't he have packed up and cleared out by now?"

"If he were the murderer I should say he would be careful to do no such thing. His uneasy conscience would inform him that if suspicion as to the cause of death arose, his disappearance from the neighborhood might very well call attention to him. But enough of speculation. Was that a spot of rain? We had better turn and walk back to the farm. Meanwhile, let me outline a plan of campaign."

As they strolled back through the darkness, Mr. Lewker's deep voice ravishing the stillness with its measured periods, Hilary realized that she had forgotten an important aspect of her companion's qualifications as an amateur detective: his former connection with the British Secret Service. He had, it seemed, a certain influence with Sir Frederick Claybury, who as head of Department Seven had been Lewker's immediate chief during the war. Department Seven had a dossier section which was almost as efficient as that of Scotland Yard itself, and rather wider in its range. Filthy proposed to telephone Sir Frederick and ask him to seek information about three persons: Professor Ferriday, with reference to the story about the insurance of his assistants; Raymond Cauthery, regarding his activities as Communist and Aristo; and Wenceslaus Pyecroft, in the matter of his record as a Communist.

"With luck, we shall get that information tomorrow," Lewker told her. "I am going to walk down to the Ogwen phone box now and ring the Chief at his private address. I happen to know he is always at home on Tuesday evenings."

"How do you know they'll be able to get anything about those three? Your Department Seven hasn't got everybody in England taped, surely?"

"I have no doubt about Cauthery and the professor. They were engaged on important work for the government, and Department Seven takes an almost morbid interest in such persons. 'Who ran to catch them when they fell, And kissed the place to make it well?' Department Seven.

Pyecroft is another matter: If, however, he was Communist enough to carry banners in processions which, according to Harold, he was—he'll be in somebody's books and the Chief can get hold of his dossier. The thing that is worrying me is whether Sir Frederick can be persuaded to give me the dope—I believe that is the *mot juste* over the telephone."

They had reached the garden gate, and the lit windows of the farmhouse flung their cheerful orange glow into the darkness close at hand. Filthy came to a halt.

"If anyone inquires after me," he said, "pray inform them that an after-supper walk, beneficial in that it involves an automatic massage of the lower stomach, will return me to Dol Afon much refreshed at half-past ten." He squeezed Hilary's arm lightly and released it. "Remember—we need the true reason for Mildred's behavior of Sunday night."

With that he turned and walked away into the darkness. Hilary went slowly into the house. In the pitch-dark hall with its mingled odors of past cooking and present mackintoshes she stood still for a few moments, considering her program. She couldn't quite avoid a feeling of resentment that Lewker should have saddled her with a most distasteful job. To start hurling awkward questions at a girl whose lover had been killed less than two days ago was bad enough, but when one had—well, not exactly discouraged the attentions of the said lover it was extremely unpleasant. Honest with herself as always, she had to admit that her behavior hadn't been all it should have been. Perhaps it was a just punishment that this difficult part of the inquiry she had herself set on foot should fall to her lot. Had Filthy, she wondered, meant her to realize this when he gave her the task? Probably he had. The idea had a vaguely Prospero-ish touch that she found irritating; it is never agreeable to have someone else point a moral for us. But after all she had practically invited Mr. Lewker to tell her what to do, and to Hilary Bourne that meant that her loyalty was given. She would go through with the job.

She went along the passage and popped her head into the sitting-room. Wreaths of blue tobacco smoke thickened the yellow lamplight, especially above the table where Uncle George and Professor Ferriday were playing chess; Aunt Mabel was frowning over the darning of a sock and Harold Jupp and Michael were reading. Michael looked up quickly at her entrance.

"Mr. Lewker's gone for a stroll down the road," she announced to the room in general. "I felt tired, so I came back."

Michael Rouse closed his book and opened his mouth to speak. Aunt Mabel forestalled him.

"If I were you, dear, I'd go to bed. Mildred's there already. I'm sure you need all the sleep you can get when nerves have been tried rather highly."

"I expect you're right," said Hilary. "Anyway, I'll take your advice. Good night, all."

As she closed the door behind her she saw Michael getting hurriedly to his feet. She hastened down the passage towards the stairs; just lately she had felt an inclination to avoid speaking to Michael at all costs. But before she had turned the corner he came out into the passage behind her and closed the sitting-room door.

"Hilary!"

She stopped dead, and answered without turning round.

"Yes?"

"Must speak to you."

He was striding towards her. Hilary turned to face him. He was close to her, a square dark bulk smelling of tweed and tobacco smoke. He made no attempt to touch her, but it was as if his whole personality spoke to her with inaudible voices; she seemed to hear his need of her, his love for her; she knew that she had only to take a step forward, to speak his name, and his arms would be round her. And yet she could not take that step. Between them stood the gray ghost of Raymond Cauthery, its agonized mouth forming the sound that echoed in her thoughts—*Don't!* . . .

Michael was still standing silently there in front of her.

"Yes, Michael?" she said in a whisper that was half-fearful; was he going to tell her, to confess that he had—

"Just wanted to say—" His gruff voice checked itself. She heard the little click as his teeth came together.

" Good night," he finished lamely, paused an instant, and then swung on his heel and went back to the sitting room.

Hilary turned away and climbed the dark stairs. She felt now even less inclination for her task of interrogating Mildred. At any rate, she told herself, she would let it depend on whether the girl was awake or not; she could hardly wake her up just to ask her whether she had really been poisoned two nights ago. Besides, she could approach the matter more naturally in the morning, when they were both getting up.

She pushed open the door of the room she shared with Mildred. It was in darkness. She felt her way to the dressing table, found the matches, and lit the candle with as little noise as possible.

Mildred occupied one of the pair of old-fashioned iron bedsteads which Mrs. Morris had fitted with comfortable mattresses. She was lying motionless with her back to Hilary and the bedclothes pulled round her ears, and made no reply when Hilary spoke her name. That settled it, then. The inquiry could be postponed till next morning.

In spite of her depressing remembrance of Michael and his odd behavior, Hilary's spirits rose at this welcome postponement. She hummed a little tune to herself as she undressed, and by the time she had got into pajamas she was unconsciously singing, under her breath, the words of the tune:

"O don't deceive me, O never leave me,
How could you use a poor maiden so?"

"For God's sake *stop* singing that thing!"

Hilary, on the point of blowing out the candle, jumped and looked round, gaping in sheer astonishment. Mildred was sitting bolt upright in bed, her face red and angry, her dark hair unbecomingly tousled.

"I don't know how you dare, coming in here and singing—that horrible song of all others," she went on harshly, the words tumbling from her like a mountain stream that has burst the farmer's dam. "After the way you behaved with Raymond from the moment you came here, and everything, to stand there and sneer at me with those words—"

"But look *here!*" Hilary almost shouted in her consternation. "I'd not the slightest intention of sneering, I swear it. I didn't even think about the words of the song, and anyhow I thought you were asleep—"

"Well, I wasn't asleep," retorted Mildred sullenly, though she began to look a little ashamed of her outburst. "You might have guessed I haven't had any sleep to speak of the last two nights. I lie awake thinking and listening to you snoring."

"I don't snore," Hilary snapped indignantly.

"Yes, you do. Like a dog growling over a bone. It's awful."

Hilary's sense of humor came to her aid, and she had some trouble to avoid laughing outright. Mildred was serious in her resentment and it wouldn't do to be amused. She went over and sat on the foot of Mildred's bed.

"I'm sorry about this," she said gently, "but I'm rather glad you said that about me and Raymond Cauthery. I know I behaved shamefully, and I've been wanting to tell you how much I regret it. I'm awfully sorry, Mildred—"

Mildred beat both hands on the bedclothes and gave way to another outburst, though this time her anger seemed to have undergone a reverse.

"Why should you be sorry? It wasn't your fault. It was Raymond's fault—all of it, everything. I knew Raymond. You weren't the first he'd run after since he said he loved me. He ran after any good-looking girl who'd spare a glance for him. Oh, he's dead, I know, and I'm supposed to speak nothing but good of him. Well, it wasn't entirely his fault either. He was too attractive. He was irresistible to girls. I *know.*"

She came to a sudden stop, kneading the sheets between her fingers and staring at them unseeing. Privately Hilary thought she was being absurd, and she resented the implication that she had been irresistibly attracted to Raymond Cauthery. But she felt certain that there was something more behind Mildred's agitation than appeared from her words. This might be her chance to get at the truth of Sunday night's disturbance.

"Well, I don't see that there's any need to get all worked up about it now," she said with deliberately irritating lightness. "We're all shocked and sorry about the dreadful accident, of course, but there's no point in dwelling on it. Try and relax your mind. Raymond's death was a terrible blow to you, but you mustn't let it—"

"It isn't that," muttered the other. Suddenly she threw herself back on the pillow and burst into violent sobbing. " You don't know—you don't know," she wailed.

Hilary reached out and placed a hand on the shaking shoulders. This seemed to be her cue; she hated herself for doing it, but she must make a shot in the dark.

"Perhaps I guessed, even if I don't know," she said quietly. "It's something to do with Sunday night, isn't it?"

The sobbing stopped abruptly.

"You—guessed?" the girl said in horrified tones. "Has anyone else—"

"Only me," Hilary assured her, suddenly overcome with pity for this strangely frightened creature. "Look here," she went on impulsively, quite forgetting her detective duties, " I don't want to pry, but if it would help you to tell me anything—well, perhaps I could be some sort of use."

Mildred grasped convulsively at her hand.

"You can't help me," she gulped. "Nobody can. I—I'm a ruined woman." She began to sob again.

"That's just nonsense," said Hilary firmly. "You're alive and healthy and very pretty. You just can't be a ruined woman. Who says so?"

" F-Father. He said so that night, when I told him and Mother about—about me and Raymond. He's scarcely spoken to me since. I think he'd have turned me out for good if it hadn't been for Mother."

Hilary was silent. She began to have an inkling of the truth, and it was not in her to press for further revelations. But Mildred, once started on her confession, was plainly determined to go through with it.

"I know it was a dreadful sin," she whispered tearfully, "and I was awfully weak. Raymond—you know how irresistible he was—we—he wanted—I let him—"

"I understand," said Hilary quickly, squeezing the hot damp hand she held. "It isn't the first time that's happened in human history, you know."

"Raymond said he was buying an engagement ring," Mildred gabbled on unheeding. "He said it would be a very short engagement. It didn't seem so very wrong. But when—when I saw him with you—I mean when I thought he didn't want me, I was afraid. I thought if I told Father he might do something about it. I went to their room that night and told him and Mother what had happened. Father—I thought he was going to hit me. He gripped my arm awfully hard and that made me cry out. He said I had committed a deadly sin and was no daughter of his. He said—"

"Listen," Hilary interrupted in a firm voice. "Your father may be a good clergyman and a first-rate mountaineer, but he's an old woman in some ways. What you did was wrong—that can't be denied. But to call it a deadly sin is just balderdash and bunkum. There are dozens of worse sins than being weak enough to give in to someone you love. *Did* you love Raymond when this happened?"

"I th-think so. No, I'm sure. It was only afterwards, when I started to find out the sort of man he really was, that I began to think I didn't really care for him as I ought to."

Hilary put an arm round the girl's shoulders.

"And there's not going to be—you're not going to have a baby?"

"No. It's all right. That was what I went to see the doctor in Bethesda about. Mother thought I'd better."

"Your mother doesn't talk about deadly sins and turning you out?"

"Oh, no," said Mildred, choking in her haste to defend Aunt Mabel. "Mother's a darling. She seems to understand. But Father—oh, it was just awful. He's got the most frightful temper about some things. You know why he went out early that morning, and didn't come in to breakfast? It was because he'd said he'd kill Raymond for—for leading me into sin. He didn't mean it, of course—he was in a kind of religious frenzy when he said it. But he'd have knocked him down or something if they'd met."

Hilary realized with a start that she had acquired some highly significant information. She thrust the thought behind her almost angrily and set herself to complete the comforting of Mildred. She was pretty sure that the girl had not been in love with Cauthery at the time of the latter's death, and that it was almost entirely the Reverend George Jupp's righteous horror and threats of damnation that had brought her to this state.

"Look here, Mildred," she said, "I think you're a year or two older than me, but perhaps I'm the one with more experience. I mean, I've worked for my living for two years with other girls, and one learns quite a lot, you know. Lots of girls—and lots of men—wouldn't think what you've done is anything much to worry about. Let's admit you've lost something you'd rather have kept until you got married. But that's all. When you meet the right man you'll tell him that once you fell in love, and the rest of it, and if he really loves you it won't matter a damn to him."

"You really think so?" whispered Mildred, gazing at her with eyes red-rimmed but filled with renewed hope.

"I know so. Why, there's a girl in the office where I work—daughter of a Dean. She's engaged to marry a Commander R.N., D.S.O., and frightfully handsome. She's had dozens of passionate *affaires* before, if she's to be believed, and she says when she told him he just said he preferred a woman with experience—it showed she wasn't making a mistake in taking him for a permanent skipper."

"Oh, Hilary"—Mildred clasped her convulsively—"it's awfully relieving to hear you talk so matter-of-factly about it."

"Well, it is a matter of fact, isn't it? Now just see if you can't get some sleep. You must be needing it badly. And as for Uncle George—well, he's your father and when he goes off the deep end you'll have to be meek and tolerant. When all's said and done, what you did was wrong, and you can regard that as your punishment, if you like. But for goodness' sake don't let it get you down. You can hold up your head—and remember lots of women don't even have the joy of a lover at all."

Heavens! she thought. I'm talking like a female novelist. But it seems to have done the trick.

Mildred had snuggled down under the bedclothes. She certainly looked a good deal happier, and lay quietly holding on to Hilary's hand for a little while. Presently her regular breathing told that she was asleep.

Hilary, feeling rather cold and exhausted, blew out the candle and climbed into her own bed. Mildred's words about Uncle George's threat were buzzing in her brain, but one doesn't pour out one's youthful wisdom for the comfort of a distressed sister, and play the detective at the same time, without using a good deal of mental energy. In five minutes sleep was closing the shutters of her mind. Her last conscious thought was of the Dean's frolicsome daughter who was to marry the gallant Commander; she was Hilary's first literary invention, and Hilary was rather proud of her.

CHAPTER FOURTEEN

Some oracle
Must rectify our knowledge.
THE TEMPEST

MR. LEWKER stepped briskly down the track from Dol Afon in the early morning sunshine. His bald head and new-shaven jowls projected from an old gray sweater, and his hairy knees were revealed by a pair of very baggy khaki shorts, a concession to the unseasonable warmth which even at half-past eight was beginning to make itself felt. Tryfan and his peers rose nobly into a clear sky of palest blue and there were diamonds scattered in the meadow grass; but Mr. Lewker's eyes were unseeing this morning and he frowned at the gray stones of the track as he walked. As he rounded the corner where the outcrop of rock hid the continuation of the track he lifted his head and exchanged the frown for a grin. Hilary was sitting there, as he had expected, elbows on trousered knees and chin on fists.

" 'One turf shall serve as pillow for us both,' " boomed Filthy, lowering himself carefully to sit beside her. "Good morning. Permit me to observe that while—as the song says—it's dabbling in the dew that makes the milkmaids fair, sitting on damp grass may not have the same effect."

" 'For this be sure tonight thou shalt have cramps,' " retorted Hilary irrepressibly, smiling at him and immediately growing serious. "Filthy," she went on earnestly, "do you really think Uncle George is capable of murdering anyone?"

"Of killing a man," he amended gravely, "yes. We all are, given a particular set of circumstances. But I fancy you are beginning at the guard's van of a train of thought, so to speak. Let us look at the engine—no, you are quite right. Metaphor before breakfast should be a punishable offense. I take it you have some new facts for me?"

Hilary nodded. " Yes—but it's—well, a bit awkward to talk about. Let's walk on down the track, shall we? I can tell you better if we're on the move."

"Willingly, my dear."

They got up and went slowly in the direction of the main road. As they walked Hilary told briefly but not without hesitation of her interview with Mildred the night before. Filthy listened without interruption until she had finished.

"I see," he said at last. "We presume, then, that Mrs. Jupp's tale of

Mildred thinking she had been poisoned was a hasty improvisation intended to explain Mildred's agonized scream. I remember we displayed a certain incredulity when she told us at first that it was merely indigestion. And Uncle George, who could not trust himself to face Cauthery without offering him violence, went off for a walk up Cwm Tryfan a few hours after threatening, in 'a kind of religious frenzy,' to kill him."

The girl said nothing. They reached the gate where the track debouched on to the road: turned, and began to walk slowly back toward the farm.

"All the same," Hilary said suddenly, "it doesn't prove anything."

"We are still a long way from proof," agreed Lewker heavily. "Probabilities are mounting up, however."

"Probabilities aren't facts, and you said yourself it's facts we want."

"True. But a witness testifies that Uncle George declared his intention of killing—or his desire to kill—Cauthery. I would add my own strong impression that he considers sexual sin the apotheosis of evil and would, in the case of Cauthery and his daughter, be quite capable of seeing himself as an instrument of divine punishment."

Hilary kicked a pebble out of her way with impatient violence.

"I don't see that words spoken in a frightful rage, or your impressions, are evidence," she said obstinately. "Anyway, let's forget it until after breakfast. What happened about your phone call?"

"I spoke to the Chief, who was extremely affable, possibly owing to my blandishments, possibly because he had just been drinking port—he has acquired a priceless vintage just recently, he tells me. He agreed to squeeze all the information I asked for out of Department Seven by eleven o'clock today, at which hour I am to ring the Department's number."

"That's better," Hilary approved, "Those sorts of facts'll get us somewhere."

"Thank you, Watson. But I still think your own work of last night was most useful."

"I hope it won't be. Look here, I've thought of something we ought to have done before. Wouldn't the Great Detective have rummaged about among the dead man's possessions—searched his room for clues, and so on?"

"You are quite right. As a matter of fact, I have made a note to do that after breakfast this—"

He stopped speaking abruptly and sniffed the air with a frown. They had come to the place where the track rounded the rocky outcrop. From the farther side of the miniature crag floated the unmistakable fragrance of Dibdin's Cut Plug. Three more paces brought them face to face with Michael Rouse, who was sitting in a nook of the rock smoking stolidly.

"Good morning," said Filthy cheerfully, wondering how much of their conversation Michael had overheard. "You are the very man I wanted to see."

"Morning," grunted Rouse. He got to his feet, glancing quickly at Hilary and away again.

"I think I'd better go on to the farm," the girl said hurriedly. "It's almost breakfast time—"

"And are we not also flesh that lives by flesh?" boomed Lewker. "We will walk together in the direction of our bacon." He linked his arm in Hilary's and the three of them began to walk up the track. "How expressive is that delightful phrase about saving one's bacon! The maker of it clearly realized that life and bacon are practically inseparable. If it were not for the singularly pungent odor of your tobacco, Michael, I believe we should smell Mrs. Morris's frying rashers even from here. I gather, by the way, that Ogwen Cottage was able to supply you with Dibdin's the other morning."

"Yes," Rouse said shortly.

"That was fortunate. But regarding that same day, there is a matter upon which you may be able to enlighten me. You know, perhaps, that I am a member of the Foothold Club, which is affiliated to the British Mountaineering Council. The B.M.C. have asked that a detailed account of all climbing accidents should be prepared by some responsible person and sent to them. I am taking it upon myself to do this, and I would like to give the exact time of Cauthery's accident, if possible. I apologize," he added to Hilary, "for bringing up this sad matter again, but I want to be as accurate as I can."

Oh lord! thought Hilary. He's trying to catch Michael out in some way. What a sickening business it all is!

"That's all right," she said aloud, tonelessly.

"Good. Michael, you must have heard Miss Bourne's whistle almost as soon as she blew it. Did you happen to notice the time?"

"Sorry. Wasn't wearing a watch."

"Hum. Perhaps we can get it in some other way. We five—you, Mrs. Jupp, Harold, Professor Ferriday and myself—left Dol Afon at nine-forty. Mrs. Morris chanced to look at her kitchen clock as we set out and remembers it pointed to eight-forty, her husband having religious scruples about altering his clocks to British Summer Time. You went along the road with Mrs. Jupp, and then on to Ogwen Cottage, just over a mile. You would get there about ten o'clock?"

Michael grunted a dubious affirmative.

"Then your phone call and tobacco-buying would take you how long?"

"Lord knows. Say ten minutes."

"Ten past ten. You started back to go over the North Ridge. Which way did you go?"

"Cut over the hillside above the road." Rouse appeared uninterested but willing to help. " Idea was to beeline over North Ridge and down Bastow Gully to the Heather Terrace. Must have taken me more than half an hour to get to where I was when I heard the whistle. I was going fast. But better not take it that I heard the first whistle. It was very faint. Might have been the tenth or twentieth repeat I heard."

"True," nodded Lewker thoughtfully. " And that might explain the somewhat odd circumstance that you arrived at the top of the Milestone slightly *after* Professor Ferriday, who was considerably farther away when he heard the whistle."

"That, and the fact that I had to get down three hundred feet of steep rock. I told you that before."

Hilary's quick ear caught the note of defiance in Michael's voice, and she found herself clenching her fists tightly as she walked. But Lewker seemed not to notice it.

"So you did," he agreed. "Then we can only say the time of the accident was about eleven o'clock. I wish we could get it a little closer than that. Did you pass Mrs. Jupp on your way across the hillside? She might be able to help us if she noticed the time."

"No. She was sitting a long way below my line of traverse. Didn't see anyone except Derwen Jones. He was high up on the slopes going over to Cwm Bochlwyd."

To Hilary's relief the clamor of Mrs. Morris's breakfast gong sounded from the farmhouse. They were only a few yards from the garden gate, and she hurried in front and opened it.

"Do come on!" she called over her shoulder with forced cheerfulness. "Porridge doesn't keep hot forever."

" 'Havewithyou. I'll not miss the grace,' " boomed Filthy, quickening his pace and pushing Michael before him.

Hilary's first glance, as she seated herself at the breakfast table, was for Mildred, and she was relieved to see that the girl looked a good deal more cheerful than on the previous day. She was chatting quite normally with her mother, and replied without embarrassment to a curt remark from Uncle George—the only time he addressed her during the meal. Hilary supposed it was an encouraging sign that the big clergyman would speak to his daughter at all; she felt that the Jupp family was at any rate on the road back to harmony. Then she remembered that neither Uncle George nor Mildred was eliminated from Filthy's list of suspects. It was surely unthinkable that Mildred could have murdered Cauthery—Hilary was certain of that after last night's outpouring of confidences. And yet that was only her own impression, and she had been severe with Filthy about counting impressions as evidence. However convincing Mildred's words and manner had been it was still possible that her confession was a clever covering-up of fear and remorse for the killing of her lover; she might have believed, at that time, that she was going to bear the child of a man who was about to desert her. Yes, motive was there, with means and opportunity. . . .

"Pepper! Pepper! Hilary, you're jolly well half asleep." Uncle George's roar broke in upon her thoughts.

Hilary's smile as she passed him the pepperpot was mechanical; she had remembered that of all those seated round the table the Reverend George Jupp was the only one who was known to have both a cause and an expressed desire for the murder of Raymond Cauthery. That was, of course, if Mildred hadn't made up the story of his threat to shield herself—but then, he was her own father, and it was too horrible to think that she could deliberately throw suspicion on him. Hilary shivered uncontrollably and helped herself to toast and marmalade. It was ghoulish to be munching away like this and imagining the worst of one's fellow breakfaster; unconscious of their doom, she thought moodily, the little victims play. Only one of them, though, was to be the victim—and it might not, after all, be anyone of the Dol Afon party. She hoped fervently that it might turn out to be Derwen Jones or Wenceslaus Pyecroft, preferably the latter, who as the suspect least familiar to her was the most desirable as a murderer.

Still in this very un-detective-like vein, she asked herself which of the people sitting round the breakfast table she could bring herself to consider—failing Derwen or Pyecroft—as a murderer. They were listening to Uncle George's highly colored account of a climbing holiday in Corsica and she was able to consider them one at a time: Aunt Mabel, Mildred, Michael, Harold Jupp, Uncle George, Professor Ferriday—the professor, with his thin lips curled in a slightly sardonic smile and his little black eyes glinting mischievously, looked for the moment oddly cunning and secretive. Hilary liked Professor Ferriday. But she had to admit that if one of those six people was the murderer of Raymond Cauthery the professor, setting aside all evidence and logic, was to her mind the least unlikely.

Hating herself for the thought, she tried to dismiss it by listening to Uncle George, who was concluding his story.

"And believe it or not, Ferry, we were on the summit of Monte Cinto at exactly one and a half minutes past eight. Good going, eh?"

"Not only good, but remarkable," said the professor dryly. "I should imagine such speed allowed you no time for appreciation of the beauties of your peak."

"All very well for you to carp, old feller," returned Uncle George good-humoredly. He addressed the table at large. "This—this ageing hypocrite made a new record for the end-to-end traverse of the Welsh three-thousand-footers in nineteen-thirty. When he was forty-seven, mark you. I'll guarantee he hadn't much time for the scenery on that trip. Fourteen peaks in eleven hours!"

Lewker cut in as the professor opened his mouth to retort.

"Talking of times," he boomed, "I am anxious to establish the exact time of that unfortunate accident, if possible." He told of the report he proposed to send to the British Mountaineering Council. "I suppose, professor, you didn't happen to notice the time when you heard Miss Bourne's whistle?"

"I fear I did not," said the professor apologetically.

"I did, though," Harold Jupp announced with satisfaction. "At least, I looked at my watch a second or two afterwards—when we decided to go back down Grooved Arête, Mr. Lewker. It was five minutes to eleven exactly."

"Thank you," said Filthy casually, noting the time in his little red-covered book. "I take it your watch keeps good time?"

"Gains a second in four days, that's all," returned Harold proudly.

Hilary, chancing to glance at Aunt Mabel, saw her looking oddly at Lewker. Was it imagination, or was she really paler than she had been a moment before?

"Mr. Lewker," she said, with the slightest trace of anxiety in her voice, "you seem very particular about the time of that—that dreadful accident. Is it really necessary to be so exact?"

" 'Good madam, grant my petty vanities,' " quoted Filthy lightly, putting away his notebook. "Accuracy is a foible of mine, and this being a sort of semiofficial report—but let us forget the matter. I am sorry to have brought it up on such a lovely morning."

"It *is* lovely, isn't it?" agreed Mrs. Jupp in her normal manner. "What's everyone doing today? "

Uncle George coughed portentously. "Ferry and I are driving into Bethesda. Certain arrangements—the—er—interment—"

"Of course," said Aunt Mabel hurriedly. "And I have some shopping to do. Perhaps, Mildred—"

"I'll come with you, Mother," Mildred said.

"Thank you, dear. Perhaps Hilary would like to come too. We could squeeze her in, George, couldn't we?"

Hilary hastily said she would have loved to come but had already promised to walk up to Cwm Bochlwyd with Mr. Lewker.

"I thought we might call on young Pyecroft," Filthy explained to Uncle George. "I believe we omitted to thank him for his services on Monday."

"An excellent plan," approved the clergyman in his head-of-the-party manner. "Thanks, Lewker."

Michael Rouse, who was frowning at the pipe he was endeavoring to clean, glanced up at Hilary. In his blunt and stolid countenance his light blue eyes held a mute appeal that tugged at her heartstrings.

"Hilary," he began; and stopped awkwardly. Harold struck into the pause.

"I say, Rouse, don't forget you promised to show me that thing that might be a *Lycopodium.*"

This, it appeared, was a specimen which, from Rouse's description, might turn out to be the rare *Lycopodium annotinum,* on the slopes below Gallt yr Ogof. The other agreed reluctantly to lead Harold to the spot after breakfast.

"Plate drill," commanded Aunt Mabel briskly, and began to collect into a pile the empty plates passed round the table to her. "This young Pyecroft you speak of," she added. "Is he very tall and thin, with long black hair and glasses?"

"Yes," said Harold. "Why?"

"Well, I think he's likely to be camping still. You see, I was talking to Gwennie in the kitchen before breakfast, and last night she went with her young man to a meeting in Bangor where this Pyecroft got up and spoke. Pass your empty cups up this end, please, and then I'll ring for Gwennie."

"What sort of meeting was this, Mrs. Jupp, do you know?" inquired Lewker.

"Oh, a Communist meeting. Derwen Jones is a Communist, you know. Gwennie's quite proud of the fact that he's the only one in the valley." She rose from the table. "Apparently Derwen had met Pyecroft at some rally in Cardiff last year. Though why a veterinary surgeon, which he intends to be, should want to cure horses while a lot of commissars stand over him with knouts, I *can't* think."

With this notable comment on the Soviet system of government she rang the bell, and the party drifted out of the parlor. Lewker caught Hilary's eye and managed to detain her until the rest had gone out of the room.

"Cauthery's room," he murmured. "Come with me and have a look at it."

"All right. But we're a bit late doing it, aren't we?"

"We are. Gross laxity on the part of the Great Detective. I suppose it has been tidied up by now."

"Well, Aunt Mabel was in there yesterday collecting his clothes and things, but I happen to know Gwennie hasn't done the room out yet."

"Good." He glanced cautiously out of the parlor window. "One, two, three, four, five—they are all out in the garden except Rouse. Come along."

They went quickly down the passage and up the stairs. As Hilary, who was in front, turned the corner onto the landing, she almost cannoned into Michael Rouse. He gave a startled grunt, avoided her eyes, and pushing rather rudely past Lewker hurried on down the stairs.

"Our young friend seems to lack something of his usual courtesy this morning," commented Filthy, opening the door of the room which had been shared by Cauthery and Harold Jupp.

There were two beds, and Harold's was untidily heaped with bedclothes and pajamas and a tattered book on botany. The other was neatly made. A small table with a large faded crimson tablecloth stood against the wall close to it, corresponding to the marble-topped washstand with basin and ewer that stood near Harold's bed. Lewker went first to the big chest of drawers on the far side of the room.

"Just keep an eye on the garden, my dear, if you please," he requested. "I would rather Harold didn't find us here. Let me know if he comes into the house."

Hilary went to the window obediently. Lewker pulled open the drawers one after the other. Half of them were empty and the rest contained underclothes, Harold's by their untidy arrangement, except one which housed a jumble of ties, money, books and peppermint drops—also, presumably, Harold's. He crossed quickly to the table and lifted the tablecloth. There was no drawer, but beneath the table was a large tin without a lid, evidently intended as a receptacle for waste paper and rubbish. It was empty.

"Someone's been burning paper in the fireplace," said Hilary suddenly, deserting her post.

"So they have. Back to your window, Sister Ann." He went and knelt by the grate. "Yes. And not only paper but certain nonburnable substances. An old razorblade, a bootlace and a tobacco tin. One may deduce that the contents of yonder tin have been emptied here and a match applied."

He spied a scrap of paper still unburned, put a hand into the ashes to pull it out, and gave an exclamation. At the same moment Hilary turned from the window.

"Harold and Mrs. Jupp—just coming into the house," she whispered.

Lewker stuffed the scrap of paper into his pocket and hurried her out of the room, giving her a little push in the direction of her bedroom. As he closed his own bedroom door Harold's footsteps were coming up the stairs. He sat on the bed and examined the charred fragment from the fireplace without much hope of gathering any fresh help from it. It appeared, however, to provide him with food for intensive thought, for after a first scrutiny he sat perfectly still for five minutes scowling at it. Then he placed it carefully in his red-covered notebook and went downstairs with a somewhat heavy step.

Ten minutes later Hilary and Lewker set out to walk along the lake to Ogwen Cottage. Mrs. Jupp called after them that lunch was to be at one-thirty and Mrs. Morris, overhearing her, poked her head out of the kitchen door to add that it wass rice pudding like Mr. Lewker wass so fond of. At Lewker's suggestion the two avoided the main road and took the faint track that runs along the other shore of the lake, squelching through beds of moss softer than the softest featherbed where water sparkled up round their boot-soles at every step, then scrambling along ice-smoothed slabs of silver-gray rock that sloped steeply into the glassy waters of the lake. Llyn Ogwen was a magic mirror this morning, in which the greens and blues and grays of the peaks that dreamed above in the morning sunlight were reflected and intensified, the tiny silver rings made by rising trout serving only to call attention to the multitude of details reproduced so miraculously clear on the unruffled surface.

At a spot where the rocks came down to the water's edge in a little crag fringed with greening bilberry plants Lewker called a halt, and they sat down out of sight of distant Dol Afon on the water-rounded stones beneath the crag. Hilary drank from the clear water and sat back with a sigh, shaking her fair hair from her face. She had discarded her wind-jacket and was wearing a green shirt with her slacks. Lewker, watching her, was impelled to quotation.

"You nymphs, call'd Naiads, of the wind'ring brooks,
With your sedged crowns and ever-harmless looks,
Leave your crisp channels, and on this green land
Answer your summons," he boomed in measured tones.

Hilary smiled up at him. "*Tempest,* Act Four. That's the first time you've quoted Shakespeare today, and it's nearly half-past ten."

"I make up for my remissness with an extra long one. Also an apt one." He took the charred paper from his notebook and held it out. "'Answer your summons,' Naiad, and tell me what you make of this."

Hilary took the fragment and examined it curiously. It was the right-hand edge of a sheet of stiff white notepaper, about two inches wide and eight long, irregularly charred down the left edge and obviously part of a brief typewritten letter. What remained of the letter ran as follows:

IAL.
LLY Branch
N.W. 1

27, 1949
ved no reply
requesting you
in order without
immediately,
ther steps
lly,
ger.

As soon as she had read the disjointed words Hilary looked closely at the right-hand top corner of the fragment, then held it up to the sunlight, then turned to Lewker.

"I can tell you one thing about this, anyway," she announced. "It's a bit of one of our S46 forms. I've seen hundreds of them—and here's the stationery number, S46, very small at the top."

"And what," asked Lewker, "is an S46 form?"

"It's the small notepaper used by the managers of the Inland Bank branches. I usually help with the post at the end of the day's work in the bank at Manchester, so I've put lots of these into envelopes. It looks," she added, scrutinizing the fragment again, "as though this came from our Piccadilly branch, unless there's another branch in W.1 ending in LLY."

"Very good. And can you reconstruct the letter?"

Something in his voice made Hilary afraid. She handed the paper back to him.

"I'd rather you did that," she told him.

"Hum. Commercial phraseology is hardly my line, but I will do my best. I should say it ran something like this. 'CONFIDENTIAL' (underlined in red). Then the heading—'Inland Bank Ltd.,' Piccadilly Branch, London, W.1 April 27, 1949. Dear Sir, We have received no reply to our letters requesting you to put your account in order without delay. We are now obliged to ask you to do this immediately, otherwise we shall take further steps in the matter. Yours faithfully, So-and-so, Manager.' In the vanished left-hand bottom corner, I think, we should have read 'R. Cauthery, Esq.' and his London address. Can you suggest any other interpretation?"

"No-o," admitted Hilary doubtfully, wondering how this new item could help the investigation and on whom it might throw suspicion. "I suppose this was the letter Raymond got on Sunday—the one that was sent on from London and Mrs. Morris forgot to give him."

"Presumably it is."

"And it means, of course, that Raymond was short of cash. He'd just burn it—he was like that."

"I think," said Lewker slowly, "that he was even more casual about destroying it. He merely crumpled it up and threw it into the tin under the bedroom table."

"But it's been burned, and—"

"A hurried attempt was made to burn it—by Michael Rouse. You remember," he went on, forestalling Hilary's protest, "that we were discussing a search of Cauthery's room when we came upon Rouse before breakfast. He overheard us—I would like to know how much he heard—and went straight from the breakfast table to the bedroom. He had no time to spare, so he tipped the contents of the tin into the fireplace and lit them. We met him coming away from doing it."

"But that's all guessing!" Hilary burst out indignantly. "Anyone might have burned the papers. Michael might have been upstairs for—for any other reason."

"His bedroom is downstairs," Filthy reminded her. "And so—O Wales, Wales!—are the—er—usual offices. Everybody else was in the-garden. And the ashes in the fireplace were still warm. We can only deduce that Mr. Rouse thought it would be a good idea to destroy any possible evidence that might be in the tin, and did so. Only that and nothing more."

There was a short silence. A wheatear alighted on the edge of rock above them and flew off with a shrill *whit-yee*, its white rump like a blown snowflake in the sunshine.

"Come," boomed Lewker, hoisting himself to his feet. "In twenty minutes I must have speech with Sir Frederick Claybury in London."

"But why?" demanded Hilary. "Why should Michael burn Raymond's letters?"

"That," said Filthy gravely, "is what we have to discover."

CHAPTER FIFTEEN

ANT. *He misses not much.*
SEB. *No, he doth but mistake the*
truth totally.
THE TEMPEST

AT THE WESTERN END of Llyn Ogwen, where the Nant Francon falls away suddenly towards the sea and the Ogwen river plunges down its rock wall to the green strath, Ogwen Cottage stands snugly against a little crag with Tryfan and the Glyders peering down its chimneypots. In a grove of firs some hundred yards away is the Youth Hostel, beside which stands the red telephone kiosk, contriving, in spite of the main London to Holyhead road a stone's throw from it, to look out of place on a mountain pass that still retains something of its wildness.

A shepherd, lean and wrinkle-faced, in his Sunday-best of stiff-looking black, was sunning himself on the roadside wall as Hilary and Lewker approached; he was doubtless waiting for the morning bus that runs from Bangor to Llanrwst, crossing the pass at Ogwen at eleven o'clock every day. He gave them a shy 'good morning' as they passed through the gap in the stone wall leading to the phone box.

"We're late," remarked Hilary, looking at her wristwatch. "It's a minute past eleven already."

"That need not trouble us unduly, I think," said Lewker, pulling open the door of the kiosk. "Sir Frederick is regrettably casual about times for a man in his position. It would be a good idea," he added, "if you came in here with me. You should be able to hear Sir Frederick's voice—a very clear one—and that will save me the trouble of retailing his information to you afterwards."

"I'll be a bit warm with two of us in and the sun sizzling down," Hilary pointed out.

"Never mind. 'We two alone will sing like birds i' the cage.' " He pulled her in after him. "I trust the local exchange speaks English."

He lifted the receiver and dialed 'O.' The girl heard a man's voice, with a strong Welsh accent, replying.

"Exchange here. Good morr-ning!"

"Good morning," Lewker returned affably. "Do you think you could get me Trunks?"

"Trunks? I can, sir, indeed. And what iss the weather up at Ogwen this morning?"

"Brilliant sunshine and very warm for the time of year."

There was a groan from the other end of the wire.

"It would be that—and me with a half-day to go fishing in the lake. It's cloudy skies them trout want, sir. Here's Trunks, sir."

A less human voice took over. Lewker asked for a Whitehall number and was told to have three-and-elevenpence ready, and a further three-and-ninepence if he wanted an extension three minutes. There followed a long wait which was rendered less tedious for the occupants of the phone box by the necessity of digging out of their various pockets six shillings, two sixpences, and eight coppers. Fortunately they were able to provide the sixteen coins between them before the call came through. In a surprisingly short time Lewker was speaking to the Chief of Department Seven, a cheerful baritone voice whose clear enunciation made every word audible to the girl. She listened in breathless silence to the following conversation.

"That you, Filthy? You're late. Big Ben struck the hour just four and a half minutes ago."

"I know, Sir Frederick. I merely wished to give you time to get back from the saloon bar."

The noise of the Llanrwst bus going past on the road drowned Sir Frederick Claybury's retort, but judging from Lewker's tongue-clicking it was a vulgar one.

"All right, Chief," he boomed. "Let us to our fell business. Have you anything for me?"

"I have, you bald-headed nuisance. My myrmidons have dug out some details which I shall now pass on to you, contrary to all the regulations of Department Seven. First, R.C.—I'll skip the age and description and so forth. Was a mild Communist before he began to work for the Gov under your other subject, whom we'll call the prof. Hence we've kept an eye on him. This Aristo foolery of his seems harmless enough. Apparently he's a sincere anti-Communist now. Spends a good deal more than he earns and has lately been borrowing pretty heavily. You asked if he has any known enemies. Well, there's nothing in our dossier to that effect, but I'll come back to that point later. That finishes R.C., except that he's reported to be holidaying somewhere near where you're speaking from. Seen anything of him?"

Lewker pretended not to hear this, and Hilary deduced that he had said nothing about Cauthery's death to Sir Frederick.

"Thanks, Chief," he said. "What about the prof?"

"You're a secretive old devil. I'd give a fiver to know what you're up to. Well, the prof's a pretty important bloke to certain highups in the military line, and we've looked after him like a mother. He's on holiday too, but his lab is closely guarded. An odd bloke—sort of idealist, I gather. Been carping about the Gov's miserly allowance for his work and so on. There was some suspicion in official minds that he might try to get money from other governments, our friends behind the Iron Curtain, for instance, but there's been no proof of it so far. It would finish him if there was, of course—Official Secrets Act and so forth. He seems to be the kind of man who wouldn't let that stop him, though. Regards his precious work as God's gift to all humanity and to hell with his own nation if it won't give him the dibs to finish the job. That sort of thing. *He's* a bloke who might have enemies, if you like."

"What about that insurance business I asked about?"

"Nothing in it, old man. We've been into it fully. A silly Yellow Press tale, founded on sweet nothing and—"

Here the exchange cut in with the news that Lewker's three minutes were up and there was a crowded interval while three shillings, a sixpence and three coppers were pushed into their slots.

"You're lavish with the cash these days," chuckled Sir Frederick at the other end. "I hope you think it's worth it. Now for your last subject, W.P., the Feast of Stephen bloke. This department had nothing on him, but my lads found something for you. He's a red-hot Communist and used to be in the same branch of the party as R.C. This is where R.C. crops up strongly again. Good King W. was working in a civil service department in those days, an excellent worker with not a stain on his escutcheon. They were prepared to turn a blind eye to his politics even when the purge began. Well, when R.C. deserted the party he wrote to W.P.'s bosses—the people up top—telling them W.P. was in the pay of Russia and advising them to sack him. As a result the people up top made enquiries and W.P. was sacked. That help you?"

"It may do. Is that all?"

"Not quite. W.P. seems to have got to know who did the dirty on him, because about three months ago R.C. got a sort of threatening letter, which he took to the police in considerable agitation. It was a silly sort of letter, all wind and high-falutin'—no definite threat to kill or injure, you understand. The bobbies advised R.C. to take no notice of it, but they put the matter up to the Yard and the Yard traced the letter to W.P. They had him up and gave him a lecture that scared him stiff. No action was taken apart from this, and that's the last that's been heard of the matter. W.P.'s present whereabouts are unknown—and so much for Buckingham."

"And was W.P. in the pay of Russia, do you know?"

"No more than any of these red-flaggers are. Though, mark you, there's no telling what a featherbrained lad will do once he's got bitten with that brand of tarantula. These idealists, Filthy, are the most dangerous cusses that ever—hullo, there goes your other three minutes. You've got all I can tell you—good luck with it."

"I am exceedingly grateful, Chief. You shall have the full story some day, I promise you. Good-bye."

Lewker set the receiver on its rest and the two, perspiring gently, burst out into the sunlight and fresh air.

"You heard all right?" Filthy demanded, mopping his brow.

"Every word," Hilary told him, "except what he said about your saloon bar crack."

"That, my child, was by no means relevant to our investigation. The rest, on the other hand, was very much so. I suggest, however, that we do not discuss it immediately but let it simmer in the mind while we walk up towards Bochlwyd."

He led the way up to the rock steps and iron gate that gave access from the barnyard of Ogwen Cottage to the moorland above. The sun smote down with summer heat through the still air, but Lewker set a fast pace that left little breath for talk. Y Garn, the Glyders and Tryfan shimmered in the heat; the dampness of the boggy hollows where the track to Bochlwyd branched was welcome to Hilary's feet. As she plodded steadily in Lewker's wake she turned over and over in her mind the various details of Sir Frederick Claybury's report, trying to spin them into a pattern that would spell one name—that of the murderer. But for all her spinning the only thing that emerged was a bewildered conviction that the problem had become more complicated; there were new facts and increased suspicions, but instead of converging on one person they pointed in different directions. If she accepted one of them, the rest refused to fit in. Wenceslaus Pyecroft was now provided with a strong motive, and he had actually threatened the dead man, afterwards turning up on the very site of the murder. That couldn't be coincidence. But if Pyecroft had killed Cauthery, why on earth should Michael Rouse behave in such a suspicious manner?

Then there was this business about Communists and Russia. Derwen Jones, it seemed, was a Communist, and had previous acquaintance with Pyecroft. How could that be made to fit in with Michael's burning of a letter from Cauthery's bank, for instance? Russia had been mentioned in connection with Professor Ferriday, too. Was the U.S.S.R. the thin connecting link of all the isolated facts?

Filthy was making tremendous speed up the steep track that mounted beside the Bochlwyd cascades. Hilary broke silence to enquire rather querulously whether he was trying to make a record. He turned a red and streaming face to answer her.

"We hurry," he puffed, "because our time grows short. Ere suppertime, as Prospero, says, I must perform much business appertaining."

They climbed on swiftly. Cwm Idwal fell below and Tryfan's west face lifted close at hand above the steep pastures. At the top of the precipitous slope, where the ground flattened and Llyn Bochlwyd spread its placid waters under the far buttresses of Glyder Fach, they paused to splash the waters of the issuing stream over their faces. Then round the lake's edge and up to the boulders where they had found Pyecroft's camp three days earlier. The green tent was still there, but as they came up to it they saw that, as on that previous occasion, it was open and empty. Pyecroft's hospitable notice addressed to passing 'comrades' was hung on the tentpole.

Lewker scrambled on to a nearby boulder and scanned the neighboring hillsides. Except for distant grazing sheep they appeared deserted, and his shrill whistle brought no response but a faint echo from the crags high above.

"We draw a blank," he announced, getting down from his perch. "Now what should the Great Detective do?"

"He might search the tent," suggested Hilary doubtfully.

"Yes. A base trade, ours. However—" He stooped on hands and knees and crawled into the tent, while Hilary peered in from behind him.

"Hum. Sleeping-bag, *Das Kapital* again, billy-can—empty—electric torch, oddments of clothing, canvas bag containing bread, butter, coffee and tinned food, small haversack full of paper presumably for lighting fires—ha! What have we here?"

He pulled out of the haversack a green paper-covered book. It was *The Five Red Herrings*, by Dorothy Sayers. Lewker chuckled.

"Can it be that our Wenceslaus descends on occasion from *Das Kapital* to detective stories?"

"He picks the best, anyway," observed Hilary.

"Truly said. Should we, I wonder, attach any importance to this discovery? I think not." He replaced the book in the haversack, returned the other things to their places, and crawled backwards out of the tent. "I fear," he added, standing up and brushing off some breadcrumbs that were adhering to his hairy knees, "that we are wasting valuable time here."

"D'you mean you've decided that Pyecroft didn't do it?" asked the girl eagerly.

"By no means. You are being altogether too Watsonish, my dear. Pyecroft, on the evidence, is a prime suspect. I mean simply that tomorrow is Thursday, on Friday the party disperses after the funeral, and our murderer has not been discovered. He, or she, is still no more than a shadow in the Milestone Cave. And I do not see that we can get any forrader by our present methods."

"Then we've made no progress at all."

"There you are out. We have gathered a small army of facts, but it is a mutinous army. It refuses to march against any single enemy. Observe." He raised his stubby fingers and ticked off names as he mentioned them. "Rouse—Pyecroft—George Jupp—Derwen Jones. We have established means, opportunity and ample motive for each of them, and none of them has an alibi. We cannot even eliminate entirely Mildred Jupp or her mother."

He sat down heavily on a boulder and lit a cigarette. Hilary's heart sank. Subconsciously she had been expecting her companion to find among the contradictory clues some line that would lead straight to the murderer—who would not, of course, be Michael Rouse. Lewker drew at his cigarette in silence for some moments and seemed to find comfort in it.

"Well," he said at last, "so far we have been working under a handicap unknown to most detectives. We have not been able to put direct questions to our suspects. We shall have to throw off that handicap now."

"You mean we'll have to tell everyone?"

"I do. It will put the murderer on his guard, naturally—if he is not already aware of our doings. Rouse must have guessed what we are about, for one. But we shall be able to get everyone's own story of his or her movements and their reasons for them, and we must look for discrepancies there. One other thing I want to clear up first—"

"The timetable," Hilary put in swiftly.

"Yes. We have the time of the murder fixed with admirable accuracy. I wish now to fill in as many ascertainable times as possible, if only by estimate as we did with Michael this morning. I will admit it is a net dropped into an unlikely pool, but we may catch someone in it."

Hilary nodded, her gray eyes looking far away across the silent cwm.

"I'm glad you're going to do the timetable," she said, "because I've spotted something—at least, I think so—and it depends on a timetable. When the professor was climbing up Green Gully, and you and Harold were on Grooved Arête—"

She got no farther with her exposition, for at that moment there was a crescendo of barking on the boulder-strewn slope above them and two Welsh sheepdogs, lean, long-tailed, sharp-eared beasts, came charging down upon the tent. A shrill whistle from behind the dogs checked their fierce approach and turned their threats to canine apologies. They crept nearer by shy degrees, writhing their bodies and wagging their tails in an ecstasy of friendliness. The whistle bad come from Derwen Jones, who now appeared on the grassy crest above the tent and seemed to be on the point of hurrying away again.

"Good morning, Mr. Jones," called Lewker, standing up. "Can I have a word with you?"

Derwen made no reply, but after an instant's hesitation he came striding down the hillside with the long unfaltering pace of the mountain shepherd, his untidy red hair flaming in the sunlight. His lean face was grimly set as he came to a halt in front of Lewker, and after a curt glance at Hilary he did not look at her again.

"I expect you came to pay a visit to your friend Pyecroft," boomed Filthy affably. "So did we, but it seems he is not at home."

Derwen folded his arms slowly and made no reply. Under shaggy red brows his eyes were steady and inimical.

"I am glad we met you, however," continued Lewker, proffering a cigarette which the other refused with a gesture, "because I wanted to ask you—"

"Something about that smashup on Milestone Buttress, I'll be bound," interrupted the shepherd harshly. "You can save your breath, mister. I know nothing about it, see?"

"Now what," said his interlocutor softly, "what put that idea into your mind, Mr. Jones?"

Derwen jerked his head impatiently.

"Oh, I saw you and this young lady messing about on the Buttress yesterday. You wouldn't do that, day after accident, 'less there was something funny up. I thought it was a bit queer myself, a good climber like him falling off easy stuff like that. I know the place—" He stopped abruptly.

"Yes. You have climbed the Milestone Buttress yourself, I gather."

"I have that—and more than once," Derwen said defiantly. He thrust his head forward until his eyes glared into Lewker's at a range of less than a foot. "See here, mister. If you poke and pry long enough, you'll find out I told young Cauthery I'd beat the life from him if I caught him with my Gwennie. I meant it, see? And I'll tell you another thing. You know what an alibi is?"

"I think I may say I do."

"Well, I've got one, see?"

"Then," said Lewker gently, "you can tell us what time the—um—accident occurred?"

The other stared, looked confused and then defiant.

"Yes, I can, within a bit. I saw Mr. Pyecroft running across to get help, as I was coming down from Cwm Bochlwyd. That must ha' been not long after eleven."

"That is not an alibi, Mr. Jones."

"I'm coming to that. When I was up in Bochlwyd I walks up to Bwlch Tryfan after a young ram, see. It was mist up there. I comes of a sudden on a big chap kneeling behind a rock, seemed to be praying, and I see it's Mr. Jupp that's staying at Dol Afon. He gets up when he sees me, looking a bit awkward-like, and to make believe I hadn't seen him praying I asks him the time. He pulls out his watch and shows me. It was ten to eleven."

"I see. And what did you do then?"

"Why, I thanked him and cleared off. Now, mister, find me a man that can get from Bwlch Tryfan to Milestone Buttress in under half an hour and I'll give you a hundred quid."

He stepped back, whistled sharply to the two dogs who had been lying panting in the shade of a rock, and swung on his heel.

"Wait a little, Mr. Jones," urged Lewker. "You may be able to help us further. You are a Communist, I hear?"

"And proud of it," Derwen flung over his shoulder. He paused and turned for a parting shot. "And when the day of revolution dawns, mister, we'll have all you crimson amateur tecs strung up, see?"

In a dozen strides he was gone over the hill crest. Lewker, rubbing his chin meditatively, watched him go.

" 'A mad-brain rudesby, full of spleen,' " he murmured. "And quite the rudest Welshman I have ever had the misfortune to encounter."

"But he gave us some important evidence," cried Hilary eagerly. "Uncle George is out of it—Derwen gave him an alibi."

"Hum. I am not sure that Derwen's tale is thoroughly watertight. That alibi—a double one if Mr. Jupp confirms it—came remarkably pat. Why, I wonder, should Uncle George display his watch instead of telling him the time?"

"Because he was all worked up with praying and couldn't trust himself to speak," Hilary suggested.

"You might be right—"

"Well, for goodness' sake let's assume I am," she said impatiently." You admit yourself the facts point all ways. Why not do a bit of guessing—call it working on probabilities if you like—for a change?"

Her companion seated himself again on his boulder with a sigh of resignation and took out his notebook and stub of pencil.

"Very well, we will try it. We will ignore the possibility of booby traps, consider all alibis copper-bottomed, and give Aunt Mabel's gammy leg its full due."

"I consider Mildred to be in the highly improbable class, too."

"Very well. Give me a moment." He scribbled busily for a minute or two and then handed the notebook to Hilary. "You asked for it, sweet coz."

In Lewker's tiny but legible scrawl she read the following:

ABERCROMBIE LEWKER HILARY BOURNE	*Out. Eliminated by mutual consent.*
GEORGE JUPP	*Out. Derwen gives alibi.*
DERWEN JONES	*Out, assuming G. Jupp confirms.*
PROFESSOR FERRIDAY HAROLD JUPP	*Out. Booby trap not allowed.*
MRS. JUPP	*Out. Gammy leg.*
MILDRED	*Out. Hilary—woman's intuition.*

Possibles—

PYECROFT. *Opportunity proved; was in vicinity of Milestone Buttress shortly after murder.* BUT *has been given no opportunity of producing an alibi. Means proved; asserts he is no climber, but can undoubtedly climb well enough to get down into Milestone Cave. Motive now appears quite adequate.* BUT *does not strike me as the type to commit a well-planned murder.*

ROUSE. *Means, Motive and Opportunity all A1. Proved to have attempted to destroy evidence. Has guts, resolution, and is a far more likely suspect psychologically than Pyecroft.* NO BUTS *against Rouse.*

"I object," Hilary said as soon as she had finished reading this summary. "Michael's motive isn't A1 at all. Compared with Pyecroft's, it's thoroughly C3."

"If we are to guess," said Lewker thoughtfully, "I could fit him with another motive."

"How?"

"You might build it up yourself, using imagination and three other items—the half-burned letter, what we heard over the telephone, and Rouse's obvious attachment to Professor Ferriday."

Hilary pounced on the name.

"The professor! That was what I was starting to tell you when Derwen Jones turned up. I want him as a third possible."

"But you ruled out the booby-trap idea."

"I know. But at breakfast I was watching them all and wondering which of them—leaving out your wretched facts—really looked as though he could murder anyone, and I decided only Professor Ferriday did."

"My dear, innocent, illogical young woman!" Filthy threw up his hands. "Do you not realize—"

"Wait a bit. I thought some more about the professor while we were walking up here. I think you've left him out too easily. Filthy, how long was it between the time the professor disappeared into the mist at the top of Green Gully, and the time he shouted down about the distress signal?"

"That is not easy to say. It might have been ten minutes or twenty."

Hilary leaned forward earnestly.

"Look here, then. Suppose he raced down the North Ridge at top speed. Remember he made a mountain speed record when he was forty-seven, and he's amazingly fit still. He might have scrambled down the Milestone to the Cave, done the—the deed, raced back again and shouted down to you. I know it'd be a pretty close thing for timing, but it might have been done like that."

Lewker wagged his head doubtfully.

"You forget two things. One, that we have so far found no motive for the professor. Two, that both Harold and I heard your whistle barely ten seconds before he called down to us."

"Yes—but suppose it wasn't my whistle you heard," said Hilary triumphantly. "The professor had one—he could have blown it in a muffled sort of way just before he called to you. I don't believe you could hear a whistle on Milestone Buttress from where you were climbing, anyway."

"You still have no motive. And uncertain as I am about the time available, I very much doubt whether it was enough to allow even the fastest mountaineer to go down the ridge to Milestone Buttress and back. However, we will settle the matter this afternoon when we complete our timetable." He rested his notebook on his knee and began to write on a blank page. "Meanwhile, Mahomet shall come to the mountain. Have you a pin, my dear?"

Hilary produced a safety-pin, and Lewker, tearing out the leaf from his notebook, pinned it to the bottom of Pyecroft's 'Mountain Comrade' notice.

Dear Mr. Pyecroft (it ran), *Will you meet me by Adam and Eve at six-thirty this evening? I wish to discuss with you an aspect of the recent " accident" which directly concerns you. Abercrombie Lewker.*

" Those inverted commas should bring him," remarked Lewker complacently. "It would not do to interrogate him at Dol Afon, and there is no better place for the discovery of truth than a mountaintop."

"Suppose he doesn't get back here before six-thirty?"

"We must hope he does." He looked at his watch. "Come, Hilary, son of Wat. We must go down. And we'll go by way of Ogwen Cottage again, because I want to get some cigarettes."

"You sound quite cheerful again," said Hilary rather reproachfully as they left the tent and began to retrace their steps.

"That is probably because I have our future program clearly in my mind now. This afternoon, to the East Face to work out a timetable. This evening, interview with Pyecroft. Tomorrow morning, unless we have found a sure solution, we call a meeting behind locked doors at Dol Afon and try the direct interrogation method—our last card."

"And if that fails?"

"If that fails, my dear, you will see that we have no alternative but to go to the police."

Hilary made no reply to this, and they did not speak again until the stones of the Idwal track were underfoot and Ogwen Cottage lay before them.

"We shall barely be in time for lunch," Lewker said as they came down to the road. "Walk on, please—I will buy my cigarettes and catch you up."

Without giving her an opportunity to demur he vanished through the front door of the cottage. Hilary was halfway along the lakeside road when he came up with her.

"Did you get the sort you wanted?" she asked as he fell into step beside her,

"Oh, yes. Yes."

Lewker's manner was grave and abstracted, and Hilary forbore further conversation for a while. They had reached the milestone above which rises the Buttress when he spoke without turning his gaze from the road ahead.

"Forgive me for asking this. Feeling and affection in us humans can change in a few days. Do you still feel that if Michael Rouse proves to be the one who killed Raymond Cauthery the world would come to an end?"

Hilary walked on for ten paces before replying.

"I'm sorry," she said it last, tonelessly. "I can only tell you this. Once I thought I was in love with Michael. Now—I don't know."

Her companion made no comment. But the girl's troubled face decided him, for the first time, to keep to himself a matter bearing on their investigation. For the lady of Ogwen Cottage had assured him that she never stocked pipe tobacco, that Dibdin's Cut Plug was a brand unknown to her, that she had been alone at the Cottage on Monday morning and was certain that no young man with red hair had called there.

Michael Rouse had lied about his movements during the hour prior to Cauthery's death. Why?

CHAPTER SIXTEEN

Make the rope of his destiny our cable,
for our own doth little advantage.
THE TEMPEST

"PHE-EW! Regular heat wave," panted Harold Jupp as he dragged himself out of a scree-filled cleft on to easier ground. "If I'd known we were in for such a sweat bath," he added, collapsing on the flat shelf of the Heather Terrace beside Lewker, "I'm jiggered if I'd have come on this mystery trip, Where are we bound for, Mr. Lewker?"

Mr. Lewker mopped his streaming brow and waved a hand feebly.

"Wait, laddie," he begged, "until I am off the boil."

Harold nodded and rolled over on his back, gazing up at the sunlit precipices of Tryfan's East Face that soared in huge perspective into the blue afternoon haze overhead. Summer, one would have said, had come to the mountains and come to stay. The two who lounged and sweated on the Heather Terrace, however, knew their mountains better than that. They knew that while today might be warm and windless enough to make sunbathing at three thousand feet a pleasure, tomorrow or the next day might find wind and mist driving like a charge of fiends over the ridges, soaking the mountain walker to the skin and chilling him instantly, smiting his stumbling feet from the true path and lashing him relentlessly when he tried to creep into shelter. It is this mountain trick of changing in a few hours from smiting benevolence to screaming, insensate ferocity that causes half the so-called mountaineering accidents; when lightly clad and inexperienced "hikers," setting out from the sheltered valleys without proper clothing or reserve food to cross some apparently easy ridge, are found next day or the day after dead in a gully far from their proper route. For mountains punish ignorance with a heavy hand, and it is not only the careless rock climber who comes to grief among them.

This afternoon, for an hour or two at least, the early season smiled on the crags and cwms of the Ogwen mountains, and the majority of Uncle George's party were slumbering in the sunshine of the farm garden or idling with a book in the meadows nearby. It had taken some ingenuity on the part of Lewker to get himself, Harold Jupp and Hilary away from Dol Afon without having to answer awkward questions as to their destination, but he had managed it. Harold, who had planned an afternoon's lounging by Ogwen Lake after his morning botanizing with Rouse, had been rather reluctant to accompany them, and it was only Lewker's hint that matters of import were in hand that had persuaded him. So far he had been told nothing of the actual program, and it was Lewker's purpose to tell him no more than was necessary; though he feared that Harold was sharp enough, behind his stodgy exterior, to put two and two together.

"Have you stopped simmering yet?" demanded his youthful companion suddenly. "Because I'm all agog, whatever that may mean. Is this some sort of game? Why didn't Hilary come with us? Where do we go from here?"

Filthy decided on a man-to-man approach. "Look here, Harold," he boomed, sitting up and looking serious. "I know I can trust you, or I would not have brought you up here. Before I go on, I want your assurance that what we say and do this afternoon will be kept absolutely to yourself. I need your help in one or two experiments, but I cannot yet reveal my reasons. Tomorrow, I promise you, you shall hear the whole story. Till then I must keep silence."

"All right," said Harold after a moment's hesitation. "I'm on, though I'm jiggered if I know what you're up to. And what's Hilary doing? Is she in on these experiments?"

"I warn you that I cannot answer questions, laddie. This one, however, shall be answered. Hilary is proceeding via the North Ridge track to the top of Milestone Buttress, where at four-thirty precisely—our watches are synchronized—she will blow a blast on her whistle. I wish to satisfy myself that a whistle on the Milestone can be heard on Grooved Arête, so by that time you and I must be at the point on that climb whence we heard the distress signal on the day of Cauthery's accident."

"But—"

"In addition," Lewker went on quickly, "I wish to establish as closely as possible the times of our movements on this face of the mountain on that day, and certain other times. In particular, I shall want you to see how quickly you can get from the top of Green Gully to Milestone Buttress and back again."

Harold's mouth had been slowly opening while Lewker spoke, and his eyes were round and rather frightened. It was plain that the implication of this program was not lost on him. He gulped and then burst into speech.

"You don't think—you can't mean—gosh! Was there something phony about Raymond's accident, Mr. Lewker?"

Filthy made no reply. He got to his feet and picked up the rope he had been carrying. Harold stood up slowly; his round face, which had been red with the exertion of the long slog up to the Heather Terrace, was rather pale and troubled.

"I'll try and keep the questions under," he muttered. "And I'll do what I can to help—but I don't like it, Mr. Lewker."

"Neither do I, laddie," returned Lewker. "However, concentrate on the work in hand. We are going to finish Grooved Arête this time."

They tramped in silence up the uneven rake of the Terrace, rounding the projecting pillars of the mountain, until they came to the shallow trough of Green Gully and the bold rib which is the start of Grooved Arête. Here they were in the cool shadow of the thousand-foot precipice above, for the sun caught only the higher crags in its westering rays.

Lewker uncoiled the rope and handed one end to Harold. Then he took notebook and pencil from his pocket.

"We will use your watch as our timekeeper," he announced. "What is the time now?"

"Three-fifty." Harold's voice had recovered its normal slow, flat tones. "I remember you asked me the time just as we left the farm—it was two minutes past three then, wasn't it?"

"Yes. Forty-eight minutes is good going. I tried to hit the pace at which Professor Ferriday led us up here on Monday. You will recall he went fairly fast."

"He did," said Harold feelingly.

Filthy scribbled in his notebook.

"On Monday, then, we left Dol Afon at nine-forty. Estimated time of arrival at foot of Grooved Arête, ten twenty-eight." He crammed the book into his pocket. "Now for the next section. Tied on? Good. Let me know if you think we are climbing faster or slower than last time."

He began to climb, working his way up the steep rock like a squat bald-headed ape. He had changed his shorts for climbing breeches, for knees are apt to suffer in grooves and chimneys. Slowly they rose above the Terrace, talking little except when the climbing demanded curt question and answer. " Hauling in. . .that you ? . . . Come along . . ."

Lewker reached the top of the second pitch and took in the rope as Harold climbed up to join him.

"Time?" he demanded as soon as the other was safely on the ledge.

"Half a minute past four."

"Call it four o'clock. Now—this is where we looked up and saw the professor disappearing into the mist in the upper reaches of Green Gully. Where would you say he was when we last saw him?"

Harold gazed upward with knitted brows.

"Just about by that triangular rock that sticks out," he said at length, pointing. "The mist was trailing over the heathery face on the left of it, I remember."

" Yes. That is my own impression. He probably made a detour there to avoid the twenty-foot chimney that is out of sight from here." He pulled out his notebook again. "Ten minutes. Then on Monday at ten thirty-eight Professor Ferriday was climbing past that triangular rock. Very well. On we go."

They climbed slowly by thin ribs of rock and steep well-scratched grooves. Over on their left, from the direction of the Pinnacle Rib, came faint and cheerful shouts from another climbing party. Harold boggled over a slab with delicate holds, and remarked that he had done it more quickly last time. When they stood together on the ledge that was the limit of their ascent on the fatal Monday it was exactly twenty-past four.

Here Lewker sat down, lit a cigarette and once more got out his notebook.

"Twenty minutes added," he observed, "gives us a time for Monday of ten fifty-eight. Actually it was ten fifty-five by your watch when we paused here and heard the whistle. Three minutes is a small error in the circumstances."

"I must say," complained Harold, sitting down with his legs overhanging a forty-foot drop, "that I don't see the point of all this. We knew what time the distress signal was given already."

"We did. Now we know a few more times. In due course, laddie, all will be made plain. For the moment, as the excellent Friar Laurence observes, 'be patient, for the world is broad and wide.' Have some chocolate."

They sat munching in silence for a few minutes, Lewker frowning at his notes and Harold staring out over the sun-drowsy spaces of blue air. Then the former shifted on his uncomfortable seat and peered thoughtfully up at the impending crags above.

"When we heard the professor shout from the mist," he said, "did you notice anything about his voice?"

"His voice? I don't think so." Harold cogitated. "It was faint, of course, and the wind blew it about a bit."

"What about its direction?"

"Well, it was overhead, naturally—and now you mention it, it was rather to the right of us."

"To the right? As though he were a little way down the North Ridge from the top of Green Gully, somewhere near the top of Nor' Nor' Gully, for instance?"

"Yes."

"Hum. I thought the same." He looked at his watch and then at Harold's. "A minute short of half-past four. We had better prepare to let the sound of whistling creep in our ears."

They sat silent while the seconds ticked away. Punctually on the half-hour the long high note of a whistle, very far away but clearly audible, sounded on the still air.

"Right," said Lewker briskly, getting up. "That concludes our second experiment."

"It was blowing a bit on Monday," Harold pointed out, "and today's unusually still."

"Also today's whistle was blown on the top of the Buttress, not in a niche halfway down its face. However, we have established that a whistle can be heard at that distance. It remains to finish the climb."

They turned to the remaining and more interesting upper section of the Arête. Popular and free from severe difficulties as it is, Grooved Arête demands care and concentration in its top pitches. One cannot make the long step that leads to the Haven, creep precariously across the slithery overhang of the Slab, or clutch and scrabble in the Chimney, and at the same time meditate upon times and possibilities, however suggestive. Harold, for one, was so engrossed with the business of following in the wake of his oddly-shaped but remarkably agile leader that he was for a moment puzzled, when they clambered over the final pinnacles of the North Tower towards the sunlit summit ridge, to account for Hilary Bourne's presence there. The girl was lying face downwards on a flat projecting slab just above them, peeping over its edge to watch the last few feet of their climbing.

"How did it go?" she inquired as Lewker hauled himself over the edge beneath her and turned to belay Harold.

"Excellent well, i' faith." He threw her a quick glance and a nod. "We heard your whistle."

"Oh. Then—"

Lewker frowned and—his hands being occupied with the rope—jerked his head to indicate the grunting Harold twenty feet below. Interpreting this to mean that Harold had not been fully informed as to their purpose, Hilary said no more until he was up beside them on the ridge.

"Gosh, I enjoyed that," he gasped, joining Lewker on Hilary's slab. "Thanks, Mr. Lewker, for a grand climb. I enjoyed every—"

He stopped, the enthusiasm fading ludicrously from his face as he remembered the horrid suspicions and speculations that had ridden his mind on the lower pitches.

"I enjoyed it myself," said Lewker easily. "Though I rather think we ought to post a notice at the foot of the Arête warning subsequent parties that they will find the strenuous pitches well greased. I must have lost half a stone."

"You can afford it," Hilary told him unkindly.

" 'The truth you speak doth lack some gentleness.' But—to change the source of quotation—you shall comfort me with apples. I heard you begging some from Mrs. Morris before we started out."

Hilary unstrapped the small rucksack she had carried up and took out three apples and a packet of biscuits. The three sprawled on the warm rock and ate, to the accompaniment of desultory conversation. By tacit consent all mention of the afternoon's "experiments" was avoided, and the talk, led by Lewker, ran upon climbs and climbers of the past; men, now famous, who had scrambled joyfully on these very crags in years gone by. Filthy, who had begun his mountain apprenticeship early, could remember meeting some of them—Mallory, Aldous Huxley, Herbert Samuel, L. S. Amery, and some others whose names are only famous in the tradition and literature of mountaineering. His reminiscences served to while away twenty minutes, and prevented the voicing of the questions which Harold was obviously aching to ask. At the end of that time Lewker stood up briskly and announced himself ready for further exertion.

"This, laddie, is to be a joint effort," he told Harold. "I am, on the whole, a faster climber than you, while you excel on more level ground. Our object is to make the fastest possible time from that triangular rock we noted in the upper reaches of Green Gully to Milestone Buttress and back. I shall do the Green Gully section as far as the ridge, where I want you to take over and do the Milestone part. It will be a grueling job for you, I fear. Are you game?"

"I'm game all right," Harold retorted, " but I'm pretty certain you're barking up the wrong tree. The—man couldn't have—"

"We will not discuss that, if you don't mind. Are you ready, Hilary? Our base is now the top of Green Gully."

They made their way down by the well-scratched track that rounds the North Tower on its west side, thus avoiding an abrupt little step in the cock's-comb of the ridge, and came to a comparatively level platform of heathery peat and rock. Below, the remainder of the North Ridge could be seen sweeping down in successive shoulders, golden in the late afternoon sunlight, outlined against the green of the valley meadows fifteen hundred feet lower. The ordinary track up Tryfan was plainly seen, winding down the crest until it disappeared with a westerly trend in the direction of Milestone Buttress, which was out of sight. A few yards down the ridge from the platform where they stood was the deep-cut notch caused by the emergence of the Nor' Nor' Gully, and on its far side, just above the track, rose a little knoll of smooth rock. Lewker called Harold's attention to the knoll.

"Do you think," he asked, "that it might have been from there that the professor called down to us on Monday?"

"It might be."

"Right. That knoll shall be your finishing-point, laddie." He stripped of the light wind-jacket he was wearing. "You, Hilary, are appointed timekeeper. What is the time now?"

"Twenty to six."

"So late already? However, we shall do it. When I shout, you will know that I am down by the triangular rock and starting to climb up. Take the time then."

Harold and Hilary watched him as he scrambled down on the east side of the crest. Easy rakes and ledges of heather and bilberry took him down for fifty feet or so and then he disappeared into the steeper descent of Green Gully. A few minutes later his booming voice echoed in the crags and Hilary glanced carefully at her watch. In a surprisingly short time they heard the scrape of bootnails close beneath them, and Lewker's crimson face rose out of the depths. He rushed like a charging bull up the easy slope and flung himself exhausted on the platform beside Hilary. Harold was already on his feet and without a word set off at top speed down the ridge.

"Right to the summit of the Buttress, then straight back!" Filthy called after him.

"O.K.," came the faint reply, and then Harold was out of sight and earshot.

"Three and a half minutes," Hilary reported.

"Hum. The professor might have climbed it in three but not, I think, in less."

"Filthy—*could* he have done it?"

"I refuse to make any conjecture until my timetable is complete. Meanwhile, I have one small item to add to our collection. While you were acquiring apples and biscuits from Mrs. Morris I buttonholed Uncle George and—with no little ingenuity—introduced into our conversation the remark that Derwen Jones had met him on Bwlch Tryfan on Monday morning."

"And he denied it?" asked the girl eagerly.

"He admitted it, though with some embarrassment. I did not, naturally, mention the circumstances we heard of from Derwen."

"Then that puts them both out of it—unless, of course, they're in cahoots. But I just can't imagine that."

"Perhaps not. But watches can be altered. Derwen might have been an unconscious accomplice in a false alibi."

Hilary nodded quickly. "I see—Uncle George does the murder at five to eleven, races over Tryfan in the mist to Bwlch Tryfan, gets there—say—at twelve o'clock, alters his watch to ten minutes to eleven, and shows it to Derwen Jones." She stopped and frowned. "But then—how did he know Derwen was going to turn up so conveniently?"

"How indeed? And if it was really twelve o'clock, and it could hardly have been earlier, when Derwen encountered him, how could Derwen have got down from there in time to see Pyecroft hurrying off for the stretcher? Besides, even a man as free from the trammels of time as a mountain shepherd could hardly be relied upon to accept a time that was more than an hour earlier than it should have been."

"So we'll have to rule out both Uncle George and Derwen. Better put your windproof on again. It's getting chilly."

Lewker complied absently.

"Yes," he muttered, frowning. " I suppose their alibi must be allowed. But it is an affair of time, and questions of time seem to crop up all over this business. Even that book we found in Pyecroft's tent—"

"The Five Red Herrings?"

"The same. That excellent story depends for its solution upon a right interpretation of the evidence of times."

"But Pyecroft—if you're suggesting the book put some idea into his head—hasn't even tried to give himself an alibi," Hilary pointed out.

"He is, as yet, presumably ignorant that he is suspected." He heaved a deep sigh, rolled over on his stomach, and fingered the coils of rope that lay untidily on the ground beside him. "Tell me this, Hilary. I promised that until you gave your permission this matter should not be handed over to the police. If nothing comes of this experiment, if we cannot find Pyecroft guilty, if our conference of all the possibles tomorrow produces nothing—do you agree that then we should go down to Bethesda Police Station tomorrow afternoon and tell our story?"

There was a long pause before Hilary answered. The huge shadows of the peaks were stretching across the velvety green of the far valleys now, and the sun was dropping slowly towards the long bars of purple cloud that had crept up the western sky behind Foel Goch. The red-gold rays still shone upon their high-flung platform, but there was a suggestion of clammy chill in the air; the brief abortive summer was almost over, and tomorrow might bring rain.

"Yes," the girl said suddenly. "There's nothing else to be done, of course. You've done a lot, and I'm most awfully grateful to you for not going to the police at once."

She got to her feet with some abruptness and walked away down the ridge for a little distance. Lewker let her go. She must know as well as he did that this attempt to bring the professor into the position of a prime suspect might easily fail; that unless something definite could be proved against Wenceslaus Pyecroft, Michael Rouse stood out as the murderer by every test short of actual proof. Lewker felt a strong sympathy for Rouse, who was (in his theory) not a criminal by choice but a murderer from the highest motives. But if one is to excuse murder on the ground of motive, would not every murderer be able to produce a plausible excuse?

A hail from Hilary interrupted his thoughts, and he went to join her where she stood on the knoll of rock above the top of Nor' Nor' Gully. Below on the North Ridge track the tiny figure of Harold could now be seen climbing towards them. He was coming up at a good speed but they could see him make an occasional stumble.

"He's been a long time," commented the girl. "It's nearly quarter-past six, and we've got to meet Pyecroft at six-thirty."

"Don't tell Harold that, my dear. Give the lad plenty of praise—he will appreciate yours more than mine. After all, we have rather imposed upon his good nature."

Harold, panting hard and putting on a final spurt, clambered up the rocky path beneath them and sprawled breathless at their feet. Hilary checked the time by her wristwatch.

"Thirty-three minutes—good work, Harold," she cried. "You must be pretty fit. I should have collapsed halfway back."

Harold turned a very red but pleased countenance to her, but was incapable of speech. Filthy added his own congratulations, pausing in making a notebook entry to do so, and offered him a piece of chocolate which he had been keeping in reserve.

"No, thanks—I'll have a—glucose tablet," panted Harold, pulling out his tin. "I timed myself going down," he went on when he had recovered his breath.

"It was fourteen and a half minutes to the top of the Milestone—

eighteen and a half coming back. Is that any use?"

"You have been absolutely invaluable, laddie, and I am most grateful. Particularly for your abstention from questions at this stage."

"But I'll hear all about it tomorrow?"

"I promise you that. Now—there are two more items on our program. One of them can be carried out by Hilary and myself. The other I would like you to do for me when you are sufficiently recovered."

Harold sat up, and, conscious of Hilary's admiring gaze, swung nonchalantly to his feet as one to whom a half-hour race over a mountain is nothing.

"I'm ready right away," he said carelessly. "What is it?"

"Only this. You have a watch. Go down the North Ridge at an easy pace—imagine yourself a newcomer to mountains unable to move fast over rough ground—and time yourself from here to Dol Afon. 'That,' as Prospero, says to Ariel, 'shall be thy charge: then to the elements Be free, and fare you well!' "

Harold, looking slightly disappointed, waved a hand and set off, followed by Lewker's reminder that for the information of Dol Afon he had spent the afternoon with them botanizing on Tryfan.

When he was out of hearing Hilary turned a reproachful face on her companion.

"That was all eyewash," she accused. "You just wanted to get him out of the way."

"So I did. We could hardly have him present at our conference with Pyecroft. Before that momentous interview, sweet coz, consider with me this timetable of mine."

He spread out his red-covered notebook and Hilary looked over his shoulder. The timetable was neatly et out:

PARTY ON EAST FACE, Times.

Monday		
(a) Left Dol Afon	*9:40*	*Ascertained; Mrs. Morris*
(b) At foot of Grooved Arête	*10:28*	*Estimated by test*
(c) Prof. reaches triangular rock in Green Gully	*10:38*	*ditto*
(d) Whistle and Prof's shout heard by A.L. and H.J.	*10:55*	*Ascertained; H.J.'s watch*
(e) Interval between (c) and (d) = 17 minutes.		
Wednesday		
(f) Time front triangular		

rock to top of Green Gully	*3½ mins.*	*Test, A.L.*
(g) Time to Milestone and back to top of Nor' Nor' Gully	*33 mins.*	*Test, H. J.*
(h) Total, which ought to agree with (e) above	*36½ minutes*	

Hilary studied this table with care. There was no avoiding its conclusion; but she grasped at the only straw of error.

"I know the professor's a good bit older than Harold or you," she said, "but you're both not very quick goers, and it's admitted he's very spry for his age. Wouldn't it be possible—"

"Consider, O son of Wat," Lewker begged her. "Neither Harold nor myself are record-breakers. But we took, going all out, more than twice the time that the professor would have had at his disposal. No living man could have covered that distance in seventeen minutes. Consider, finally, that we allowed no time in our test for the descent to the cave, the probable waiting, the murder, and the re-ascent. The climb down to the cave might take no more than two or three minutes, but the rest—an overwhelming impossibility." He closed the notebook with a snap and thrust it into his pocket. "Professor Ferriday joins Uncle George and Derwen Jones."

"Three eliminated, two improbable, and—and two possibles, left," Hilary summed up bravely. She picked up an end of the rope and began to coil it neatly. "I suppose we won't need this again."

"No," said Lewker slowly. "It has failed to hang a man today."

CHAPTER SEVENTEEN

If he be not born to be hanged,
our case is miserable.
THE TEMPEST

WENCESLAUS PYECROFT was at the trysting place before them. As Lewker and the girl clambered up the ridge to the summit they saw his tall figure, looking strangely attenuated beside the bulky shapes of Adam and Eve, silhouetted motionless against the orange glow of a threatening sunset. He did not move as they approached, and Lewker saw that he was set in a heroic pose reminiscent of the late Mussolini, with arms folded and thin legs astride.

"Good evening, Mr. Pyecroft," he called. "I am sorry we are a minute or two late—"

"Ay come here," broke in the other, his bleating voice resentful, "Ay come here of may own accord—mark that—and Ay am kept waiting."

"Well," returned Filthy good-humoredly, "you could hardly have found a more magnificent place to wait in." He indicated a comfortable rock to Hilary and sat down himself with his back against the massive side of Adam. "Just look at that wealth of color," he continued enthusiastically, waving his hand towards the distant summit of Y Garn. "That fine frenzy of flame and smoky cloud, with the darkening peaks standing bold and black, like the murderers in *Macbeth,* against the—"

"Ay am still waiting," Pyecroft interrupted again coldly.

"Bless me, so you are. Do sit down, Mr. Pyecroft, and tell us why you killed Raymond Cauthery."

Hilary gasped involuntarily. This was letting out the cat with a vengeance. To her amazement the thin figure before them did not immediately collapse or even display great astonishment. Pyecroft started, but recovered himself at once. He threw back his head, shaking the lank hair from his brow and setting his spectacles aflash in the lurid light from over the sea.

"Ay am accused," he said shrilly. "Therefore Ay shall remain erect. Say what you have to say and Ay will give you may answer."

Filthy eyed him for a moment in silence, frowning.

"You seem to expect this charge," he remarked gravely. "Did you know that Cauthery had been murdered?"

The other seemed a trifle disconcerted.

"Ay did not. Ay know the man was a double traitor. Ay know the police, the servants of the Kepitalists, are watching me, following me, spreading the tale that Ay once threatened the man Cauthery. Ay know, from your demand that Ay should come here for questioning, that you had coupled this tale with may presence on Tryfan on the day of the eccident. That is all Ay know."

He settled his feet defiantly and tightened his folded arms. Lewker rubbed his chin.

"I see. Tell me, Mr. Pyecroft, what do you mean when you call Cauthery a 'double traitor'?"

"He was a member of the Party," snarled Pyecroft, "and he betrayed us." As he went on he seemed to be swept away on the flood of his anger. "He was in a position to do a great work for the cause of World Brotherhood. He had already started that work. Then he turned from us, the ret, and used the—the work he had begun for his own ends, the sordid, Kepitalist end of—Manny!"

He spat out the last word as though it soiled his lips. Lewker leaned forward quickly.

"Can you prove that?"

"Ay can't. But Ay have may suspicions—" He bit off his words suddenly and refolded his thin arms with an air of determination. "Come, sir! Ay am suspect of murder. Ay demand to hear your reasons."

"Very well, Mr. Pyecroft. But I wish you would sit down comfortably. No? Then here are my reasons. You admit yourself that Cauthery was a traitor to the cause of Communism, of which you are an enthusiastic protagonist. He was engaged in attacking Communism. He procured your discharge from your job. You wrote him a threatening letter which he took to the police. You were in the Tyn-y-coed Hotel and overheard Miss Bourne telling me that Cauthery was to be one of a climbing party in the Ogwen district this week. You were spying on Cauthery from the North Ridge of Tryfan on Sunday. You appeared in the immediate vicinity of Milestone Buttress within an hour of the time Cauthery was killed." He paused and stared severely at Pyecroft. "This is circumstantial evidence, Mr. Pyecroft, but it is a weighty accumulation. No doubt you have an explanation of your behavior. May I ask if you have also an alibi?"

Hilary thought that Pyecroft looked somewhat shaken by this indictment. She had been puzzled to reconcile this defiant and not unimpressive person with the querulously bleating youth who had been rescued from the chimney below the North Ridge three days before. Now she saw that he had screwed himself up to this pitch of resolution and was fighting hard to keep his dignity. She felt rather sorry for him.

"Ay am not to be intimidated," he announced in reply to Lewker's question. "Ay can produce both explanation and alibi, though Ay must say Ay don't see why Ay should produce them to you."

"There is no reason why you should," Lewker said quietly. "Tomorrow, in all probability, the information we possess will be in the hands of the police."

Pyecroft drew his breath sharply and audibly.

"Raight-ho, then," he said hurriedly, dropping his melodramatic manner. "Ay'll explain. After what Cauthery did to me and the Party, Ay felt like killing him. Ay was in a—a kind of frenzy when Ay wrote that letter you found out about. Afterwards, there were—er—certain developments that made me realize it was a very foolish thing to do."

"The police warned you?" suggested Lewker unfeelingly.

"Well—yes. It was quite by chance that Ay was in the Tyn-y-coed that evening, on may way up here. Ay had been thinking about Cauthery and when this young lady mentioned his name it gave me quaite a start. Ay went on thinking after you'd gone, and Ay decided"—he paused and gulped—"Ay decided it would be a good scheme to see Cauthery and tell him that Ay—er—bore no malice."

He was afraid, Hilary thought, that the other would see him first and report his presence to the police, or something.

"Thet's why," Pyecroft continued, "Ay was watching for him on Tryfan that day, when Ay got jemmed in the creck. Then Ay came down to your farm on Monday to see him, but he'd gone off to climb on Tryfan."

"So you followed, knowing he was going up Milestone Buttress?"

"Ay didn't follow him. Ay decided to come back again in the evening. Ay walked away from the farm and halfway up Cwm Tryfan. Ay was sitting there by the stream when Ay heard voices above on the East Face, and saw you and two other men on the Heather Terrace. Ay watched you start to climb. Then there was the whistle, and some shouting, so Ay came up a scree gully on to the treck that goes from Heather Terrace round the bottom of North Ridge, heard you running, and waited for you. That's all."

He looked from Lewker to Hilary as he ended, challenging them to find fault with his statement. Lewker considered him gravely.

"Very plausible, Mr. Pyecroft;" he boomed. "I would point out, however, that though you say you saw us on the Heather Terrace, we did not see you in Cwm Tryfan. If you had been seeking an opportunity to kill Raymond Cauthery, your movements, in so far as they are confirmed by witnesses, would have been equally natural."

"Would Ay have waited there after doing it?" demanded the other, his voice rising shrilly. "Would Ay have offered may help?"

"A subtle murderer would have done just that, Mr. Pyecroft. Unless you have a witness to confirm your statement that you were by a stream in Cwm Tryfan when that whistle was blown—"

"But Ay can *prove* it!" Pyecroft almost shrieked the words. Behind his strong-lensed glasses his eyes were wide and glaring. With an effort he regained his composure and turned to Hilary with one trembling hand outstretched.

"Ay call this young lady to witness the statement Ay now make," be said dramatically. "Ay had may binoculars with me that day. Ay watched you through them, on the Heather Terrace. There was you, Mr. Lewker—Ay believe that is the name?—and a young man in a laight-colored jecket, and a small thin man in green, who went up a gully by himself, climbing much faster than you others. He went quaite out of saight in the mist. When Ay heard the whistle you and the other man were nearly halfway up the face. There!" He glared triumphantly from one to the other of his listeners. "Could Ay have told you all that if Ay'd been murdering someone on Milestone Buttress?"

Hilary, for one, found his plea a reasonable one. Forgetting for the moment that to accept Pyecroft's alibi would mean leaving Michael Rouse in the position of prime suspect, she hoped Filthy would spare the young man further inquisition. But Lewker was inexorable.

"I cannot find," he said harshly, "that you have proved your alibi. You had ample opportunity later to observe what clothing the three of us were wearing. It could have been no very difficult matter to deduce that the thin man in green—Professor Ferriday—had climbed alone, and faster than we others climbed, from the fact that he had reached the top of Milestone Buttress before we—"

"But it's true—Ay swear it is—you've got to believe it!" Pyecroft's control was completely gone, and he was gibbering uncouthly. "Ay'm not capable of killing a man—Ay haven't even got the nerve for climbing—"

"Wait." Lewker's booming voice cut him short. "It is always possible," he went on with sudden affability as the other ceased his shrill protests, "that our suspicions do you a grave injustice, Mr. Pyecroft. In that case we shall owe you an apology. You will have behaved—if I may say so—with much fortitude under an unjust charge."

The specious friendliness in the actor's tone completed Pyecroft's downfall. His lips trembled uncontrollably, he gulped several times, and taking off his glasses with a shaking hand he strove feverishly to conceal in the business of wiping their misted lenses that a large tear was running down his beaky nose.

"You must realize, on the other hand," Lewker continued smoothly, "that the matter is a very serious one indeed. It should, of course, have been laid before the police earlier. For reasons into which I shall not go at the moment, however, we postponed this duty while certain preliminary investigations were made. It cannot be left there any longer."

Pyecroft, not trusting himself to speak, nodded.

"Tomorrow those concerned in the matter—for there are others besides yourself—are meeting at Dol Afon to discuss it. Among those present, I hope, will be your acquaintance and fellow Communist Derwen Jones."

He glanced keenly at the other as he spoke, but if he had hoped for a sign he was disappointed. Pyecroft merely sniffed dolorously and nodded.

"I think," Filthy went on, "that as one who has fallen—however mistakenly—under suspicion you should be present at that meeting. It will be half-past nine. You understand, of course, that there is no compulsion in the matter. You are perfectly at liberty to inform the police of my—"

"Ay will be there," Pyecroft said, recovering his voice. "Ay—Ay think Ay'd better go back to may tent. Er—good naight."

He turned away, replacing his glasses awkwardly as he did so.

"Good night," responded Lewker gravely.

Pyecroft, his lank form silhouetted against the smoldering fires of sunset, stumbled across the rocky plateau of Tryfan summit and disappeared over its western edge. Hilary and Lewker watched him go in silence.

"Well," Hilary said when he was out of sight, "I think Wenceslaus Pyecroft's a bit cracked, if you ask me. The sort of chap you couldn't tell what he might do if he got worked up."

"Ungrammatical, sweet coz, but acute. I see in our spectacled friend one of those dangerous sentimentalists who believe that what they do for the best must always be right. Their special standard is a faulty syllogism: 'I subordinate myself to an Ultimate Good, therefore all I do to that end is right; therefore I do no wrong; therefore any nation, law or person that thinks otherwise is wrong! Of such stuff are Communists made—and murderers."

Hilary nodded vigorously. She had remembered Michael's perilous position in the red-covered notebook now and was anxious that Pyecroft should not be eliminated.

"He could commit a murder," she said, "and feel himself so justified that it'd be as if he hadn't done it. He'd be able to convince himself that he hadn't done it, in fact."

Her companion struck a match for his cigarette, and the brilliance of the little flame made her realize that the twilight was already upon their lonely summit. Beyond the dark giants that guarded the Nant Francon the westerly cloud banks had built their dam of smoky purple higher and higher against the sunset flood until the sea of color was almost hidden behind it. Lewker's deep voice struck oddly upon the mountain silence. "There was a clever Frenchman who once said 'Beware of that man; he believes what he is saying!' He might have added: 'And beware still more of the man who can tell a lie and convince himself that it is truth.' " He shifted his broad shoulders against the monolith at his back. "All the same, friend Pyecroft's manner was uncommonly convincing."

"It was just acting—only very good acting because he'd convinced himself as well. You gave him plenty of warning, you know. He'd bags of time to get up his part."

"He gave an accurate account of the positions of our East Face party at the time the whistle was heard," Filthy pointed out.

Hilary turned to him eagerly, her fair hair catching and holding a last glint of gold from the dying light over the sea.

"You said yourself he might have deduced your positions. Look here—suppose he wasn't down in Cwm Tryfan at all but hiding somewhere quite near you, in the rocks, just above the Heather Terrace, for instance. He could have watched you start your climb, and seen the professor start up his gully. That would be about half-past ten by your timetable. He'd have twenty-five minutes to get to the Milestone and do the murder, wouldn't he? You must admit that's a possibility."

"Oh, I admit it," said Lewker in so bitter a tone that Hilary jumped. "Possibilities, probabilities—they are all we have." He stood up and held up a pudgy hand with the unconscious drama of gesture that never deserts the professional actor. "We have collected damning facts enough for half a dozen murders, yet I, like Hamlet—

> "A dull and muddy-mettled rascal, peak
> Like John-a-dreams, unpregnant of my cause,
> And can say nothing."

He flung away his half-smoked cigarette and walking moodily round the vertical flank of Adam stood there with his back to Hilary staring down the sheer crags of the East Face. The deep basin of moorland far below was brimming with twilight now. The lonely voices of the sheep floated up from the darkening pastures; peace and melancholy mingled inseparably in their faint far crying. From the dim shafts of rock that fell dizzily away at his feet came the sudden brief *crark* of a raven. One would scarcely have said that there was much comfort to be derived from a contemplation of this wild scene, but when Lewker turned from it he seemed to have regained his usual imperturbable good humor.

"Well," he boomed, "the Great Detective is at fault. Were I really a Great Detective I should at this point sense a hidden discrepancy in the facts I had collected. I should pass the facts in review before my supernormal intelligence and pounce upon the discrepancy. And it would lead me straight to the murderer. But that doesn't seem to be in my script. I shall have to throw up the part after all."

Hilary slipped a comforting arm through his.

"Come along—let's go down to Dol Afon," she said. "Perhaps something will turn up tomorrow."

"Your part is Watson, not Micawber," he remarked, giving the arm a squeeze. "But you are right about the advisability of descent. I must have a bath before supper."

They left Adam and Eve brooding motionless over the darkling valleys and set off down the North Ridge. Lewker, in the lead, set so fast a pace that Hilary was hard put to it to keep up and conversation was impossible. They came down the last slopes to the road in semidarkness, with a few drops of rain falling like muttered threats from the overcast sky, and reached the farmhouse with plenty of time to bathe and change before the evening meal.

After supper, at which no one seemed inclined for talk and even Uncle George was curiously subdued, Lewker refused an invitation from Professor Ferriday to make up a bridge four and strolled out alone into the farm garden. He stood there for a while, frowning at his thoughts and the darkness. The rain had so far held off, but the feel of it was in the faint night wind that came cool on his cheek out of the west. High overhead Tryfan, its peak not yet capped by mist, reared a darker bulk against the starless sky. Away to the left a fast-moving speck of light appeared on the valley floor—the night bus from Llanrwst whirling its unseeing passengers along the Holyhead Road to Bangor, while Adam and Eve—those strange twins who had watched over this valley long before man learned his power of life and death—looked down impassively from their timeless heights. The light grew swiftly to a short caterpillar of glowing windows, passed, and left the darkness darker than before. And that, mused Filthy dolefully, was just what all his laborious discoveries had done.

He went slowly into the house and up to his room, where he undressed and got into bed. But not to sleep. In the inmost recesses of his mind a tiny voice had begun to nag at him. At first he could not interpret it, but it was persistent and bothersome. Some vital thing he had left undone in his search for evidence? A question he might have asked which would have solved his problem in a flash? Or—could he after all be worrying over that hidden discrepancy he had rather bitterly jested about with Hilary? Yes—there was *something,* something he had seen, or heard, or touched, or even smelt, which would not fit into the ascertained facts. And it must be found.

He sat up and lit his candle; reached for the red-covered notebook and turned first to his timetable. He had had a curious feeling that times were of importance in this case. But though he stared at it and read it through and through for twenty minutes the only result was an uncomfortable feeling that its compilation had been a childish waste of time and energy. One by one he scanned the other notebook pages containing his carefully made records. There was Mildred's story as Hilary had told it, Hilary's own detailed story of her climb with Cauthery, the notes of the telephone conversation with Sir Frederick Claybury, Pyecroft's tale told to him this evening which he had written in before supper—suggestive detail in profusion but no discrepancy, nothing to prove that any of the suspects had lied.

Except Michael Rouse. Rouse had lied about his tobacco-buying visit to Ogwen Cottage. Lewker could think of a reason for that lie, but his reason had nothing to do with the murder.

He flung the notebook on the floor in disgust, blew out his candle, and lay staring up at the darkness. He tried now to make his mind a blank, to let that nagging voice have the field to itself. But in spite of his efforts his imagination began to paint a series of pictures on the viewless canvas of the dark, pictures that arranged themselves perversely in pairs.

Uncle George; swearing, with shaking hand and face convulsed, to be revenged on the man who had seduced his daughter. Uncle George; rising abashed from his knees on Bwlch Tryfan to show Derwen Jones the time by his watch.

Mildred Jupp; coming round the base of Milestone Buttress shortly after the murder, to receive with curious self-possession the news of her lover's death. Mildred Jupp; pouring out her troubles to Hilary and revealing her father's threats.

Professor Ferriday; on Bristly Ridge, lightly mooting his ingenuous idea of an undetectable mountain murder, and, later, jokingly suggesting Cauthery as a suitable victim. Professor Ferriday; shouting down from the mist-wreathed North Ridge a few seconds after the faint shrilling of Hilary's whistle.

Derwen Jones; in the dark kitchen garden, threatening Cauthery with a violent death if he caught him with Gwennie again—and afterwards striding away from the barn where the two had been flirting. Derwen Jones; tactfully asking an embarrassed Uncle George for the time, at ten minutes to eleven.

Michael Rouse; stalking moodily into the farmhouse after warning Hilary against Cauthery. Michael Rouse; stolid, quiet, and honest-seeming, the Michael who had somehow caught and held the loyalty of Hilary Bourne.

Wenceslaus Pyecroft; appearing suddenly out of the mist close to the scene of the fatality, unable to face the thought of seeing or touching the murdered man's body. Wenceslaus Pyecroft; nervous, hypersensitive, stuck in a chimney he had tried to climb with unnailed boats. (A third picture intruded itself here—Pyecroft the Communist, addressing a meeting in Bangor, and his acquaintance Derwen Jones attentive in the audience. It faded quickly.)

Mrs. Jupp; limping stealthily up the scree between her 'viewpoint' and the slope of Tryfan, climbing the easy traverse into the mist. This time the picture would not form. . . .

Lewker's weary mind relaxed. Slowly all stress and perplexity faded from it as fatigue of body took its healthy charge. And there, in the half-life between sleeping and waking, he saw the truth.

Instantly he was fully awake and groping for the matches. The candle grasped at the tiny flame, flickered and nearly went out as he dived over the side of the bed to find his notebook, wavered like a nervous spinster as he hastily flicked over the pages.

Yes—there it was. How had he managed to miss it? And the other things? One by one they fell into place. There could be no mistake now. Confirmation would be needed—a phone message, here, a telegram—assurance doubly sure. But he had the murderer securely in his grasp.

Triumph gave place to graver feelings as the full realization of his discovery and what it entailed came upon him. He was about to bring grief to people he had come to know and like; he was about to rob a fellow human being, who but for him might have lived a happy and useful life, of existence. But Abercrombie Lewker, a sentimentalist in some ways, was a realist in this, that he knew Justice for a thing greater than man. There was no faltering in his decision, and within five minutes of his discovery he was sound asleep, leaving the candle alight on the bedside table.

The candle burned slowly and with a steady flame. It was a fine tall candle, erect and sturdy. When the dawn light crept over the crouching hills round Dol Afon it was cold and dead.

CHAPTER EIGHTEEN

Their understanding
Begins to swell, and the approaching tide
Will shortly fill the reasonable shore
That now lies foul and muddy.
THE TEMPEST

OVER the pass between the hidden summits the rain came driving from the sea, mottling the leaden surface of Llyn Ogwen and hurrying on in thin silver shafts to drum a goblin tattoo on the windowpanes of the Dol Afon sitting-room. Inside the room ten people had managed to dispose themselves in varying degrees of comfort, and the atmosphere, laden with the smoke from after-breakfast pipes and cigarettes, had a spurious air of snugness. The gray light that filtered in through the window scarcely illuminated the nine faces that were turned expectantly toward Lewker, who was sitting at the table close to the window. Filthy had the momentary impression of nine shadowy masks challenging him to strip one of them from the face of a murderer. He ran his eyes quickly round the crowded room.

Aunt Mabel occupied the most comfortable of the worn armchairs by the fireplace, with her knitting needles clicking busily. In the other her husband sucked jerkily at his pipe, and just behind him, perched on an aged piano stool in the corner, were Mildred Jupp and Hilary.

These four formed a group on Lewker's left. On his right Professor Ferriday shared the horsehair sofa with an extremely self-conscious Wenceslaus Pyecroft while Harold Jupp swung a leg nervously from his seat on the sofa's antimacassared arm. Near the door, almost opposite Lewker, Michael Rouse and Derwen Jones sat on kitchen chairs; their faces were respectively stolid and sullen beneath oddly similar red hair.

Before breakfast Lewker had walked down to Ogwen Cottage in the rain and used the telephone box for one call and a telegram. The former had brought the confirmation he had expected; for a reply to the latter be would have to wait. And now the stage was set for the last act, and Lewker, in whom—consciously or unconsciously—an ineradicable stage-sense took charge wherever he found himself, was resolved to play his chosen part of the Great Detective according to the best traditions. With the eyes of his audience upon him he took from his pocket the red-covered notebook and laid it on the table beside him. Then he looked up and spoke, without pomposity but in the unmistakable tones of the tragedian.

"Until five days ago, I was a complete stranger to all of you here. I am the more grateful that you acceded so willingly to my request, as yet unexplained, that we should all meet in this room to discuss a very grave matter."

"Well, we certainly hope it's worth listening to," began Uncle George with an attempt at jocularity which was instantly quelled by a glance from his wife.

"I would rather say it must be listened to. I locked the door of this room, as you saw. That was to insure freedom from interruption. I am expecting a telegram, but apart from that I think we shall be undisturbed. And I must ask you all—" he looked round the room— "to maintain absolute secrecy about what passes here this morning until we have decided among us what steps are to be taken. The matter is one of life and death."

No one spoke. Aunt Mabel's knitting needles ceased their clicking for a moment and then resumed. Pyecroft cleared his throat, and blushed as the noise grated loudly upon the silence. Lewker, having made his impressive pause, continued in the same grave, even tones.

"A chance word let fall by Miss Bourne just after the inquest on Raymond Cauthery led me to make certain investigations on the actual scene of the accident. As a result of these I established beyond any possible doubt that Cauthery's fall to death was not accidental, though it had been ingeniously contrived to appear so."

He paused again, and this time the silence was as though the nine listeners had been stricken with complete paralysis. It lasted only a moment, and Uncle George, was the first to find his voice.

"What on earth—you don't—upon my word!" he gobbled. "This is preposterous, Lewker! Are you trying to suggest that—that someone or other—confound it, man, do you realize what you're saying?"

"I am saying that Raymond Cauthery was murdered, Mr. Jupp. I will give you my reasons—"

"May I ask," Professor Ferriday's high precise voice broke in, "why, if the circumstances warranted this extraordinary suspicion, you did not at once report the matter to the police?"

"Or to me—or to me?" bellowed Uncle George, very red in the face. "As—er—the leader of our party here, I consider you should have told me at once. Why was I not told?"

"George! " said his wife; her glance at him held more than a trace of fear. "I think this is some dreadful joke of Mr. Lewker's." She rose, gathering her knitting. "If you don't mind, I shall go—"

"Please, Mrs. Jupp." Lewker's voice was authoritative. "I assure you I am very far from joking. I must ask you to stay and hear me out. You will understand why in a moment."

Aunt Mabel hesitated, bit her lip, and sat down again. Automatically, her gaze fixed on the man at the table, her fingers groped again for her knitting.

"I may have erred in not going to the police immediately," he went on steadily. "I take full responsibility for that. However, let me remind you that less than two days have elapsed since these suspicions were aroused. I have reason to believe that this delay will not impede the course of justice. As to my reasons for not informing you, they shall be made clear now."

With his notebook open for reference he began to describe concisely the discovery in the Milestone Cave and the inevitable deduction made.

Hilary, sitting uncomfortably beside a tense, wide-eyed Mildred, realized that he was going to spare her as much as he could and was grateful. In front of her Uncle George (she could only see the crimson back of his neck and an indignant bristle of beard) was blowing out his cheeks at intervals with a plopping noise. Beyond him she could see Michael hunched on his chair, his square jaw clenched on the stem of his pipe, frowning at the floor; Derwen Jones, with arms folded, scowling into midair; Harold Jupp, pale and restless; Pyecroft, biting his fingernails and gazing wildly round the room through his thick-lensed glasses; the professor, thin lips tightly compressed, small black eyes fixed unwinkingly on Lewker's face. Aunt Mabel's needles provided a continuous faint machine-gunnery to her husband's heavier explosions. Her eyes came back again to Michael. His red hair stuck up in an absurd little tuft at the back of his head. A fragment of the "Nimrod" variation from Elgar's *Enigma* drew its lovely thread across her mind; the Liverpool Philharmonic orchestra had played it when she had sat beside Michael that time, and his hair had, stuck up just the same then. . . .

Was she in love with him? She didn't know. She knew only that Filthy's confident manner woke a dreadful apprehension in her. There had been no opportunity for her to question him this morning, but somehow she guessed that he had found the murderer of Raymond Cauthery. And who could it be but Michael?

"You must all see, then," Lewker was saying, "that, setting aside a highly improbable coincidence, whoever perpetrated this crime must have had intimate knowledge of the Milestone Buttress and of the movements of Cauthery and Miss Bourne on that morning. The murder need not have been planned in advance, but the murderer must have known that Cauthery would climb the Buttress on Monday. And that was known to no one but Mrs. Morris and her daughter and those who are in this room."

"Rot!" exploded Uncle George in a shout that rattled the china dogs on the mantelpiece. "Obvious, arrant nonsense! Why, we all know each other, we all—"

His glare, roving round the room, lighted upon Wenceslaus Pyecroft, and his voice trailed away ludicrously. Professor Ferriday nodded slowly.

"We shall have to admit the justice of Lewker's conclusion, George," he piped, "if we admit the premises he has described." He turned to the actor. "I take it, then, that we are all suspected of murdering my unfortunate assistant?"

"Not all. I mentioned Mrs. Morris and Gwennie Morris, as knowing the movements of the Milestone Buttress party. Not only were they even more unlikely as perpetrators of a violent murder than the rest of us, but they were, as each could testify, in the kitchen of Dol Afon during the whole of that morning. I think you will agree with my decision to rule them out at once. Miss Bourne was a possibility, of course. She had opportunity, and she has admitted that a few minutes before Cauthery's death she had used force to repel his attempt to make violent love to her." Michael Rouse's chair creaked loudly. Mildred's hand found Hilary's and clutched it tightly.

"On the other hand," went on the expositor, "had it not been for Miss Bourne's hint there might have been no indication that the death was other than it appeared. Furthermore, she has—overcoming a very natural repugnance—given invaluable help in narrowing down the field of possibility and thus establishing the innocence of certain persons. We may therefore eliminate her. Of the remaining possibles it was at the outset apparent that three—myself, Harold Jupp, and Professor Ferriday—were out of the running by reason of our positions on the

East Face when the faint sound of the whistle indicated the state of emergency on Milestone Buttress. The time by Harold's watch was then ten fifty-five. Harold and I were roped together and halfway up Grooved Arête. The professor had been out of sight in the mist above Green Gully for a considerable time—about seventeen minutes, as we later established by an experiment at which Harold, though kept in ignorance of my reasons, assisted me."

Harold looked as though he was trying to render himself invisible by self-compression. Professor Ferriday met Lewker's glance with a grim little smile.

"If I had possessed wings and a reasonable motive," he said, "I might have been your murderer."

"Exactly, professor. You disappeared into the mists at ten thirty-eight, by our careful computation. To have committed the murder you would have had to get to the Buttress, carry out your plan there, and be back above us on the North Ridge by ten fifty-five. The mere journey down to the Buttress took Harold Jupp, at his fastest speed, over fourteen minutes, and the double journey thirty-six and a half minutes. You were therefore eliminated."

Harold Jupp let out his pent breath in an audible sigh of relief.

"Thank you," said the professor with a wry twist of his lips.

"I tell you all this in some detail," Lewker said, looking round the circle of intent faces, "so that you may see that, however mistaken I have been in trying to conduct this investigation myself, I have done my best to be thorough. This experiment with times, by the by, is a little out of place in my statement, for there were others who were not obviously limited by time. For instance—"

"Look here, Lewker," Uncle George broke in impatiently, "if you've got an accusation to make, make it and let us decide whether your grounds have any basis in fact. There's no point in going into a lot of useless detail. It's extremely trying for my wife and daughter. You may not know it, but these last few days have been a greater trial for them—and for me, I may say—than for any of you, for a reason I can't reveal."

"I know that reason, Mr. Jupp," Lewker said gravely.

"You—" The big clergyman fell back in his chair, his face suddenly white. "Lewker—I beg of you—"

"I shall not divulge it. I must remind you that eight persons in this room have been unjustly suspected of murder, Mr. Jupp. I owe it to each of them, and to myself, to explain how this came about. In your case I know that Cauthery had treated your daughter in a way that seemed to you unforgivable. It may have seemed so to your wife and daughter also. I know that you yourself uttered a violent threat against Cauthery, that you went out before breakfast that morning and were on or near Tryfan at the time of the murder, that you did not return until just before lunch—two hours after the murder."

Uncle George stared speechless for a moment, then dropped his graying head on his hands.

"God forgive me that threat," he muttered, "but I didn't kill him."

"Of course you didn't, George," said Aunt Mabel sharply. She turned fiercely on Lewker. "You've no business to make such ridiculous accusations. My husband talks violently at times, but he wouldn't hurt a fly!"

"Forgive me, Mrs. Jupp," said the actor gently, " but I made no accusation. The facts, as I gave them, are incontrovertible—as is the fact that you yourself were almost within hail of Milestone Buttress during the vital period, and yet state that you did not hear the distress signal."

"Oh, very well," she retorted, jerking her head impatiently. "I did it."

There was a hissing intake of breaths. Hilary felt Mildred's hand contract with almost painful force round her own. She saw Uncle George lift his head and stare incredulously at his wife with his mouth open; he seemed incapable of speech. A heavier shower thrashed against the windowpanes and the room grew suddenly darker, as though some shadowy figure had obscured the gray light. Aunt Mabel seemed unconscious of the sensation she had produced.

"Yes," she went on with a sort of controlled fury, knitting very fast as she spoke, "nobody saw me, did they? I haven't got a what-is-it—an alibi. I dragged my arthritic leg up the side of Tryfan and down that slippery rock, murdered poor Raymond, and then dragged myself back to finish my painting. That's as likely as what you say about George. Isn't it?"

Lewker's pouchy countenance softened for the first time that morning to something approaching a smile.

"I must consider your statement as rhetorical irony, Mrs. Jupp," he said quietly. "I believe that is how you intended it. You have, as you say, no alibi, but I doubt whether you are able to do the amount of climbing required. The work you did on your watercolor that morning showed concentration which, I think, you could not have given to it had you been preparing to kill a man. The wind, as you could have pointed out if you had wished to, was blowing from the west at sufficient strength to bear the sound of whistling away from you. You are, on the whole, a less likely murderer than your husband, who—"

"He didn't do it neither," said Derwen Jones loudly and so suddenly that everyone jumped. "What about me asking him the time, that I told you about?" he added, scowling at Lewker.

"I was about to come to that. I must explain first that Mr. Derwen Jones comes into our inquiry on the score of a justifiable grievance he entertained against Raymond Cauthery." Here Derwen muttered something unintelligible under his breath. Lewker disregarded him. " This grievance was sufficient to make Mr. Jones offer extreme violence to Cauthery in my hearing. Further, Mr. Jones was on the mountainsides west of Tryfan, rounding up the Dol Afon sheep, on the morning of the murder."

"I saw his dogs and heard him whistling them about half-past ten," said Aunt Mabel, who was still pale but had regained her composure. "They were moving away towards Bochlwyd."

"Thank you, Mrs. Jupp. We have to note, however, that during the ascent of the Buttress, perhaps ten minutes before the murder, Cauthery told Miss Bourne that he had just seen a redheaded man clambering up the scree on the west of the Buttress. That man would have been able to get up the flanking rocks on that side and down the top pitches of the climb in time to be in the Milestone Cave before Cauthery got there—if he were a good mountaineer. And Mr. Jones is a good mountaineer."

Uncle George raised a hand and seemed about to speak. Lewker went on more quickly, forestalling him.

"It seems that by chance Mr. Jones came upon Mr. Jupp in the mist on Bwlch Tryfan and asked him the time, in response to which he was shown Mr. Jupp's watch, which pointed to ten minutes to eleven. That appears to give both of them an alibi—oddly enough, for the very time we have noted as the time of the murder. It is by no means a perfect alibi, and we have still to consider one who has no alibi at all. That is Miss Jupp."

Mildred's hand twitched violently in Hilary's. Hilary squeezed it reassuringly.

"It's all right," she whispered. "He knows you didn't do it."

"Miss Jupp's motive for killing Cauthery," continued the booming voice evenly, " is one which has inspired more than one recorded murder in the past. She went out shortly after Cauthery and Miss Bourne drove away from Dol Afon, and was next seen when she came round the foot of the Buttress to where Professor Ferriday and I were waiting with Cauthery's body."

Oh, *blast* him! thought Hilary savagely. Must he rub it in like this? Then she remembered that Filthy had to be scrupulously fair to all those who had been suspected, including the murderer; remembered, too, that Mildred was not altogether blameless for the suspicion that had fallen upon her and on her parents. But the suspense was becoming unbearable. He hadn't even mentioned Michael yet, and there was only Pyecroft left besides Michael. . . .

"I may say," Lewker was proceeding, "that I did not attach much importance to the rather odd behavior of Miss Jupp when she received the news of the accident. People vary greatly in their behavior on such occasions, and at that time Miss Jupp—as I later came to know—was sustaining a heavy emotional burden. But it should be clear that I was not able to remove her then from the list of suspects."

He paused and flicked over the pages of his red-covered notebook.

"I pass now," he added, "to a gentleman who has come here of his own accord this morning—Mr. Wenceslaus Pyecroft."

Pyecroft, who had been listening open-mouthed and with increasing bewilderment to Lewker's successive summings-up, became suddenly galvanized into life. He shot up like a jack-in-a-box from his seat beside the professor, threw out one arm stiffly with fingers extended, and exclaimed in a kind of stifled shriek: "Ay did not kill Raymond Cauthery!"

He remained in this dramatic posture for so long that Hilary began to think it was an epileptic seizure. Then, apparently realizing that he was making the Fascist salute, he hurriedly clenched his fist, glancing at Derwen Jones as he did so, and subsided in a state of demoralization on to the professor's knee. Upon his tremulous and confused apologies Lewker's deep voice superimposed itself.

"I do not think I am making an unfair estimate of the late Cauthery's character when I say that, so far from having regard for other people, he took a certain delight in injuring them or their feelings at no particular risk to himself. There are people like that. Mr. Pyecroft had been dealt a severe blow, gratuitously as some would think, by Cauthery, who had not only deserted the cause of Communism but had denounced Mr. Pyecroft as a devotee of that cause. Mr. Pyecroft injudiciously wrote Cauthery a letter vowing to be revenged on him—a letter which is in the possession of the police. When, therefore, we find him in the mist above Milestone Buttress within an hour of the murder we cannot but consider him as a suspect."

Professor Ferriday leaned forward.

"How," he piped curiously, "did you acquire this information about Pyecroft's letter and Raymond's action in informing on him?"

"I have been in touch with my friend Sir Frederick Claybury of Department Seven," Lewker told him. "He gave me this and other information."

"I see," said the professor thoughtfully. "Pray forgive the interruption."

Lewker nodded curtly and looked directly at Pyecroft.

"Mr. Pyecroft. I want you to answer an important question. During our conversation last evening you made an incomplete statement. You said that when Raymond Cauthery was a Communist he undertook a certain task for what you term 'the cause of world brotherhood,' and that when he executed his ideological *volte face* he used this 'task,' in some way, for his own personal profit. If I assure you that your reply will not go beyond the walls of this room and will almost certainly free you from suspicion of Cauthery's murder, will you tell us exactly what that task was?"

Wenceslaus Pyecroft hesitated, but only for a moment. It has been the strength of every great tyranny that the evil instinct which leads men to seek security in complete subordination can become more powerful than the love of life itself.

"Ay refuse," he quavered stubbornly.

"Very well. We may be able to get at it in another way later on." Lewker's tones were ominously quiet. He turned now to the rest of his audience. "To conclude the case against Mr. Pyecroft, I will mention the following points. His visit to Dol Afon on Monday morning, ostensibly to speak with Cauthery, could have been for the purpose of finding out where he was going that day. What could be easier than to wait in hiding, until Cauthery had driven away and then emerge to ask for him at the farm? Cauthery was the leader of the Aristos and editor and promoter of their monthly review, an organ not only anti-Communist but advocating a return to a ruling aristocracy. To Communism his death, one imagines, would be doubly an occasion for rejoicing—and Mr. Pyecroft is an active and devoted member of the Communist Party. We may note in passing that during his stay in this district he has addressed a Communist meeting at Bangor, and that Derwen Jones, another of those on whom suspicion has fallen, is also a Communist."

Derwen Jones, who had begun to rise slowly to his feet on the mention of his name, burst out wrathfully.

"*Diawl!* What are you getting at, mister? See here—d'you think the Party'd soil its hands with a dog like Cauthery? By tamn, you can lay off that game—"

"Sit down, Mr. Jones." The deep voice was not raised, but it held menacing authority. Derwen hesitated, scowled and sat down. "I will explain again that I am trying to give my reason for suspecting a number of innocent persons in turn of a brutal murder. I have shown that Mr. Pyecroft had a very strong motive—more than one motive, indeed—for killing Cauthery. On the other hand, he has produced an alibi. He says that he was watching our party on the East Face at the time the whistle blew from Milestone Buttress, and in support of this statement he adds a correct description of our appearance and positions at that time. Again we have an imperfect alibi, for he could have observed us from another spot nearer the Buttress and even made a good guess at our positions from later events. For the moment I leave the matter there."

Lewker turned a page of his notebook and smoothed it down with a stubby forefinger. In the short silence the rattle of Aunt Mabel's knitting needles sounded unnaturally loud.

"I come now," said the actor slowly, "to the last name on my list. Michael Rouse."

It was Hilary who clutched Mildred's hand now. She could not bring herself to look at Michael, but she knew he would be chewing stolidly on his pipe-stem and frowning still at the floor. She kept her eyes fixed on Lewker's face. He looked up, met her gaze, and looked away quickly, sending his glance round the room.

"You have seen, I hope," he said, "how this tangle of motives and doubtful alibis prevented me from saying with any degree of certainty 'This is the murderer.' My one hope was to detect some sort of deliberate deception, a lie or subterfuge relative to the time or place of the murder, which would point to one person. The alibis I have described cannot—be they true or false—be broken. They are perfectly consonant, as you will agree, with each person's own story and with his or her known movements. So, at any rate, they appeared to me. Michael Rouse, though I believe he has known for some time of my suspicions, has made no attempt to provide himself with an alibi. Unless"—he looked inquiringly at Rouse—"he can produce one now?"

Michael did not look up. Deliberately he took his pipe from his mouth, wagged his head in stolid negative, and replaced the pipe.

"No alibi," Lewker resumed, "but that might be considered a sign of innocence. Or, of course, it might be simply that an alibi was impossible of arrangement. Now if we accept the joint alibi of Messrs. George Jupp and Derwen Jones, it means that the red-haired man seen by Cauthery on the scree above the Milestone Buttress was—as a practical certainty—Michael Rouse. We know he reached the top of the Buttress, after the 'accident,' almost as soon as Professor Ferriday, and was therefore not far away at the time of the murder. He himself states that he was on the crags two or three hundred feet above when he heard Miss Bourne's whistle. Jealousy has before now led to murder. But Michael Rouse does not strike me as the type of young man to murder another from such a motive. I looked for, and found, some indication of another and stronger motive. First, however, it must be stated that Rouse made a deliberate attempt to mislead in the matter of his movements prior to the murder. He told me that he had been to Ogwen Cottage that morning and had bought some tobacco—Dibdin's Cut Plug. I ascertained myself that he had done no such thing. Not only that, but his statement at the breakfast table that he had no tobacco left and must go to the Cottage to buy some was not true. He has been smoking Dibdin's Cut Plug for the last three days. He is, in fact, smoking it now."

With a great effort, for she felt as though her muscles were held immobile in the grip of any icy cold, Hilary forced herself to turn and look at Michael. He had not moved in the slightest. His face was completely impassive, and the curl of blue smoke from his pipe was the only sign of life about him. She wanted to run across and shake him, to cry in his ear that he must explain, explain—tell them his reason for lying, if he had one. If he had one. . . .

"It is clear," Filthy was saying with maddening deliberation, "that the fact that he did not go to Ogwen Cottage that morning is no very large point in the case against him. If he had gone there, he would still have had ample time to get to Milestone Buttress and be in the Cave before Cauthery reached it. The only conclusion we can reach is that he made this tobacco-buying an excuse to get away by himself. He accompanied Mrs. Jupp along the road as far as her sketching viewpoint—"

"He helped me over the wall," Aunt Mabel interrupted challengingly. "And I know very well Michael wouldn't do a horrible thing like killing Raymond."

"He helped her over the wall," Lewker pursued, unmoved, "walked on round the next corner, climbed over the wall himself, and doubled back along the rocky hillside above Mrs. Jupp—there is good cover there—to make his way up the scree beside Milestone Buttress. The facts will not bear any other interpretation."

"Yes, but he might have—" Hilary stopped short in sheer amazement at the sound of her own voice.

"Please go on, Miss Bourne." Lewker's tone was very gentle.

"Well," she found herself saying quite steadily, "Michael warned me the night before that—that Raymond was a bit of a wolf. A lady-killer, you know," she added for the benefit of her elders. "I was angry and wouldn't listen. But don't you think he might have—made that excuse so that he could keep an eye on us, sort of?" she finished in a rush.

"That is very possible. It is a possible sequel that he also overheard, from an observation post in the Cave, Cauthery's violent love-making and your rebuff. Do you deny that, Mr. Rouse?"

Hilary's hand went to her pale lips and her eyes flew to Michael. He had not moved, but there was a dull color in his cheeks. He made no response to Lewker's question, and the latter went on with his relentless exposition.

"More significant is the fact that he attempted to destroy a letter that was in the murdered man's room. Since no one else has received a letter here, that was the letter which Cauthery received belatedly on Sunday. I say ' attempted to destroy' because its contents were not completely obliterated. Sufficient remained to reveal their meaning."

For the first time Rouse showed a sign of perturbation. He moved his feet with a grating sound and looked up quickly.

"The letter was from the manager of a bank," Lewker continued, "the last, it appeared, of a series, warning Cauthery that unless he paid money into his account immediately further steps—legal proceedings or foreclosure on a mortgage, one assumes—would be taken. Now the following morning Cauthery, as Miss Bourne informs me, sent off an express registered letter from Capel Curig post office and appeared in higher spirits thereafter. You will recall that the bank's letter had been delayed and was urgent. Is it a farfetched assumption that Cauthery had sent off a remittance to put his account in order? And if we assume that, where could he have got the money? For banks do not send such letters where small sums are in question."

"You need go no further into the matter," came Professor Ferriday's dry tones. "He got it from me."

Lewker nodded, but his eyes were on Michael Rouse, who was gazing hard at the professor as though he was trying to hypnotize his chief.

"I had guessed as much," he boomed. " Cauthery came to your room the night before his death. He was there when Miss Jupp's outcry disturbed us all. I saw him coming out, and he volunteered the unlikely statement that he thought the outcry had come from your bedroom. You lent him the money, then?"

"Yes. I gave him a check. The poor boy was very worried."

"May I ask whether it was for a large amount?"

The professor raised his eyebrows.

"I see no necessity to answer that question," he said coldly.

"Very well. Was Cauthery in the habit of borrowing money from you?"

Professor Ferriday's wrinkled face screwed itself into a grimace of contempt.

"All this can have no possible bearing on my late assistant's murder," he piped. "It appears to me, Lewker, that you are—as the phrase goes—flogging a dead horse. What are you trying to suggest? That Raymond was blackmailing me?"

Lewker sat back in his chair. "Just that, professor," he said steadily.

"Indeed. No doubt you can tell me what dark secret he had discovered in my lurid past."

"I can at least make a good guess."

The scientist sat back in his turn and eyed the actor with a sort of humorous sorrow.

"My dear Lewker," he said, almost with affection, "this is indubitably not your *métier*. Conjecture is surely not an instrument to be used by even an amateur detective. I make a temporary loan to one of my assistants and you cry 'blackmail!' I did not expect such childishness from you. You can produce no shadow of proof."

"I should inform you, professor, that I have sent a prepaid telegram to the Piccadilly branch of the Inland Bank requesting them to reply giving the total of checks drawn by J.M. Ferriday paid into Cauthery's account during the last six months."

The professor smiled pityingly.

"I fear you will be disappointed. Banks do not give away such information."

"You may be right. However, I will pursue my childish conjectures, if you will tolerate them for a few minutes more. They relate now to information supplied by Department Seven, which, as you probably know, watches over your scientific labors with close care; to a hint given me by the Communist Wenceslaus Pyecroft; to certain words spoken by yourself in my hearing; and to Michael Rouse's reason for attempting to destroy the bank's letter. Let me first draw attention to the admitted liaison maintained between the U.S.S.R and the Communist Party in this—yes, Mr. Rouse?"

Michael Rouse had straightened his hunched back and taken his pipe out of his mouth. He made the gruff throat-clearing noise which was his customary preliminary to speech.

"All right," he said briefly. "I killed him."

CHAPTER NINETEEN

Let us not burthen our remembrances with
A heaviness that's gone.

THE TEMPEST

MICHAEL'S hand was large and rather horny-palmed, clasped over Hilary's where it lay on his shoulder, and a good deal warmer than her cold fingers. Hilary had no recollection of getting up and crossing the sitting room, but she must have done so, for here she was standing behind Michael's chair with a most unmaidenly hand held in his and the state of her affections not only certain at last but brazenly proclaimed. For Aunt Mabel's face of incredulity, for the professor's look of amazement and sorrow at his assistant, she had no eyes. These were but shadows in a world where only she and Michael and Lewker had reality—Lewker, whose unimpressive figure had taken on the mantle of Prospero, with power of life and death over the man she loved. She kept her gaze fixed on his face.

Mr. Lewker, of all the company, seemed completely unperturbed by Michael's admission. He looked, thought Hilary bitterly, dreadfully complacent. He folded his thick fingers over his paunch, nodded slowly at Michael, and gave utterance to the first quotation he had produced that morning.

" 'Now does my project gather to a head,' " he boomed in Prospero's words.

> "My charms crack not; my spirits obey; and Time
> Goes upright with his carriage."

Then he appeared to remember that he had to deal with a confession of murder and leaned forward with a graver air.

"Now, Mr. Rouse. You killed Raymond Cauthery?"

"Yes." Michael's voice was quite steady.

"You acted as has been suggested—climbing up the scree and down to the cave, waiting there, and hitting Cauthery with a splinter of rock as he climbed up?"

"Yes."

"You did this because you overheard the passage between Cauthery and Miss Bourne in the niche below?"

"Yes."

"It is an unconvincing motive, Mr. Rouse. Why did you try to destroy Cauthery's letter after you overheard my expressed intention to search his room?"

Michael considered for an instant before replying.

"Thought it might give you the wrong impression."

"You thought it might lead me to the conclusion that Cauthery was in urgent need of money. Why did you wish to keep this quiet?"

"Well—because—"

"Mr. Rouse." Lewker's spread hand came down on the table. "It will save time, spare distress to—um—certain persons, and convince me of a sufficient motive, if you will admit you knew that Cauthery was blackmailing Professor Ferriday."

"I protest," piped the professor at once.

"This is a matter that can be proved sooner or later," added Lewker, disregarding the interruption.

Michael looked straight at Lewker, avoiding his chief's eye, and spoke more quickly than usual.

"It's true. I can't prove it, but I think it's been going on for some time. Since Cauthery started this Aristo business."

"Since Cauthery left the Communists, in fact."

"Yes. In those days he was all for Russia. I used to think he was trying to convert the professor. Then—"

"One moment, Mr. Rouse." Lewker's little eyes were gleaming now. He switched his gaze from Rouse to Wenceslaus Pyecroft. "Mr. Pyecroft, Raymond Cauthery became a Communist while he was engaged on experimental work—for a counter to the atomic bomb—in Professor Ferriday's laboratory. He was required by his party to persuade the professor that more funds for his work could be obtained by giving the U.S.S.R. certain information. Am I right?"

Pyecroft half rose, his thin face working with fright and indecision.

"Ay—Ay can't divulge Party secrets," he quavered. "Ay should not be asked—"

"That will do, Mr. Pyecroft. Professor, I will recall to your mind a conversation we had on the summit of Glyder Fach last Sunday. You gave me to understand that you placed your work on this new discovery above all considerations of patriotism or rival ideologies. You went so far as to say that, as the surgeon about to assist at the birth of a universal boon, you would not refuse the offer of an American or a Russian to pay for your surgical instruments."

Professor Ferriday threw up his head.

"Well?" he demanded,

"The chief of Department Seven informs me that—as you yourself told me—you were dissatisfied with the allowance made by the British Government for your experiments. He added that there was some suspicion in official minds that you might attempt to get additional funds from foreign governments. Let me remind you, and all of us here, that what is said in this room will not go beyond it. Now, professor—"

A knock at the door cut him short and made everyone start. To Hilary it brought a sudden realization that there was another world outside this little dark room; she tightened her hold on Michael's hand, and was comforted greatly by the answering pressure. Lewker went across to the door and unlocked it with a key taken from his pocket. He took an orange envelope from some invisible person, locked the door again, and returned to the table. Nine pairs of eyes followed his movements and watched as he tore open the envelope and read the telegram it contained. A brief smile—it might have been of triumph—flickered on his pouchy countenance as he turned to the professor.

"This, professor," he boomed, waving the form, "confirms my expectations. Now, perhaps, you will admit the truth of Rouse's statement—a statement which is doubtless the main reason for the murder of Raymond Cauthery."

The professor's skeletal brown hand covered his eyes for a moment. Then he looked up,

"I rely," he said quietly, "on the secrecy of all present here. I did, under Raymond's persuasion, release certain valuable information to the agents of Soviet Russia, in return for sufficient money to enable me to expand my work. At a later date Raymond threatened me with exposure, which would have meant imprisonment and the end of my experiments. To keep his mouth shut I had to pay him considerable sums, as you have no doubt seen from that telegram. I had no idea that my other assistant was aware of this."

"I wasn't," Michael said, with an odd look at his chief. "I only suspected it. But I heard him go to your room the night after he'd got the letter. I thought then he was at it again."

"And so," Lewker's boom took up the tale, "you decided to kill him, Mr. Rouse. Your devotion to your leader is obvious and exemplary. You had determined on this murder, then, before you overheard the incident on Milestone Buttress?"

"Yes."

"Hum. You behaved rather carelessly for an intending murderer, did you not?"

"Did I?" The question was casual, almost weary.

"Indeed you did. You allowed yourself to be seen by your victim when you were climbing up the scree to get into position for the deed. You made no attempt at all to provide yourself with an alibi, though one might have been contrived with a little ingenuity. You did not think of destroying evidence until you overheard my conversation with Miss Bourne."

"Didn't know anyone would suspect it wasn't an accident," muttered Rouse.

"Yet, I gather, your job requires a first-rate brain. Consider, also, that you placed Miss Bourne, for whom you seem to entertain some affection"—his glance dwelt for an instant on the interlocked hands—"in a position of danger. Suppose the rope had not caught in that notch, suppose she had not been properly belayed in her niche, Cauthery's fall might well have dragged her down and killed her also. Did that not occur to you, Mr. Rouse?"

Michael said nothing. There was a wretched pause, and then Uncle George stood up. He had recovered his robust coloring and though his bearded face was very solemn he appeared relieved and confident.

"Need we go on with this, Lewker?" he demanded loudly. "You've made your case out in detail—congratulate you on your labors, and so on—and we've all heard Mi—er—Mr. Rouse's confession. We must all feet a certain sympathy with him. The fact remains, however, that he has indubitably committed a murder. There's no course open to us but to—to let justice take its course."

" You mean," Lewker said softly, "that we must hand Michael Rouse over to the police in Bethesda?"

A little, horrible silence followed. Hilary, tense and agonized, looked desperately round the room at them all. Mildred had gone to stand by her mother; their faces were pitiful as they looked towards Michael. Uncle George stood complacently stern, a good man doing his unpleasant duty. Harold Jupp had his eyes shut and his face screwed up. Derwen Jones and Wenceslaus Pyecroft looked equally embarrassed and anxious to get away. The professor's face was hidden in his hands, but he looked up as Lewker spoke to him.

"You agree to that course, professor?"

The scientist made a gesture of helplessness.

"I must. What else can I do? I would ask only that if it be possible to do so the blackmail motive should be omitted from the information you give to the police. To make that public might mean—the end of my work, which is of the first importance. Could that be done, Lewker?"

"I suppose it could," replied the actor expressionlessly.

"You can count on me," said Michael gruffly.

Professor Ferriday turned his head towards his assistant, but Hilary, watching him, saw that he did not lift his eyes to meet Michael's.

"You will understand why I cannot express my gratitude, Michael," he said in a low and rather hurried voice. "What you did, you did to help me. I shall not forget that, my dear boy."

Lewker gave vent to a choking sound, instantly suppressed; it was lost in the louder throat-clearing of Uncle George.

"Hrrm! I think, Lewker, these good people should now be allowed to depart. You and I could then confer as to the—er—further procedure."

Pyecroft and Derwen began to shuffle to their feet. Mrs. Jupp, sniffing violently, was folding her knitting. The professor passed a handkerchief over his face and started to rise.

"Wait." Lewker made the word ring in the little room. The general hushed movement ceased. Hilary felt a sudden stab of hope; Filthy hadn't finished—was there something still unrevealed? She racked her mind desperately but could find no loophole of escape for Michael.

"I have done a great deal of talking this morning," Lewker went on apologetically, "and no doubt some of it has appeared unnecessary. What I have to say now is entirely necessary, and I must ask you all to listen to me for a little longer. I do not expect to bore you."

He paused, staring down at the red-covered notebook that still lay open on the table. Uncle George, after looking as though he was going to protest, sat down again and the others followed his example.

"You will have observed," boomed the actor, without raising his eyes, "that on the evidence of Michael Rouse and Professor Ferriday there is one person who had a stronger motive for murdering Cauthery than Rouse himself possessed. That person is Professor Ferriday. You would admit that to be so, of course, professor."

The professor, staring at Lewker, raised his thin eyebrows; but the other still frowned at his notebook.

"Of course," he said dryly after a moment.

"Thank you. I said earlier that my one hope for a solution of this business was to detect some deliberate deception which would point unmistakably to one person. Michael Rouse's tobacco-buying deception, which you have heard described, told us only that Rouse wanted an excuse to be near Milestone Buttress instead of going straight to the foot of his climb with Professor Ferriday. You noticed, of course, that this deception was carried out very halfheartedly—amazingly so for a man using it as part of a plan of murder. Very well. Let me next recall to your minds the detailed account I gave you of events on Milestone Buttress just before the murder."

Uncle George gave a noisy cough which plainly expressed his impatience of this further dissertation. Clergymen are among those who do not enjoy a busman's holiday. It may be this dislike of sitting quietly while others orate at length that is at the root of their traditional antagonism to the theater. Lewker's voice had been flat and devoid of expression for the last few minutes; now he began to build up a kind of crescendo which forced even Uncle George to lean a little forward expectantly.

"Cauthery had begun the climb and passed out of Miss Bourne's sight. As she waited there at the foot of the Buttress she saw a green bus passing on the road below, traveling east. That bus was the Bangor to Llanrwst morning bus, a daily service. It passed Ogwen Cottage—as I had occasion to notice while I was telephoning yesterday morning—a little after eleven. In point of fact it is due there at eleven-five. If it was on time that bus would pass Milestone Buttress two minutes or so later. I have confirmed, from the bus company itself and from an observer at Ogwen Cottage, that on Monday morning the bus was if anything a little late. When Miss Bourne saw it, therefore, the time could not possibly have been earlier than seven minutes past eleven."

Hilary felt as a blind man who receives sight by a miracle must feel. She saw—and all things around her were new and beautiful, She wanted to shout her discovery in Michael's ear, to whirl him round the room in a dance of escape, of freedom. . . .

But Lewker was booming on to his climax.

"Ten minutes from the foot of the climb to the place where Cauthery met his death is a short allowance, but we will call it that. To be absolutely within the safety limit, we can say that Cauthery's fall must have taken place later than eleven-fifteen. Yet we on the East Face heard a whistle blown at ten-fifty. On the North Ridge at ten-fifty the professor shouted down to us that it was a distress signal from the direction of Milestone Buttress. Tell me, professor—who *blew that whistle twenty-five minutes before the real signal?*"

He was looking straight at his man now, his gaze hard and unwinking. Hilary had never seen his rather comical features so set and stern. Professor Ferriday shrugged his thin shoulders.

"This is all perfectly absurd," he said contemptuously. "Your data must be faulty, my dear Lewker. There was only one whistle blown."

"On the contrary, my dear Ferriday, this is the one part of my investigation of which the data are indisputable. Those times are testified to by witnesses—and would convince any jury. The first whistle, and your shout, occurred at ten minutes to eleven. The murder, and Miss Bourne's signal, took place at least twenty-five minutes later. I will tell you—"

"Ferry!" Uncle George was on his feet. "Don't stand this! Tell him he's mad—answer him, man!"

He was shouting at the top of his voice, but there was appeal, and fear, in his bellowing. The professor's tongue flickered rapidly over his lips.

"Ridiculous," he said a little hoarsely. "Rouse has confessed to the murder."

Lewker took him up swiftly.

"Rouse has confessed—yes. You were prepared to let him die for your crime, professor. The murder of Raymond Cauthery, a blackmailer, was a crime for which I could find excuse. But the attempted murder of Michael Rouse—for such it amounts to—is a thing indefensible. Miss Bourne having treated his warning with scorn, Rouse determined to be on hand in case of trouble. He knew Cauthery's ways. Hence his actions that morning. I think he decided to watch from near the top of the Buttress and satisfy himself that Miss Bourne did not need a change of escort when she finished the climb. He was hiding there in the mist when Professor Ferriday arrived and went down the Buttress, but I do not think he suspected what was afoot."

"I didn't see him go down," Michael said. "He must have come along pretty quietly. Anyway, I was listening for voices, and—" He stopped and bit his lip.

"But you heard the whistle from below. You saw the professor emerge on the top slab, and you knew then what he had done. You were intensely loyal to your chief, you thought Cauthery was better dead, you believed the work Professor Ferriday was doing was a more important thing than the life of a blackmailer. You made yourself, in short, an accessory after the fact of murder, though you did not reveal your knowledge to the professor. When, later, you learned that the murder was being investigated you tried to destroy the evidence that might lead to him. When you saw this morning's exposition moving inevitably towards an accusation against the professor, you took the mistaken but in some ways creditable step of sacrificing yourself for him. Also, I think, you had in mind the importance of carrying on the work he was engaged on. Do you think that, professor?"

The professor's wizened face seemed to have deepened all its wrinkles so that he looked incredibly old.

"Rouse has confessed to the murder," he repeated mechanically, and his voice had shrunk to a piping whisper.

Lewker nodded and turned a page of his notebook.

"Harold Jupp took less than fifteen minutes to get from the spot on the North Ridge where you probably stood, professor, when you blew a whistle muffled under your coat and afterwards shouted down to us. You had twenty-five minutes, probably half an hour, to carry out your plan. You had seen, as we had, Cauthery's car pass the Dol Afon road and head for the Milestone. With your knowledge of the climb you could calculate roughly how long the two climbers would take to get up to the cave. You had, I think, planned the manner of Cauthery's death earlier, but your final decision was made on the Heather Terrace when you saw the opportunity offering itself. Mist was forming on the crags, Michael had opportunely got himself out of the way, everything was in your favor. The only risk you took was that Miss Bourne might notice the time of the accident. And that was a very slight risk indeed. As soon as you had made the false signal you ran down the North Ridge and arrived at the top of the Milestone a quarter of an hour later—at five past eleven. I think, by the by, that you must have delayed blowing your whistle as long as you dared so that the danger of the time discrepancy being noticed by Harold or myself might be lessened as much as possible. Before ten past eleven you were waiting in the Cave, with five minutes at least, ten minutes more probably, in hand. You murdered Raymond Cauthery. And there is no man so eminent or invaluable to the race that he may avoid the consequences of murder."

He closed the red-covered notebook and rose slowly to his feet.

"That evidence, professor, will be laid before the police this afternoon. I have finished what I had to say. Do you wish to say anything?"

Professor Ferriday stood up. He had recovered his self-possession. Hilary saw that he was smiling slightly.

"I see I am beaten," he said. "All the same, my dear Lewker, I am right. You are wrong. The completion of my experiments was infinitely more important than the life of one man, or two. The theorists, as you remarked during our argument on Glyder Fach summit, will have their way after all. My work is to remain incomplete because of their blind, quite unscientific theory of justice."

He came forward and stood facing Lewker across the table.

"I would prefer," he continued steadily, "to make my own final statement, or confession, to the—the higher authorities. If you will permit me, I will drive down in Raymond's car and give myself up to them. You need have no fear that I shall escape judgment."

For a long moment the eyes of the two men met and held. Then, in silence, Lewker took from his pocket the key of the sitting-room door and placed it on the table. The professor nodded and picked it up.

"Michael," he said in his precise little voice, "you know where to obtain the keys of my laboratory. You will proceed with the work we had planned."

"You can count on me," Michael said again in the same gruff tones he had used before.

Professor Ferriday went towards the door. His step faltered once, as he passed his old friend, whose face was buried in his hands. But he went out of the room without speaking again and the door closed behind him.

Three hours later an excited small boy from a farm farther down the valley brought the news to Dol Afon. A blue sports car driven by an elderly gentleman had crashed over the precipitous edge of the road beyond Ogwen Falls, where the lorry had gone over a week before. The elderly gentleman had been killed instantly.

"It's funny," remarked Hilary Bourne, reaching down from her perch on a mossy boulder to smooth the tuft on the back of Michael's red head, "how quickly all the dreadful things fade in one's memory, and only the nice things stay."

Michael Rouse took his pipe out of his mouth.

"Good job," he grunted; and replaced the pipe.

A deep voice rose from a clump of heather a few yards away like the song of a giant bee.

> "These things seem small and undistinguishable
> Like far-off mountains turned into clouds.

"It is," added Mr. Lewker drowsily, "a wise provision of Nature. Cultivate it, my children. Remember the lessons, but forget the ugliness of the teacher. Beshrew me, but I have coined a proverb."

The three were sitting in the sunshine close under the little crag at the turn of the Dol Afon track. The funeral—a double one—had taken place that morning and now it was after lunch, In half an hour they would be speeding away from the mountains on the homeward journey.

Once more the tall peaks smiled into a cloudless sky and the valley dreamed in green solitude beneath the soaring crags of Tryfan. The afternoon was warm and still, and above the murmur of streams near and far the many voices of the sheep, muted and made musical by distance, drifted peacefully to their ears.

"I think I shall only remember about Michael and me when I think of this week," Hilary said. "Oh, and Filthy's wonderful detective work too, of course. You know, even now I can think about it without going all shivery—Filthy," she added suddenly. "You knew, didn't you, what was going to happen when you gave the professor the key?"

"I did. It was the best way out, and I do not think the story need ever come to the ears of the police. A tidy ending is always dear to the heart of the Great Detective."

He sat up and brushed some bits of dead grass from his bald dome.

"It is a part," he said thoughtfully, "that I sustain with some *éclat*. But I hope never to play it again."

There was a little pause. Michael's pipe bubbled rhythmically. On the far side of the wide meadow, moving along above the wall of the main road, the head and shoulders of a bicycling youth appeared. He stopped at the Dol Afon gate and turned in, wheeling his cycle up the track and fumbling in the leather pouch at his belt.

"It's a telegraph boy," said Hilary, shading her eyes to look at him.

Michael got up and went to meet the newcomer. He returned with an orange envelope in his hand.

"For you," he said, dangling it over Lewker.

Filthy took the envelope and ripped it open. Its contents seemed to amuse him.

"So," he boomed. "Your admirable Inland Bank, my dear, regrets that it is unable to supply by telegram the information I require."

"But—look here," Hilary protested wonderingly. "You've already *had* the information. The telegram came when—when we were all in the sitting room yesterday morning. You said then that it was what you'd been expecting."

"So it was. Yes, a most opportune telegram. But—I confess it with a certain shame—it did not contain what I led the late professor to believe it contained. It was, in fact, not from the bank at all."

"Who was it from, then—or am I being rude?"

"You are never rude, my dear. It was from my wife, who has been assisting at a certain important event in the household of our friend Gideon Hazel." He rummaged in his pockets, produced a crumpled form, and held it out. "One day, perhaps, I shall receive a similar message from you."

Hilary and Michael, their heads close together, bent over him to read it. It said, simply:

IT'S A BOY

THE END

Rue Morgue Press Titles as of May 2000

Brief Candles by Manning Coles. From Topper to Aunt Dimity mystery readers have embraced the cozy ghost story. Four of the best were written by Manning Coles, the creator of the witty Tommy Hambledon spy novels. First published in 1954, *Brief Candles* is likely to produce more laughs than chills as an English couple vacationing in France runs into two gentlemen with decidedly old-world manners. What they don't know is that the two men, James and Charles Latimer, are ancestors of theirs who shuffled off this mortal coil some 80 years earlier when, emboldened by strong drink and with only a pet monkey and an aged waiter as allies, the two made a valiant, foolish and quite fatal attempt to halt a German advance during the Franco-Prussian War of 1870. Now these two ectoplasmic gentlemen and their spectral pet monkey Ulysses have been summoned from their unmarked graves because their visiting relatives are in serious trouble. But before they can solve the younger Latimers' problems, the three benevolent spirits light brief candles of insanity for a tipsy policeman, a recalcitrant banker, a convocation of English ghost-busters, and a card-playing rogue who's wanted for murder. "As felicitously foolish as a collaboration of (P.G.) Wodehouse and Thorne Smith."—Anthony Boucher. "For those who like something out of the ordinary. Lighthearted, very funny.'—*The Sunday Times*. "A gay, most readable story."—*The Daily Telegraph*. **0-915230-24-0** **$14.00**

The Black Stocking by Constance & Gwenyth Little. Irene Hastings, who can't decide which of her two fiances she should marry, is looking forward to a nice vacation, and everything would have been just fine had not her mousy friend Ann asked to be dropped off at an insane asylum so she could visit her sister. When the sister escapes, just about everyone, including a handsome young doctor, mistakes Irene for the runaway loony, and she is put up at an isolated private hospital under house arrest, pending final identification. Only there's not a bed to be had in the hospital. One of the staff is already sleeping in a tent on the grounds, so it's decided that Irene is to share a bedroom with young Dr. Ross Munster, much to the consternation of both parties. On the other hand, Irene's much-married mother Elise, an Auntie Mame type who rushes to her rescue, figures that the young doctor has son-in-law written all over him. She also figures there's plenty of room in that bedroom for herself as well. In the meantime, Irene runs into a headless nurse, a corpse that won't stay put, an empty coffin, a missing will, and a mysterious black stocking, prompting the local police to think very seriously about locking her up in a real jail. As Elise would say, "Mong Dew!" **0-915230-30-5** **$14.00**

The Black-Headed Pins by Constance & Gwenyth Little. "...a zany, fun-loving puzzler spun by the sisters Little—it's celluloid screwball comedy printed on paper. The charm of this book lies in the lively banter between characters and the breakneck pace of the story. You hardly grasp how the first victim was done in when you have to grapple with outlandish clues like two black-headed pins."—Diane Plumley, *Dastardly Deeds. With* her bank account down to empty, orphaned Leigh Smith has no choice but to take a job as a paid companion and housekeeper to the miserly Mrs. Ballister. However, once she moves into the drafty, creaking old Ballister mansion in the wilds of New Jersey, Smithy has reason to regret her decision. But when Mrs. Ballister decides to invite her nieces and nephews for Christmas, Smithy sees the possibility for some fun. What she doesn't expect is to encounter the Ballister family curse. It seems that when a dragging noise is heard in the attic it foretells the death of a Ballister. And once a Ballister dies, if you don't watch the body until it's buried, it's likely to walk. The stockings are barely hung from the mantle when those dreaded sounds are heard in the attic, and before long, corpses are going for regular midnight strolls. Smithy and a pair of potential beaux turn detective and try to figure out why the murderer leaves black-headed pins at the scene of every crime. First published in 1938. **0-915230-25-9 $14.00**

The Black Gloves by Constance & Gwenyth Little. "I'm relishing every madcap moment."—*Murder Most Cozy*. Welcome to the Vickers estate near East Orange, New Jersey, where the middle class is destroying the neighborhood, erecting their horrid little cottages, playing on the Vickers tennis court, and generally disrupting the comfortable life of Hammond Vickers no end. It's bad enough that he had to shell out good money to get his daughter Lissa a Reno divorce only to have her brute of an ex-husband show up on his doorstep. But why does there also have to be a corpse in the cellar? And lights going on and off in the attic? First published in 1939. **0-915230-20-8 $14.00**

The Black Honeymoon by Constance & Gwenyth Little. Can you murder someone with feathers? If you don't believe feathers are lethal, then you probably haven't read a Little mystery. No, Uncle Richard wasn't tickled to death—though we can't make the same guarantee for readers—but the hyper-allergic rich man did manage to sneeze himself into the hereafter in his hospital room. Suspicion falls on his nurse, young Miriel Mason, who recently married the dead man's nephew, an army officer on furlough. To clear herself of murder as well as charges of being a gold-digger, Miriel summons private detective Kelly, an old crony of her father's, who gets himself hired as a servant even though he can't cook, clean or serve. First published in 1944. **0-915230-21-6 $14.00**

Great Black Kanba by Constance & Gwenyth Little. "If you love train mysteries as much as I do, hop on the Trans-Australia Railway in *Great Black Kanba*, a fast and funny 1944 novel by the talented (Littles)."—Jon L. Breen, *Ellery Queen's Mystery Magazine*. "I have decided to add *Kanba* to my favorite mysteries of all time list!...a zany ride I'll definitely take again and again."—Diane Plumley in the Murder Ink newsletter. When a young American woman wakes up on an Australia train with a bump on her head and no memory, she suddenly finds out that she's engaged to two different men and the chief suspect in a murder case. But she's almost more upset to discover that she appears to have absolutely dreadful taste in clothing. It all adds up to some delightful mischief—call it Cornell Woolrich on laughing gas. **0-915230-22-4 $14.00**

The Grey Mist Murders by Constance & Gwenyth Little. Who—or what—is the mysterious figure that emerges from the grey mist to strike down several passengers on the final leg of a round-the-world sea voyage? Is it the same shadowy entity that persists in leaving three matches outside Lady Marsh's cabin every morning? And why does one flimsy negligee seem to pop up at every turn? When Carla Bray first heard things go bump in the night, she hardly expected to find a corpse in the adjoining cabin. Nor did she expect to find herself the chief suspect in the murders. Robert Arnold, a sardonic young man who joined the ship in Tahiti, makes a play for Carla but if he's really interested in helping to clear her of murder, why does he spend so much time courting other women on board? This 1938 effort was the Littles' first book. **0-915230-26-7 $14.00**

Murder is a Collector's Item by Elizabeth Dean. "(It) froths over with the same effervescent humor as the best Hepburn-Grant films."—Sujata Massey. "Completely enjoyable."—*New York Times*. "Fast and funny."—*The New Yorker*. Twenty-six-year-old Emma Marsh isn't much at spelling or geography and perhaps she butchers the odd literary quotation or two, but she's a keen judge of character and more than able to hold her own when it comes to selling antiques or solving murders. When she stumbles upon the body of a rich collector on the floor of the Boston antiques shop where she works, suspicion quickly falls upon her missing boss. Emma knows Jeff Graham is no murderer, but veteran homicide cop Jerry Donovan doesn't share her convictions, and Emma enlists the aid of Hank Fairbanks, her wealthy boyfriend and would-be criminologist, to nab the real killer. Originally published in 1939, *Murder is a Collector's Item* was the first of three books featuring Emma. Smoothly written and sparkling with dry, sophisticated humor, this nearly forgotten milestone combines an intriguing puzzle with an entertaining portrait of a self-possessed young woman on her own in Boston toward the end of the Great Depression. **0-915230-19-4 $14.00**

Murder is a Serious Business by Elizabeth Dean. It's 1940 and the Thirsty Thirties are over but you couldn't tell it by the gang at J. Graham Antiques, where clerk Emma Marsh, her would-be criminologist boyfriend Hank, and boss Jeff Graham trade barbs in between shots of scotch when they aren't bothered by the rare customer. Trouble starts when Emma and crew head for a weekend at Amos Currier's country estate to inventory the man's antiques collection. It isn't long before the bodies start falling and once again Emma is forced to turn sleuth in order to prove that her boss isn't a killer. Emma is sure there's a good reason why Jeff didn't mention that he had Amos' 18th century silver muffineer hidden in his desk drawer back at the shop. Filled with the same clever dialog and eccentric characters that made *Murder is a Collector's Item* an absolute delight, this second case offers up an unusual approach to crime solving as well as a sidesplitting look at the peculiar world of antiques. **0-915230-28-3 $14.95**

Murder, Chop Chop by James Norman. "The book has the butter-wouldn't-melt-in-his-mouth cool of Rick in *Casablanca*."—*The Rocky Mountain News*. "Amuses the reader no end."—*Mystery News*. "This long out-of-print masterpiece is intricately plotted, full of eccentric characters and very humorous indeed. Highly recommended."—*Mysteries by Mail*. Meet Gimiendo Hernandez Quinto, a gigantic Mexican who once rode with Pancho Villa and who now trains *guerrilleros* for the Nationalist Chinese government when he isn't solving murders. At his side is a beautiful Eurasian known as Mountain of Virtue, a woman as dangerous to men as she is irresistible. Then there's Mildred Woodford, a hard-drinking British journalist; John Tate, a portly American calligrapher who wasn't made for adventure; Lieutenant Chi, a young Hunanese patriot weighted down with the cares of China and the Brooklyn Dodgers; and a host of others, any one of whom may have killed Abe Harrow, an ambulance driver who appears to have died at three different times. There's also a cipher or two to crack, a train with a mind of its own, and Chiang Kai-shek's false teeth, which have gone mysteriously missing. First published in 1942. **0-915230-16-X $13.00**

Death at The Dog by Joanna Cannan. "Worthy of being discussed in the same breath with an Agatha Christie or Josephine Tey...anyone who enjoys Golden Age mysteries will surely enjoy this one."—Sally Fellows, *Mystery News*. "Skilled writing and brilliant characterization."—*Times of London*. "An excellent English rural tale."—Jacques Barzun & Wendell Hertig Taylor in *A Catalogue of Crime.* Set in late 1939 during the first anxious months of World War II, *Death at The Dog,* which was first published in 1941, is a wonderful example of the classic English detective novel that first flourished between the two World Wars. Set in a picturesque village filled with thatched-roof-cottages, eccentric villagers and genial pubs, it's as well-plotted as a Christie, with clues abundantly and fairly planted, and as deftly written as the best of the books by either Sayers or Marsh, filled with quotable lines and perceptive observations on the human condition. Cannan had a gift for characterization that's second to none in Golden Age detective fiction, and she created two memorable lead characters. One of them is Inspector Guy Northeast, a lonely young Scotland Yard inspector who makes his second and final appearance here and finds himself hopelessly smitten with the chief suspect in the murder of a village tyrant. The other is the "lady novelist" Crescy Hardwick, an unconventional and ultimately unobtainable woman a number of years Guy's senior, who is able to pierce his armor and see the unhappiness that haunts the detective's private moments. Well aware that all the evidence seems to point to her, she is also able—unlike her less imaginative and more snobbish fellow villagers—to see how very good Inspector Northeast is at his job. **0-915230-23-2 $14.00**

They Rang Up the Police by Joanna Cannan. "Just delightful."—*Sleuth of Baker Street* Pick-of-the-Month. "A brilliantly plotted mystery...splendid character study...don't miss this one, folks. It's a keeper."—Sally Fellows, *Mystery News.* When Delia Cathcart and Major Willoughby disappear from their quiet English village one Saturday morning in July 1937, it looks like a simple case of a frustrated spinster running off for a bit of fun with a straying husband. But as the hours turn into days, Inspector Guy Northeast begins to suspect that she may have been the victim of foul play. On the surface, Delia appeared to be a quite ordinary middle-aged Englishwoman content to spend her evenings with her sisters and her days with her beloved horses. But Delia led a secret life—and Guy turns up more than one person who would like to see Delia dead. Except Delia wasn't the only person with a secret...Never published in the United States, *They Rang Up the Police* appeared in England in 1939. **0-915230-27-5 $14.00**

Cook Up a Crime by Charlotte Murray Russell. "Perhaps the mother of today's 'cozy' mystery . . . amateur sleuth Jane has a personality guaranteed to entertain the most demanding reader."—Andy Plonka, *The Mystery Reader.* "Some wonderful old time recipes...highly recommended."—*Mysteries by Mail.* Meet Jane Amanda Edwards, a self-styled "full-fashioned" spinster who complains she hasn't looked at herself in a full-length mirror since Helen Hokinson started drawing for *The New Yorker.* But you can always count on Jane to look into other people's affairs, especially when there's a juicy murder case to investigate. In this 1951 title Jane goes searching for recipes (included between chapters) for a cookbook project and finds a body instead. And once again her lily-of-the-field brother Arthur goes looking for love, finds strong drink, and is eventually discovered clutching the murder weapon. **0-915230-18-6 $13.00**

The Man from Tibet by Clyde B. Clason. Locked inside the Tibetan Room of his Chicago luxury apartment, the rich antiquarian was overheard repeating a forbidden occult chant under the watchful eyes of Buddhist gods. When the doors were opened it appeared that he had succumbed to a heart attack. But the elderly Roman historian and sometime amateur sleuth Theocritus Lucius Westborough is convinced that Adam Merriweather's death was anything but natural and that the weapon was an eighth century Tibetan manuscript. It's murder, who could have done it, and how? Suspects abound. There's's Tsongpun Bonbo, the gentle Tibetan lama from whom the manuscript was originally stolen; Chang, Merriweather's scholarly Tibetan secretary who had fled a Himalayan monastery; Merriweather's son Vincent, who disliked his father and stood to inherit a fortune; Dr. Jed Merriweather, the dead man's brother, who came to Chicago to beg for funds to continue his archaeological digs in Asia; Dr. Walters, the dead man's physician, who guarded a secret; and Janice Shelton, his young ward, who found herself being pushed by Merriweather into marrying his son. How the murder was accomplished has earned praise from such impossible crime connoisseurs as Robert C.S. Adey, who cited Clason's "highly original and practical locked-room murder method." **0-915230-17-8 $14.00**

The Mirror by Marlys Millhiser. "Completely enjoyable."—*Library Journal* . "A great deal of fun."—*Publishers Weekly*. How could you not be intrigued, as one reviewer pointed out, by a novel in which "you find the main character marrying her own grandfather and giving birth to her own mother?" Such is the situation in Marlys Millhiser's classic novel (a Mystery Guild selection originally published by Putnam in 1978) of two women who end up living each other's lives after they look into an antique Chinese mirror. Twenty-year-old Shay Garrett is not aware that she's pregnant and is having second thoughts about marrying Marek Weir when she's suddenly transported back 78 years in time into the body of Brandy McCabe, her own grandmother, who is unwillingly about to be married off to miner Corbin Strock. Shay's in shock but she still recognizes that the picture of her grandfather that hangs in the family home doesn't resemble her husband-to-be. But marry Corbin she does and off she goes to the high mining town of Nederland, where this thoroughly modern young woman has to learn to cope with such things as wood cooking stoves and—to her—old-fashioned attitudes about sex. In the meantime, Brandy McCabe is finding it even harder to cope with life in the Boulder, Co., of 1978. **0-915230-15-1 $14.95**

About The Rue Morgue Press

The Rue Morgue Press vintage mystery line is designed to bring back into print those books that were favorites of readers between the turn of the century and the 1960s. The editors welcome suggestions for reprints. To receive our catalog or make suggestions, write The Rue Morgue Press, P.O. Box 4119, Boulder, Colorado 80306.